DETROIT PUBLIC LIBRARY

P9-DOD-960   1

driven
to be

Loved

CH

driven to be Loved

PAT SIMMONS

WHITAKER
HOUSE

Publisher's Note:
This novel is a work of fiction. References to real events, organizations, or places are used in a fictional context. Any resemblances to actual persons, living or dead, are entirely coincidental.

All Scripture quotations are taken from the King James Version of the Holy Bible.

DRIVEN TO BE LOVED
The Carmen Sisters ~ Book Three

Pat Simmons
P.O. Box 1077
Florissant, MO 63031
authorpatsimmons@gmail.com

The author is represented by MacGregor Literary, Inc., of Hillsboro, Oregon.

ISBN: 978-1-62911-568-9
eBook ISBN: 978-1-62911-590-0
Printed in the United States of America
© 2015 by Pat Simmons

Whitaker House
1030 Hunt Valley Circle
New Kensington, PA 15068
www.whitakerhouse.com

Library of Congress Cataloging-in-Publication Data

Simmons, Pat, 1959–
  Driven to be loved / by Pat Simmons.
    pages ; cm. — (The Carmen sisters ; book 3)
  ISBN 978-1-62911-568-9 (softcover : acid-free paper) — ISBN 978-1-62911-590-0 (ebook)
1. Mate selection—Fiction. 2. Man-woman relationships—Fiction. I. Title.
PS3619.I56125D75 2015
813'.6—dc23
                        2015024802

No part of this book may be reproduced or transmitted in any form or by any means, electronic or mechanical—including photocopying, recording, or by any information storage and retrieval system—without permission in writing from the publisher. Please direct your inquiries to permissionseditor@whitakerhouse.com.

1 2 3 4 5 6 7 8 9 10 11 **W** 22 21 20 19 18 17 16 15

Dedication

"Wherefore seeing we also are compassed about with so great a cloud of witnesses, let us lay aside every weight, and the sin which doth so easily beset us, and let us run with patience the race that is set before us…."
—Hebrews 12:1

To the pioneers of Pentecost:
Bishop James A. Johnson
Mother Mattie B. Poole

Thank God for the cloud of witnesses who served Him before us.

Acknowledgments

Heartfelt thanks to Ricky Whittington, Plaza Motors Benz, and Dr. Rachael Charney, SSM Cardinal Glennon Hospital. Without these individuals' granting me insights into their world, this story would not have been possible—just ask them. They answered my questions through e-mails, phone calls, and visits to their places of work. Again, thank you. If you're ever in St. Louis and need a luxury vehicle, please give Ricky a call.

As always, I thank God for allowing me this incredible opportunity to write about His goodness!

A shout-out to my family, especially my husband, who had to endure many days of my being "holed up in library mode."

Bishop James A. and First Lady Juana J. Johnson.

My mother, sister, brother, daughter, and son; my nieces and nephews; and all the readers who have supported me over the years.

A special shout-out to Mia Harris, my New Jersey captain, who is always on standby to help whenever I need information about Philadelphia, where my fictional characters the Carmens reside. I appreciate you!

To the descendants of Minerva Jordan Wade; Marshall Cole and Laura Brown; Joseph and Nellie Palmer Wafford Brown; Thomas Carter and Love Ann Shepard; Ned and Priscilla Brownlee; John Wilkinson and Artie Jamison/Charlotte Jamison; and others who were tracked down on the 1800s censuses and other documents; and my in-laws: Simmons, Sinkfields, Crofts, Sturdivants, Stricklands, Downers…and the list goes on. Love you, cousins!

CHAPTER ONE

Squinting, Adrian Cole released a slow whistle as he pulled into the parking space at St. Louis Bread Company on South Brentwood. He'd chosen the café-style restaurant for its low-key atmosphere. With a big paper to write for his strategic management course for his MBA, he felt he would be more productive there than at his condo in Maryland Heights, where he could definitely find distractions—number one, the sports channels.

As he mentally cataloged the shiny black Lexus IS's features, he confirmed the model was top of the line, although he preferred his own silver-gray fully loaded Audi A6. However, the luxury sedan wasn't the only thing that caught his eye.

A woman sat behind the wheel, and something didn't appear quite right. Even though Adrian couldn't make out the details of her face, there was no mistaking that she was in some type of distress. Her shoulders were slumped, and her head was bowed.

After turning off the ignition, Adrian grabbed his laptop and got out of his vehicle. He slowly approached her car and tapped lightly on the window, so as not to startle her. But she didn't respond. He tapped again, louder this time. Still, the lady didn't acknowledge him. Adrian debated what he should do next.

He could see the news story now: "African-American man wanted for attempted carjacking. Man is described as being six foot three, built, and of medium complexion. Witnesses say the suspect was seen trying to break into a black Lexus...." He shook his head. He needed to cut back on his crime show marathons.

With the sun beginning to set, there was just enough daylight for Adrian to make a quick sweep of the backseat and make sure the woman wasn't being held at gunpoint. *Nope.*

It appeared the damsel in distress was alive, conscious, and purposely ignoring him; so, he decided his good deed—at least his attempt at one—was done for the day. For all he knew, the woman was on the phone, arguing with her boyfriend or her husband, or learning of the passing of a loved one. Or, maybe she hadn't taken her meds and was about to go ballistic.

With a deep breath, Adrian continued across the parking lot to the restaurant. Once inside, he fought the urge to glance over his shoulder to see if the woman had driven off, was still holed up in her car, or had gotten out. By the time he picked up his tray of his favorite sandwich—a Bacon Turkey Bravo—and a cup of fresh-squeezed lemonade, Adrian had done a couple more head checks. With curiosity still gnawing at him, he slid into a booth that gave him a view of his target.

He powered up his laptop, hastily blessed his food, and took a swig of his lemonade, still spying on the black Lexus. He eyed the parking lot one more time, then chided himself. How was he going to get any work done if he was constantly looking out there? Shaking his head, Adrian tried to focus on the strategic analyses he had to complete on three companies. As he was outlining their strengths and weaknesses, his peripheral vision picked up movement in the parking lot. Adrian's head whipped up. The woman had pulled down the sun visor and was blowing her nose. He still couldn't get a good look at her, except to see that she had enough hair that she probably could spare some—whether a gift from her parents or purchased over the counter, it was definitely an asset.

He watched as she meticulously patted her cheeks, applied some lipstick, and then stepped out of the car, her four-inch heels hitting the pavement first. When she stood to her full height, Adrian guessed she was five feet seven or eight. She reached back into the car and pulled out a white jacket—a lab coat?—and draped it around her shoulders. The damsel slid on a pair of sunglasses, probably to hide her red eyes, since the sun had mostly set by now. Her skin reminded him of caramel, and the way she strutted on her shapely legs as she walked toward the restaurant said that she took no prisoners. However, just moments earlier, some type of meltdown had held her captive.

Maybe that was what prompted Adrian to change seats.

With her bag of comfort food—oatmeal cookies—and cup of coffee, Dr. Sabrece "Brecee" Carmen found a booth to hide in. As she removed her sunglasses, Brecee was about to tell the handsome stranger who appeared to be about to occupy the opposite side of her booth that she was not in the mood for company. She was already drained from her crying spell. Now she was about to add another offense to her criminal record—assault, albeit in the name of self-defense.

But when she looked into his eyes, she forgot what she had been about to say.

"Are you okay?" he asked, his voice low.

Was that the latest pickup line? Brecee thought she'd heard them all. She blinked to regain the upper edge. "Excuse me?"

He tilted his head toward the parking lot. "I noticed you were upset when I pulled up in my car."

Great. Brecee tried to mask her humiliation by sliding her sunglasses on again. Then she took a deep breath. "Oh, that? I'm fine." She tried to muster a smile, but it seemed like her lips were too heavy to lift. "I was just having a moment."

He appeared genuinely relieved. "Oh." When he smiled, she noticed the slight indentation in his jaw. It wasn't deep enough to be called a dimple, but it still enhanced an already handsome face. Of course, she could take off her sunglasses for a better look, but she feared that the glare from his white teeth, whether bleached or natural, would blind her.

Brecee had always been a sucker for a perfect smile, so she finally managed to offer one of her own.

Evidently, he took her facial expression as an invitation to join her. "Whew," he said, taking a seat. "You had me worried. I didn't know if you needed the police or an ambulance."

"I hardly have any symptoms to qualify as a medical emergency," she told him. "And anyway, I'm a doctor."

"I see that." He glanced at her lab coat.

She didn't usually wear it outside the hospital, but she'd mistakenly left her jacket with her older sister, Shae, who she had been shopping with hours earlier. "I just got a speeding ticket. It was very emotional for me."

Laughter exploded from his full lips, startling her and some nearby patrons. "A speeding ticket? You've got to be kiddin' me." The rich tone of his laughter would've been sexy if it hadn't been directed at her.

Scowling, Brecee folded her arms, leaned forward, and narrowed her eyes. "Mr...."

"It's Adrian." He extended his hand, still chuckling.

Brecee ignored it. "It was a big deal for me. I'm thirty-one, and it was my first."

"But all that over a speeding ticket?" He feigned a straight face until he bowed his head, doing a poor job of hiding his amusement. "Are you counting when you started riding a tricycle?" When he glanced up, his eyes laughed at her, even if his lips were still. "I got my first one at sixteen, and the most recent one three years ago. So, I'll up your one to my two. Feel better?"

This was not how Brecee had envisioned spending her Saturday evening—being issued her first ticket and then being laughed at by a stranger. Getting to her feet, Brecee swiped her cookies and coffee. If only she was acting in a movie and could throw the food in his face. But it would be just her luck to get caught by the same officer who'd issued her the ticket.

Adrian stood, too. The man was as tall as he was handsome, if she was in the right mind to notice. Without a wave or a good-bye, Brecee walked out, never looking back. Why did all the cute guys have to be jerks?

CHAPTER TWO

Brecee's mother always told her that her mouth was going to get her in trouble, and the warning had finally caught up with her. By Sunday morning, she was on her knees at Bethesda Temple Church, repenting of her attitude—the one that had probably contributed to her getting her first speeding ticket. She asked God to forgive her for smarting off at the officer, telling him that she had stayed within the ten-miles-over-the-speed-limit rule, and for her mood when she'd contemplated hurting the guy who'd been amused by her calamity.

If you cannot bridle your own tongue, you deceive your own heart, and your worship of Me is meaningless, the Lord whispered, bringing to mind James 1:26.

To some extent, Brecee was a people pleaser. She didn't like to disappoint her family or God. Feeling convicted, she mumbled "Amen" before getting up off her knees. She took a seat next to Shae, a celebrity in her own right as a local television news anchor and reporter. She was married to St. Louis Cardinals outfielder Rahn Maxwell, making her a double celebrity.

Even so, to the Carmen sisters, Shae was still Shae. As the two youngest, Shae and Brecee were close—very close. Being only a year and some months apart, they had been mistaken for twins by countless people. But their divergent personalities were a dead giveaway. Shae was soft-spoken, except when she was seated behind the news desk, while Brecee had a bite to her sharp tongue. She constantly struggled to overcome the habit of speaking her mind.

"You all right?" Shae whispered as she handed over her six-month-old daughter, Sabrina, whose name had been inspired by Brecee's. "You kind of lingered down there." She tilted her head toward the floor, where the churchgoers always knelt to give thanks to God for the privilege of being in

His house again. The salutation usually took thirty seconds or less. How long had Brecee been down there, repenting?

"After church, I'll tell you what happened to me yesterday when we left the mall," Brecee mumbled as discreetly as possible.

Shae lifted an eyebrow. "Something happened that you waited until today to tell me about?"

"Praise the Lord, saints, and welcome, guests," Bishop Archie said as he took his place at the podium, giving Brecee the excuse she needed to delay disclosing her woes.

"My sermon today is simply a reminder that without holiness, no man or woman shall see God. I would guess that God has a running list of believers and their excuses for why they keep coming up short in their spiritual walk with Christ." He paused to flip through his Bible. "In Hebrews, chapter twelve, God makes it clear that there is no acceptable excuse. Pick your poison: whether the offense is fornication with the same or opposite sex or a loose tongue, which the Bible says no man can tame...."

Why did Pastor Archie have to call her out like that? God knew that, as a pediatric emergency doctor, Brecee had held her tongue many times when a parent was at fault for a child's sickness or severe injury.

"If God didn't love you, He wouldn't correct you. Every trial that He allows to happen in our lives is designed to transform us into overcomers...."

Sabrina dozed off, her lips sucking the air as if it were a bottle. As Brecee stared at the precious baby in her arms, her mind began to wander. She wanted a child of her own. Some days, she got tired of giving precious little ones back to their parents. She'd even dated a few men who already had children, but she ended up liking the children more than their fathers.

Since her own father, Saul, had passed away, her other family members—especially her uncle Bradford and male cousins, but also her mother—seemed to feel it was their God-given duty to harass any suitors of the Carmen sisters. Now with three brothers-in-law added to the mix, Brecee's situation seemed hopeless. She was now the sole unmarried Carmen sister, and her whole family was waiting to see whom she would bring home next for an interrogation.

Her two oldest sisters lived in Philly, where the rest of the Carmens resided. Stacy had been married to Ted for years, and they had a son, T.J., who was five. Next was Shari, married to Garrett, with two sons, Garrison and Saul, miraculously born after high-risk pregnancies. Most recently, Shae and Rahn had married and then blessed the family with Sabrina.

Shortly before meeting Shae, Rahn had been the target of an attempted carjacking. After the Lord had spared his life, not only did he repent and get baptized with water and fire in Jesus' name; he also purchased an armor-plated car for himself. Before marrying Shae, he'd bought her an armor-plated Jaguar as an engagement gift.

And when Brecee had finished her residency at Driscoll Children's Hospital in Houston and then moved to St. Louis to be near Shae, Rahn had taken it upon himself to protect his wife's baby sister in a similar way. Brecee had refused the option of armor plating on her new Lexus, but she'd agreed to an upgraded anti-theft system. That very Lexus had been the culprit behind her first speeding ticket.

"In closing," Pastor Archie told the congregation, pulling Brecee's mind back to the present, "the Lord Jesus will continue to correct the error of your ways until you overcome that temptation. That is the only way to live holy."

I got that part, Brecee thought as the pastor gave the invitation to come to salvation.

Three men and several teenagers walked down the aisle toward the front, most of them openly crying after hearing the sermon—the very one she had shamefully zoned out on. They were baptized in water in Jesus' name before the offering was taken and the congregation was dismissed.

Brecee stood and continued holding Sabrina while Shae gathered their things. As usual, several church members approached them.

"Sister Maxwell, I got a news tip," said an older mother of three toddlers who had yet to be vaccinated because of paperwork at the clinics. Shae promised to investigate the allegations. Then a group of teenage boys got their attention and bashfully inquired about tickets to opening day at Busch Stadium. Rahn usually gave a number of tickets to the church, but he was on a road trip, so Shae assured the boys that she would check with him.

During flu season, Brecee was always hounded by worried congregants with medical questions, but she was glad to be enjoying a break right now.

When Sabrina woke and started fussing, Shae excused herself from further conversation and reached for her daughter. She smothered her daughter with soft kisses before raising an eyebrow at Brecee. "Now, what happened yesterday? We were together most of the day."

"Well," Brecee paused, glancing over her shoulder to double check they had some privacy. "After we finished shopping at the Galleria, I got a speeding ticket just for passing a car so I could get on I-40."

Shae's jaw dropped. She stopped fussing with her daughter as she tried to put Sabrina in her sweater and cap. "You're kidding me. Out of all the sisters, you were the only one with a clean record, and you've lived in three states." She paused. "I'm sorry, Sis. It's no wonder, though, considering the week you had. That was the reason we went shopping in the first place."

Brecee's eyes misted as they strolled out of the sanctuary. She didn't want to think about the three children who hadn't survived a house fire, or the child who had been severely beaten and later died. She tried to leave those images at Cardinal Glennon Hospital, where she worked.

"I tried my best to get out of it." She shrugged as they walked across the parking lot. "The sexy smile thing is overrated. The officer didn't fall for it. Besides, it hasn't work for me in years. Throwing out your name didn't help, either. All he said was, 'You do look like Shae Maxwell. I can tell you're sisters. She's my favorite anchor…blah, blah, blah,' and kept writing the ticket. He even had the nerve to mention that Rahn is starting off the season hot."

Shae grinned. "That's my baby. I can't wait for him to come home."

"Excuse me," Brecee huffed. "This is about my crisis."

"Oh, yeah." Shae grimaced. "Sorry."

When they reached Shae's SUV, Brecee helped her to secure Sabrina into the car seat before heading off to her Lexus. Since Rahn was on the road, and Shae now worked only two Sundays a month, the sisters would spend the day together. This day, they were eating lunch at Brecee's.

Paranoid about being issued another ticket, Brecee drove more carefully than ever as she exited onto I-70 eastbound to head through downtown and on to her Lafayette Park neighborhood in South St. Louis. Shae was not far behind her.

Fifteen minutes later, they parked along the curb in front of the immaculate three-story brownstone where Brecee's condo occupied the entire second floor. Once inside, Brecee brought out her portable playpen with toys for Sabrina, then got to work warming up their dinner of roast beef, garlic mashed potatoes, and steamed vegetables while Shae prepared a salad.

Brecee was setting the table when she heard Shae's cell phone play the familiar ringtone assigned to Rahn. Although Brecee knew better than to eavesdrop, she couldn't help it. She was so happy that her sister had found love again after a disastrous relationship. Brecee was a romantic at heart, and she had a cabinet filled with DVDs to prove it.

"Yes, babe," Shae was saying. "Sabrina and I are at Brecee's, and we're about to eat." She giggled at something Rahn said. "I'll tell her." A pause. "I miss you like crazy, too." Silence, then more giggles.

Having heard enough, Brecee went to check on her niece in the next room. When her stomach growled, Brecee walked back in the kitchen, jammed her fist on her hip, and cleared her throat. "Are we eating today or next week? Tell my brother-in-law hi, by the way."

"Brecee says hi, honey." More giggles. "I love you, too. Be safe." After a couple of air kisses, Shae finally ended the call. Then, sighing wistfully, she grinned, and her eyes sparkled.

Shaking her head, Brecee playfully scrunched her nose at her sister. "You and Mr. Maxwell had a whole lot of giggling going on."

Shae blushed. "What can I say? I'm married, so he can talk naughty to me all he wants when he's on the road." She went to get her daughter.

Once they were seated at the dining room table, they blessed their food before digging in.

"Mmm," Shae moaned after one taste of the mashed potatoes. "Girl, you always could throw down on these." She smacked her lips.

They chatted about family, Rahn, the newsroom, and Rahn, before Shae finally asked, "So, what are you going to do about your ticket?"

It was a no-brainer. "Girl, I'm going to court to fight it."

"Uh, Brecee? I don't think that's a good idea. You might wind up saying something and be held in contempt. Why don't we talk to Shari? She is the attorney in the family, after all. I'm sure her advice will be to let a lawyer handle it."

"You know I was considering a career in law at one point," Brecee reminded her. "I was on the debate team—"

"You're a doctor now, Brecee. Why don't you play doctor and let someone else play attorney? You know I'm right. I have no problem getting our sisters on conference call, and you know a vote would overrule your idea."

"All right." Brecee rolled her eyes. It was probably for the best. She could see herself getting her terms confused and ending up a laughingstock.

Her mind flashed to the rude guy from the restaurant. "Oh, girl, I didn't tell you that after I got the ticket, I headed to St. Louis Bread Company for some comfort food. You know how my week was, and that ticket just did something to me. Once I started crying, all the tears I had stored up over any little thing fell. As I sat in my car, minding my own business with my own pity party, this guy inside the restaurant saw me crying. Once he verified that I wasn't suicidal, he howled."

"He what?" Shae twisted her lips and narrowed her eyes, clearly curious.

Once Brecee had replayed the conversation for her, Shae dabbed her mouth with her napkin. "So, how did he look? Cute? Ugly? Skinny...you know?"

"Let's just say he had a dark chocolate skin like Philly native actor Kevin Moore, with a smile like actor Omari Hardwick and a body and a slight dimple like football player Will Demps."

"All that in one, huh?" Fanning her face, Shae winked. "Whew. I see you gave attention to detail. Sounds like eye candy...and a jerk. Too bad. It seems finding the right combination in a man is a problem."

Brecee agreed, and she was grateful when they switched subjects to other things that didn't remind her about her lack of a man to make her giggle and blush.

CHAPTER THREE

Adrian was a good guy. His mother told him that all the time, and so did every lady who tried to snag him. So why did he tarnish his reputation with an unknown woman at the St. Louis Bread Company?

That was out of character for him; but even now, Adrian tried to keep a straight face as he recounted the scene to his older cousin Dolan Cole. It was Sunday afternoon, and Adrian had stopped by Dolan's on his way home from the library, where he'd met with three classmates to update one another on what they'd done for their group project.

The two were very close, likely because most of their other family members lived in either Detroit or Oklahoma City. Plus, they both were only children.

As far as looks went, they were both buffed rather handsomely, taking after their mothers. And they had inherited light brown eyes from their paternal great-great grandfather, Marshall Cole—a contrast with their dark skin.

Adrian had always taken a laid-back approach to life. With an "I got this" attitude, he didn't lack confidence. He made a game plan and stuck to it.

When Dolan had graduated college, Adrian had become a success story on his job and had felt that an education could wait until he eventually enrolled part-time. Then, his cousin had thrown caution to the wind and married his college sweetheart, leaving Adrian solo in his bachelor status. When Dolan's daughter, Laura, had come along two years later, Adrian had been no closer to finding a sweetheart of his own.

"I agree that I could have handled the situation better with the doctor, but it was like a punch line to a joke. I wasn't expecting all that drama for a ticket." Adrian chuckled. "It's good I didn't have anything in my mouth, because I would have sprayed her down like a sprinkler."

Dolan shook his head. He didn't seem amused. Leave it to his ever-serious cousin to find nothing funny about what had happened. Adrian thought that if he were to post a video of the encounter on social media, it would probably go viral. Or maybe he was exaggerating. Anyway, he tried to keep his personal life private and use social media for business purposes only.

"If this woman is as beautiful as you say, then you blew your chances if you were trying to hit on her," Dolan said with a pointed stare.

Maybe he would have been, if he had room in his schedule for a social life. But, between work and graduate school, Adrian didn't have time for romance.

Just then, seven-year-old Laura entered the room. Her bottom lip was puckered. Something was definitely wrong.

"Excuse me, Daddy. I can't find Holly's shoes." She flopped down next to her father, snuggled under his arm, and whimpered as if it was a major catastrophe.

"Who's Holly?" Adrian asked.

"Her doll," Dolan replied. He kissed the top of Laura's full head of hair. Too bad Dolan hadn't mastered how to comb it.

Laura's soulful brown eyes could melt a person's heart, and her wide smile, albeit with missing teeth, was contagious. The girl definitely took after her mother. "I found Holly and some of your other dolls on the bathroom floor again, so I put them in your toy box," Dolan said. "Remember what I told you about leaving your toys everywhere?"

She nodded.

"Next time, I just may give them away to another little girl who wants them," he added, sternly yet gently.

"No, Daddy!" Laura jumped up. "I'll be more careful." She gave him a kiss, then bestowed some affection on Adrian before skipping away.

Dolan had his parenting skills down pat. "You have the patience of a mother," Adrian told him.

Dolan grunted, shifting in his seat. He was always uncomfortable when it came to receiving compliments about the job he was doing as a single dad, continually questioning his balance between discipline and love.

"Do I have a choice?" he finally asked.

Both men were quiet for a moment.

Then Dolan shook his head. "Who could have known Denise would have an aneurysm at twenty-eight? Twenty-eight! She gave me Laura. Every day, I learn something new, like how to be sensitive to what's important in my little girl's life. One day, she'll be a grown woman, and I want her to know how a man should treat her."

Adrian looked away. Was his cousin indirectly calling him out? "Thanks for making me feel lower than low with the doctor. I guess I owe her an apology." He stood. "I guess I'd better head home. I still have that paper to write, and I have clients coming in this week."

"All right, Mr. Car Salesman." Dolan grinned as he got to his feet and gave him a hug.

"Man, I'm not going to let you get on my bad side," Adrian told him. "How long have I been a transportation problem solver, and you still don't have it right? And we can match salaries any day."

"The comparison's hardly fair," Dolan protested. "You don't have the additional expenses of a significant other or a daughter or after-school childcare or school tuition...."

Adrian held up his hand. "I get your point. I'm sure I'll get to that place in life—later."

As Adrian drove home, the doctor's face flashed in his memory. If it wasn't for her lab coat, he wouldn't know how to find her. But a quick glance at the emblem had given him her name. Minutes after arriving at his Maryland Heights condo, he went online and Googled her. She was a pediatrician at Cardinal Glennon Children's Hospital, according to its Web site. And her Facebook profile picture was stunning.

If Adrian were in the market for a woman, she would be his first choice. He'd been a fool to laugh at her predicament. He owed her an apology, if for no other reason than to leave an open door for a future business transition. So, he texted the florist that his car dealership routinely used for special occasions and ordered flowers to be delivered the next day.

Closing his eyes, he took a deep breath. "Conscience cleared."

"How beautiful!" Brecee practically kissed the flowers exploding from the purple and yellow ceramic vase on the front desk as she strolled into the emergency department at noon on Monday just before her shift.

"They're for you." The receptionist, Veda, grinned mischievously.

"Me?" Blinking, Brecee patted her chest. "Seriously?"

When her coworker nodded, Brecee began to rack her brain, wondering who would have sent them. Any dates that her brother-in-law had set up for her with colleagues or other professional acquaintances of his had fizzled. She came up with nothing, so she gave in, reaching for the envelope and sliding out the card.

> *Our chance meeting got off to a poor start. I'm sorry I found amusement in your discomfort. That was not my intention. Can I make it up to you? Breakfast at the same bread company, or at another place of your choosing?*
>
> —*Adrian Cole*

He'd included his phone number.

"Memory refreshed now?" Veda teased.

"Yep." Brecee didn't say anything more as she stuck the card back in the plastic holder and dropped it in her purse. "It is okay if I leave the flowers here until my shift ends?"

"Of course! I'm a divorced mother of three...." Veda rolled her neck. "I can pretend that someone sent them to me. They'll be safe here, Doc."

Veda seemed always content and in good spirits. By now, Brecee should have stopped being surprised by all the baptized believers the Lord had placed in her path. God knew that Christians needed moral support now more than ever before.

Smiling, Brecee continued through the door toward the nurses' station. Adrian's note had reminded her of the latest development in the saga of her first-ever ticket.

While Shae was still visiting her on Sunday afternoon, they'd had a phone chat with their two older sisters in Philly. Of course, big-mouth Shae had told Stacy and Shari what had happened, and then Shari, a criminal defense attorney, had encouraged Brecee to check out the National Minority Bar Association Directory.

As the baby of the family, Brecee had always accused her sisters of bullying her. But, as she'd gotten older, she'd come to understand that they had her back. "Fine," Brecee had agreed. Ashley, the charge nurse, looked up as Brecee signed her name to the board to let everyone know she had arrived and was on duty. Brecee glanced at the names of the other attending doctors on shift who were supervising residents, and saw that her colleague Dr. Regina Reed, a good friend and also a sister in Christ, was back from vacation.

Once the charge nurse had briefed her on the number of patients waiting in the examining rooms and their symptoms, she went to the doctors' charting room, where they reviewed patients' notes and files.

Regina stood with a smile.

"Welcome back, stranger," Brecee greeted her. "How was your vacation after the medical conference?"

"Miami was fine. I didn't want to come back."

Brecee thought of Regina as the baby sister she never had. They were so much alike in mannerisms and appearance that many people thought they were related, but Regina had an edge. She had killer dimples, like Brecee's sister Shari.

"I'm guessing you saw that gorgeous bouquet in the waiting area," Regina said with a smirk. "What have you been up to in my absence? I was gone just seven days." She folded her arms, waiting for the scoop.

Laughing, Brecee got situated at the table and opened the first patient file. Some people could be ignored, but Regina wasn't one of them. The two of them often joked that with her gift of subtle hounding, Regina could convince an innocent person to confess his guilt.

"I can't believe you waited until I was gone to go out on a date," she added with a pout. "Which doctor this time?"

Brecee shrugged. "No doctor. Just a jerk."

"Mmm-hmm. A jerk with good taste. I want to hear all about him."

Regina's demand had to be put on hold as the Monday madhouse began. Brecee left to check on the status of a four-year-old girl who had been hit by a car, then went to confer with a resident on treatment options. Next, she was pulled away to take one call after another. Since Cardinal Glennon was a level 1 Pediatric Trauma Center, she had to facilitate the transfer of patients from neighboring hospitals who had been admitted over the weekend.

Although Brecee specialized in pediatric emergency medicine and was certified in advanced trauma life support and pediatric advanced life support, she always prayed for God to use her to save a child's life, knowing that without His aid, human methods of treatment failed.

The day got so busy that she had to skip dinner. By the time her shift ended, Brecee had treated five head injuries, four of which had required emergency surgery. On the way out the door, she glanced at the floral arrangement waiting for her. The blossoms seemed to brighten the waiting room.

As Brecee was about to grab them, another doctor pulled her into a conversation; and then, before she knew it, Brecee had walked outside and was standing at her car. Too tired to retrace her steps inside, she got behind the wheel and drove off. She would have to get the flowers tomorrow. Calling Mr. Cole would have to wait, too.

CHAPTER FOUR

Women! Evidently, Adrian's apology had not been accepted, judging by Dr. Carmen's failure to call. In spite of her snub, he'd had a pleasant, productive day at the dealership, forging relationships with several associates of a longtime client who was the CEO of a pharmaceutical firm.

With a few more verbal commitments, Adrian could finish another month strong.

The casual, low-key demeanor he'd always adopted toward his customers always seemed to work. That was Adrian's personality. He was methodical in his thinking and meticulous in his approach, but that was before Dr. Brecee Carmen. It was as if his suave demeanor had expired.

He dismissed the memory of his olive-branch gesture as he entered his condo. The selling point of the two-story unit had been the balcony off one of the two upstairs bedrooms. His place was mostly spacious, except for the kitchen—with only a bar counter area for eating, it wasn't family-friendly. Yet, it worked for him.

In the kitchen, Adrian unwrapped the leftovers of the lunch he had purchased from the Dierbergs grocery store near the dealership. He quickly arranged the slice of turkey and vegetable medley on a plate, and popped it in the microwave. While he waited for it to reheat, he stretched out on the sofa and stared at the fireplace that was demanding a cleaning after a severely cold winter.

He picked up the TV remote and pointed it at the flat-screen mounted to the wall. Another episode of *Castle* was ending, and then KMMD-TV news teased its headlines. The microwave beeped at the same time Adrian blinked. Reporter Shae Maxwell's face flashed on the screen. His jaw dropped at the same time his microwave alerted him again that his food wouldn't stay hot forever.

The resemblance between Shae Maxwell and Dr. Carmen was undeniable. It was like seeing double. Adrian recalled when the news anchor had married Cardinals outfielder Rahn Maxwell. They were considered a local celebrity couple. Now, what was her maiden name? After a few minutes, his memory came through for him. "Carmen!" He snapped his fingers. The two were definitely related, if not twins.

Adrian didn't know the details of the story Shae Maxwell was covering right now, only that a child was involved. Immediately, he wondered if Dr. Carmen was in the emergency room.

Keeping his eyes on the screen, he got up and walked backward into the kitchen, grabbed his plate from the microwave, and returned to the sofa. He chewed and swallowed without savoring his dinner.

This changed everything. It was no longer about a personal apology but possible business connections. Adrian had clients who played football for the St. Louis Rams and hockey for the St. Louis Blues, but he had yet to introduce himself to the right person within the Cardinals' camp. In his line of work, image was everything. Clients drove luxury vehicles to show their status in society or to give an impression of wealth. Now, he had to get Dr. Carmen had to accept his apology.

Adrian reached for the phone and pulled up Dolan's number and touched the screen.

He answered with a yawn on the first ring. "I appreciate your keeping me in the loop with your bonuses, but not at almost eleven at night."

"You won't believe who my crying doctor is related to," Adrian told him. "Try to guess."

"I have no idea," Dolan said dryly.

"Shae Maxwell from KMMD."

Dolan let out a slow whistle, suddenly sounded alert. "That sister is gorgeous. I had a crush on her until Rahn took her off the market. You mean to say you couldn't see the resemblance when you met the doctor? Maybe it's her sister."

"Probably, but no, I didn't." Adrian was a little irritated with himself for that oversight, too. "She had her sunglasses on for most of our conversation, and when she did remove them—briefly—her eyes and face were red."

"Okay," Dolan said, with another loud yawn that made his ear pop. "Now that you've seen the error of your ways, what do you plan to do about it?"

"Restore my good name."

"That's it?" He chuckled. "If she looks like Shae Maxwell, how can you not be interested in her on a personal level?"

"Maybe later," Adrian said offhandedly. "First, I've got to do damage control."

"You snooze, you lose, buddy," Dolan said before signing off.

After a few minutes, Adrian headed upstairs for bed. Maybe he had been on a dating sabbatical for too long, but now was not the time to start something. Not when he had so little of himself to invest in a relationship.

Plus, unlike Dolan, Adrian didn't believe in instant attraction. When it came to women, he liked to be observant and read a lady's body language. See if she was the real deal by what she said and did. How could any man know those things in the blink of an eye? Relationships took time, which was exactly what his previous dates had done—put him on a timer. Adrian Cole could not be placed in a box.

He wanted a soul mate, someone who had been set aside just for him. Now, where was that woman? That was his last thought before he climbed under the covers and drifted off to sleep.

The following morning, Adrian woke up debating whether he should reach out to Shae Maxwell. His excuse, which was the truth, was to make sure her sister had received the flowers and his apology.

Between meeting with potential clients and following up on referrals, Adrian didn't have any downtime until late that afternoon. In his office, he looked up the number for Channel 7. His heart pounded as he phoned the newsroom and waited for his call to be transferred.

"This is Shae Maxwell."

Having expected to be directed to her voice mail, Adrian was momentarily speechless. "H-hi, Mrs. Maxwell," he stammered. He couldn't say he was a fan, because he seldom watched the news; when he did, he jumped from station to station. "My name is Adrian Cole, and I've been trying to reach Dr. Brecee Carmen—"

"Hmm, so *you're* the jerk who gave my sister a hard time."

Whoa. Adrian wasn't expecting the pit bull reception. He briefly moved the phone away from his ear, but he could still hear her chewing him out, using words like "disrespectful," "unkind," and "insensitive."

Adrian cleared his throat, preparing to do more damage control. "Mrs. Maxwell, your sister was distraught, and I was genuinely concerned. In no way was I trying to be cruel."

"So, the flowers were your way of making up for your rudeness?" She didn't give him time to answer. "Well, don't expect a return call. My sister is a dedicated doctor who saves children's lives every day. She had a particularly stressful week, with several patients who didn't recover from their injuries, and she was exhausted."

Adrian dropped his head, feeling like the jerk he'd been labeled as. "I'm so sorry to hear that, and sorry I bothered you, Mrs. Maxwell. Please let Dr. Carmen know that I apologize for my insensitivity." He disconnected the call and exhaled. After two for two, he was done. Those sisters were nutcases.

⌒

Brecee couldn't believe what her sister was telling her. "Adrian Cole called you?" She had just gotten home from the hospital. Her day had been uneventful—broken limbs, some scrapes, and a few bruises, but nothing that would require surgery. Two ambulances had arrived just as her shift was ending, though.

"Yes," Shae said, "and after I got through chewing him out for messing with my sister, I felt so bad, I checked the caller ID, then sent him flowers with a note of apology."

Some things never change, Brecee thought. Shae knew how to give someone a piece of her mind without crossing the "sin" line. And whenever she tried to take on the tough-girl persona, she always felt bad afterward.

Brecee was trying to reach a point in her spiritual walk where she would no longer say the first thing that came to mind.

"Thanks for defending me, Sis. But if Mr. Cole was really interested in finding out if I received the flowers, he could have called the hospital. How did he put us together, anyway?"

"Duh," Shae said. "Everyone thinks that we look alike. Remember how Dad used to call us twins?"

"Yep. Last time he said that was fifteen years ago." Brecee sighed. "I still really miss him."

"Me, too," Shae muttered.

Brecee was beginning to wonder if this mystery man had had an ulterior motive for contacting her sister. Some of the station's viewers wanted to connect with Shae, Rahn or both for business purposes or personal reasons. "Anyway, the flowers are truly lovely," she said. "I finally brought them home tonight. I meant to call him yesterday to thank him, but it was a horrific afternoon."

"You don't have to tell me," Shae said with a sigh. "I covered the child abuse story, remember?"

Somehow, the four Carmen sisters had chosen careers that tied them to children: Stacy was a teacher, shaping young minds; Shari was dogmatic when she had to defend teenagers of criminal accusations; Shae had won Emmy awards for her news stories, involving children; and Brecee's passion was to try to fix whatever was broken or help a child recover whenever he was sick.

"Thanks for sticking up for me, Big Sis." Brecee smiled.

"Well, I thought I would let you know," Shae told her. "You can decide if you think his determination is sweet or suspicious. You did say he was kind of cute—"

"No 'kind of' about it," Brecee said, picturing his face. "He was definitely fine."

"Really? Well, if you think it's harassment, pick your poison: Shari with a lawsuit or Rahn settling things out of court." Shae paused, and Brecee could hear the blare of a police scanner in the background. "Listen, I've got to go. I'm being summoned to cover a house fire. Love you."

"Love you, too."

As Brecee made herself dinner and then enjoyed a long bath, she couldn't stop thinking about Adrian. Why had he called her sister? Shaking her head, she concluded that the man was odd.

Thirty minutes later, her phone buzzed with a text message from her sister Stacy: You know, this never would have happened if you had called the man when you got the flowers and told him thank you.

Brecee laughed at her oldest sister's bossiness. How had Shae managed to find time to tattle on her while covering a house fire?

With three sisters, there were never any secrets. Growing up, that had kept sibling rivalry to a minimum. Now, with all four of them in their thirties, Brecee found it annoying. Stacy, Shari, and Shae believed that Brecee's bark would scare all the men away. What a silly notion, considering she did go on dates from time to time. Besides, even with all the noise she made, she didn't bite. She just wanted the Lord's stamp of approval on the right man to marry and have children with. Despite her professional aspirations, she would be happy to switch roles to a stay-at-home mom, like many of her former female colleagues had done.

Our sister has a big mouth, Brecee texted back.

Let me know what happens after you talk to him.

"Right," she griped, rolling her eyes. She used the microphone to dictate her next text as she paced across her bedroom: "Stacy, the man apologized, and all is well between us."

A few minutes later, Stacy called, with Shari on the line.

"Okay," was Stacy's greeting. "For the romantic in me, call him. Who knows if the chance meeting was part of God's plan for you?"

"I'm not feeling what you're feeling," Brecee argued. "What man laughs at a woman in distress? That tells me he doesn't respect women."

"Flowers tell me he knows when he has messed up," Stacy countered.

"The breakfast invitation sounds worth a second chance," Shari added.

Shari's mention of a second chance made Brecee think of the one God had given Shari and Garrett. Brecee was still amazed by their testimony.

Regardless of the pros her sisters raised, Brecee had her cons about Adrian, and she'd never been one to back down. "Well, since Shae has a big mouth to tell you both about the phone call, I hope she tells Rahn that a strange man called her, because you know he doesn't play when it comes to his wife!"

All three sisters chuckled.

"Does Shae still have bodyguards?" Stacy asked.

"Is Rahn still her husband? Do you have to ask?" Brecee groaned. "Girl, yes. From time to time, we see them when they want to be seen. At least when they come to church, they're hearing the Word. Definitely, when we're shopping. I wish one of them had been tailing me when I was stopped by the police. Maybe he could've intercepted that ticket."

That brought the discussion back to Adrian Cole, and no matter how much Brecee protested, she was outnumbered.

"Okay, it's time for a vote," Stacy stated.

Voting was the way the Carmen sisters put an end to a discussion. They'd adopted the method when Stacy had started dating, and ever since then, whenever the conversation centered on a man, there were no secrets. Each held the other accountable to stay pure until marriage.

"Shae voted yes, by the way," Stacy said.

Twisting her lips, Brecee exhaled. "Figures."

"And my vote is, yes, you should return the man's call," Stacy added. "Shari?"

"Yes," Shari said. "This man might be part of God's plans for you."

Brecee rolled her eyes. "I think all three of you are blowing this out of proportion, but I'll make the call tomorrow before my shift."

"Uh-uh," Stacy said. "It's not even ten o'clock. Call now, and leave a message, if need be," she ordered her. "We'll talk later."

"Love you," she and Shari both said in singsong before disconnecting.

Brecee sat on her bed and stared at her phone. With her sisters' prompting, her interest was suddenly piqued to know Adrian's story. As far as meeting for breakfast, however, she had a busy week ahead. There was a one-day seminar on pediatric trauma she had to attend at the university, and she was way overdue for an oil change. She also had an early-morning hair appointment on Friday, and nothing got in the way of that.

She figured she might as well get this call over with. She could thank him without sharing breakfast. Brecee retrieved the card with his number from her purse and called him. She was surprised when he answered right away.

"Mr. Cole? It's Dr. Carmen."

"Please, call me Adrian." His voice sounded pleasant and nice. It made her smile. "You're calling either to chew me out, too, or to thank me for the flowers. Which is it?"

Already, the man was rubbing her the wrong way. But she could be just as direct. "Both. It was rude of me not to call you yesterday for the flowers.

They are beautiful." She paused, recalling the many compliments she'd received from the staff and a few patients' parents. "However, because of my busy schedule this week, I'm sorry that I must decline your invitation for a breakfast date."

"You're welcome for the flowers," he said. "We could do lunch or dinner, instead, and there is always next week."

This man was really not letting up, but she wasn't finished. "The flowers were more than sufficient to convey your apology. But I do have a problem with your calling my sister. Was it really that serious?"

"Dr. Carmen, although I would love to engage in more friendly banter, I have a paper that is due at midnight."

"Is that your way of avoiding an answer?" she pressed him as she flopped back on her bed.

"Once I made the connection between you two, I called her in hopes that she would speak to you on my behalf and get you to talk to me. Unfortunately, I didn't expect to hear from you at this hour. So, please forgive me if I seem rude, but I really do need to finish this assignment."

Why did she feel so disappointed? She had questions for him—what school he attended, his course of study, where he worked, and so on. Stacy would be crushed to learn that she hadn't gotten answers. And even more so that this man evidently wasn't interested in her.

"I understand," Brecee said. "I have a busy day ahead of me, anyway. I need to get up extra early to allow time for an oil change before heading to the hospital."

"Wait! If you bring your Lexus to Broadway Motors in Ladue first thing in the morning, I can get you in and out."

She lifted an eyebrow as if he could see her. "So, you have connections, do you?"

"I work there. I'm a transportation problem solver."

"Okay," she said slowly, repeating the title in her head. "I'm sorry, but what does that occupation entail, exactly?"

"I build relationships—business and otherwise. If a person is in need of transportation, Broadway Motors has a vehicle to fit any budget."

A car salesman? Brecee wanted to laugh out loud at him, just like he had done to her, but she didn't believe in tit for tat. There was no way for him to have known she'd had a rough week. "Ah, so it's a business relationship you're trying to build?"

"Both," he said. "I'll have breakfast waiting for you. Is eight a.m. okay?"

Just to be difficult, Brecee countered, "Seven thirty."

"Done. See you then." He disconnected the call.

What have I gotten myself into? she wondered.

Brecee knew nothing about this man, except that he had exquisite taste in flowers.

She looked forward to tomorrow, so she could find out more.

CHAPTER FIVE

Startled awake by the alarm trumpeting in his ear, Adrian sat up in bed and blinked to bring his surroundings into focus. Then he remembered what day it was, and what he had been doing up past midnight.

He would lose ten points for submitting his paper after the deadline—no excuses were acceptable, not even blaming Dr. Carmen for invading his thoughts after their brief conversation last night. However, he would be fine. Adrian worked hard and studied harder.

Begrudgingly, he rolled out of bed and dropped to the floor for seventy-five push-ups, then hit the shower.

As he dressed meticulously in a dark fitted suit and the tie that always received rave compliments, Dr. Carmen continued to occupy his mind. He was getting a second chance with her, and he was determined to make a good impression this time. Whether it would result in business or pleasure, Adrian wanted to be on top of his game, even if he'd gotten only four and a half hours of sleep. Spring break couldn't come soon enough.

Satisfied with his appearance, he left his condo, got behind the wheel of his Audi, and drove toward the ramp for I-270 southbound. He grimaced at the heavy traffic and checked the time on his dashboard. It wouldn't look good for him to be late.

After inching along for a while, he finally reached the exit for Ladue. He had twenty-two minutes and no time to spare to stop for breakfast.

Approaching the dealership, Adrian eyed the service area. There was no sign of Dr. Carmen's car, so he continued on to the plaza where St. Louis Bread Company was located.

He zipped into a parking spot and raced across the lot. A group of elderly ladies beat him to the door and flirted with him as he held it open for them. He kept a smile in place as he counted six of them. Once inside, he sidestepped the group and stood at the counter, only to stare at the menu board. Now what? Adrian had no idea whether Dr. Carmen drank regular or decaf, lattes or cappuccinos. All he remembered was her nibbling on oatmeal cookies.

The cashier peeked impatiently over his shoulder and frowned at the line that was probably building behind him. "Okay...." Adrian ordered an assortment of bagels and pastries. "Will you add two oatmeal cookies, too, please?"

"Is that all, sir?"

"Um, no. Can I also have a latte? I'll probably need three shots of espresso. And a medium roast coffee. To go."

After paying, Adrian stepped aside, keeping his eyes on his watch as he waited for his order. Thankfully, on the drive to the dealership, traffic cooperated with him. He grinned to himself when he pulled into the lot at the same time as Dr. Carmen.

Adrian climbed out of his car, lifted the bag of breakfast, and walked swiftly over to the black Lexus. "Good morning." He offered her a smile as he watched her step out, even though he was disappointed that the shapely legs he remembered were covered with a pair of hospital scrubs.

Without her high heels, the top of her head reached his chin. Her hair was pinned up in a bun. Removing her glasses was a wow moment for him. She did it with such finesse, it was like watching in slow motion. Adrian had to suck in his breath to keep from ogling, but that just gave him a whiff on her perfume. It wasn't too strong but nice and soft.

Swallowing, Adrian got his manhood under control. "I can show you to the waiting room, and then I'll drive your car to the service center."

"Thanks."

She hardly looked old enough to be anyone's doctor; and yet, despite her youthful appearance, she had an air of confidence and sophistication. And she really did look like her news anchor sister. Both were beautiful.

Tilting her head to indicate the bag of food, she smiled. "Do you need any help carrying that?"

"I got it," Adrian said as she fell into step beside him. He escorted her inside the showroom, which had yet to come alive at the early hour. As she sat on the leather sectional in the customer lounge, Adrian noticed her graceful curves that no scrubs could hide.

She looked up at him. "What?"

"Uh, nothing. I'll just get this food set up on the counter over there, and you can help yourself." With his back to her, Adrian could sense her presence as she quietly approached.

She laughed, and Adrian liked the sound. It seemed to soften the aura she exuded. "Are you feeding the entire dealership?"

He turned to her and smiled. "Nope, just you. Let me take your car back to the service department, so I can get you in and out, as promised."

Once in the garage, Adrian had to use his negotiation skills to get what he wanted.

"Baseball tickets," Gary Hite, the service manager, demanded.

"You got it," Adrian assured him.

"They better be good seats." Gary laughed, then waved a service technician over and told him to drive Dr. Carmen's car to the next available spot for an oil change.

On his way back to the showroom, Adrian stopped when he saw Dolan pull up in his Audi, courtesy of a great deal from Adrian. The two shook hands when Dolan stepped out of the car.

"Hi, Cousin Adrian!" Laura spouted from the back as Dolan unfastened the belts of her car seat. Once liberated, she climbed out and immediately gave him a hug. Looking up at him, she grinned, displaying the bud of a new tooth in the gap that had been there.

"How's my favorite cousin?" He held open the door to the showroom. "Laura, you know where the lounge is. I have something in there you'll probably like."

As Laura scampered away, Adrian turned back to her father and folded his arms across his chest. "So, what are you doing out here so early? And why isn't Laura in school?"

He wanted to get back to Dr. Carmen, but she could wait. Family was more important.

Dolan leaned closer and glanced in the direction of the lounge, then lowered his voice to say, "Laura had an irregular heartbeat at her checkup yesterday, and the doctor wanted her to have an electrocardiogram, so I took her to St. John's Mercy for the test. Since she knows where her favorite cousin works, she begged me to stop by here before taking her to school. I told her it was too early, but imagine my surprise to see your car here."

"Is she all right?" Adrian asked, feeling his heart pounding. "Do they know what's wrong with her?" The questions were forming faster than he could ask them.

"Now who's acting like a mother hen?" Dolan grinned. "Dr. Taylor didn't seem too concerned, but she wanted to rule out the cause of her arrhythmia." He paused. "So why are you here? Is there some type of early-bird special on Benzes?" he joked.

"Nope." Adrian wiggled an eyebrow. "But I did have an important person to impress. Dr. Carmen is here for a complimentary oil change, and I'm treating her to breakfast while she waits."

"You sure know how to sweeten the pot." Dolan chuckled and patted his stomach. "Suddenly, I'm thinking I didn't get enough to eat for breakfast."

Eying his cousin, Adrian knew exactly what was going on in his head. Dolan wanted to meet her. As if a starting pistol had gone off, they were suddenly engaged in an unspoken speed-walking contest to the lounge.

⌒

Brecee was perched on the sofa. She had just sent a group text message to her sisters, alerting them that she had called Adrian and was now enjoying breakfast as she waited on an oil change.

As she crunched on an oatmeal cookie, sipping on her latte loaded with expresso, she wondered how Adrian had known she needed the extra boost of caffeine. The cookies alone got him out of the doghouse.

Stacy replied first: Freebies. I love freebies. See, there was a reason you and Adrian met. Bon appétit.

Shae was next: We both live in the Show-me State now, and you know what Missourians say: "Show me." He'd better be a nice guy! But remember, the devil has decoys out there.

Shari weighed in last: God orders our steps. I hope you don't have on heels that might cause you to stumble. :)

Laughing, Brecee shook her head. Then she looked up into the face of a cute little girl with long thick hair brushed back in a fussy ponytail.

"Hello," the girl said in the sweetest voice. "What's your name?"

Brecee smiled. "Hi, there. I'm Sabrece Carmen, but everyone calls me Brecee."

"I'm Laura." The girl waved, then turned away, as if the treats on the counter had called to her. She bounced over to the food and perused the selection, then grabbed a napkin and used it to pull a bagel out of the box.

Brecee was impressed by her manners. "You can sit next to me, if you like." She patted the spot on her right.

"Okay!" Laura hurried to her side and wasted no time making herself comfortable. Then she bowed her head and clasped her hands. "Thank You, Jesus, for this bagel, and for taking the bad stuff out. Amen."

Amused, Brecee watched the girl bite daintily into the bread. This was why she'd pursued a career in pediatric medicine. She loved watching the innocence of children, and keeping them healthy, or making them better.

As the child ate, Brecee scanned her attire. Her Mary Jane shoes were hardly scuffed, and her pink pant set was neatly pressed. She looked like the model little girl—fresh, pretty, and pristine.

When Laura had chewed and swallowed, she looked at Brecee. "Are you a doctor?"

"I am." Brecee ignored another incoming text that was probably from one of her sisters.

Laura took another bite of her bagel. "What kind?"

"Your kind. I take care of little ladies like you, as well as babies and teenagers."

"I need a doctor."

"You do?" Brecee frowned at the girl.

"Uh-huh." She nodded. "Something might be wrong with my heart."

"Your heart?" She reached for her bag. Her sisters called her OCD, but Brecee didn't mind the stereotype; she didn't go anywhere without her stereoscope. "Do you mind if I take a listen?" she asked, pulling the instrument out.

The girl stuck out her chest. "My mommy died because of her heart."

"I'm sorry to hear that." Had the girl inherited a congenital heart defect of some type? She rested the chestpiece against Laura's ribs and listened. The heartbeat was slightly irregular. Where was her father? Brecee wondered if he had taken her to see a specialist yet. She would gladly refer them to one of the pediatric cardiologists at the hospital.

"It's okay, because my Mommy is asleep in Jesus," Laura told her. "God's going to blow the trumpet, and she's going to wake up like me, and we're going to see Jesus together."

This little girl must have a sanctified daddy who knew his Bible. Bravo, Lord! Laura was precious and so smart. Brecee wanted a daughter just like her one day.

She lost track of time as Laura enthralled her with conversations about clothes and toys and wanting to be a doctor someday.

Feeling eyes on her, Brecee looked up and saw Adrian and another man standing in the doorway. Both were equally handsome. When Laura jumped to her feet and ran to greet the man with a sparkle in his eyes, Brecee identified the father.

"Hello," she said, almost breathless. "You have an incredible daughter."

He grinned, and Brecee noticed that his smile was slightly crooked. "I won't argue you on that one. I'm Dolan Cole." He approached and shook her hand. "His cousin," he added, nodding at Adrian.

"Oh." She glanced at Adrian, who didn't seem too happy being ignored. But she turned back to Dolan. "I'm Sabrece Carmen, but please call me—"

"Brecee," Laura supplied. "Isn't that a pretty name, Daddy?"

"Gorgeous."

He gave her an appreciative perusal, and Brecee let him. Could this widower be a Godsend?

"I've long been a fan of your sister, but it appears by my daughter's smile that I need to switch my allegiance." He laughed, and Brecee joined him.

Adrian cleared his throat, and all three of them looked at him.

"Dr. Carmen."

Laura jumped up and down. "You can call her Bre—"

"That was for us, pumpkin." Dolan winked at his daughter.

Brecee was amused at the apparent rivalry between the cousins. She imagined they teased each other just like she and her sisters did.

Gritting his teeth, Adrian narrowed his eyes at Dolan before facing Brecee again with a smile. "Your oil change is done, and I even had them run your car through the car wash."

"That was nice of you." Brecee gave him a grin. "Thanks for breakfast. The latte was just the way I liked it. The company was great, too."

That earned her a hug from Laura.

Putting her stereoscope away, Brecee dug inside her purse for a business card, which she handed to Dolan. "I'm an emergency medicine pediatrician. Laura told me about her heart, and I can recommend one of my colleagues, if you'd like. Laura is truly a special little girl."

"Thank you," he choked, just before Adrian ushered her quickly out of the lounge to her waiting chariot.

Now that is a man, she thought.

Dolan Cole had instilled his knowledge of God, loving nature, and exemplary behavior into his daughter.

Lord, I want a man with those qualities.

As she walked away, God whispered, *Two hearts will beat as one.*

CHAPTER SIX

Adrian couldn't believe his cousin's gall. Dr. Carmen had never given him such a kind look, not even after finding out that he'd thrown in a free car wash on top of the oil change and complimentary breakfast. Then again, Dolan hadn't laughed at her misfortune, either.

After the three of them had escorted Dr. Carmen to her Lexus, Adrian stood there with his hands stuffed in his pockets and watched, annoyed, as his cousin and his daughter waved Dr. Carmen when she drove off.

Once she was out of view, Adrian nudged Dolan. "What's wrong with you?"

"What?" He had the nerve to feign cluelessness.

"You know what. You just stepped into my territory."

As Dolan helped Laura into her car seat, he glanced over his shoulder at Adrian. "When did you set up a perimeter? You're the one who said you weren't interested."

His cousin should have known better than to believe him, especially when there was a woman involved. They had horsed around plenty as children, but they'd never had a knock-down, drag-out fight. Right now, however, Adrian was tempted to deliver his first punch to the jaw. Taking a deep breath, he banished the thought. "Well, that was before today. Not only was she not crying, but she knows how to wear scrubs."

"I warned you, cuz: If you snooze, you lose." Dolan slid behind the wheel of his Audi.

Yes, he had. Adrian stepped back as Dolan started the engine. "Listen, we've never competed for the same woman…." He let the rest of his statement die on the tip of his tongue. They weren't attracted to the same type of women anyway. Hopefully, his gesture this morning would be enough to establish a business relationship with the lovely doctor, at the very least.

He decided to let Dolan do his thing. He spun around and headed back inside.

A group of his associates met him at the door with a bagel salute. They were like mice. If there was food within a one-mile radius, they could sniff out the crumbs.

"Hey, Adrian. Thanks, man," said Greg Watts, a fellow transportation problem solver, before taking another bite.

"You're welcome." Since he was there early, he figured he might as well be productive. He marched into the lounge for a cup of coffee. He would need it.

He lifted the cup from the holder, took a sip, and smacked his lips. This was not the latte with the extra spots of espresso. That's right—Dr. Carmen had taken it.

He couldn't help but wonder, in the farthest recesses of his mind, if they had more in common than their coffee preferences.

⌒

After another uneventful day at the hospital, Brecee hadn't been home ten minutes when Stacy texted, inviting her—more like commanding her—to participate in a sisters' video chat. She had just enough time to change out of her scrubs before the inquisition began.

"So, how did it go?" Stacy asked once they all their faces were showing on the computer screen.

Brecee was surprised her mother was missing. The Carmen sisters had gotten their nosiness honestly. Annette Carmen was the ringleader.

Brecee grinned. "I'm glad I went."

"See?" Stacy pumped her hands in the air. "Older sisters always know best."

"Sometimes," Brecee corrected her. She felt herself blush. "He was charming and good-looking, and he has the most precious daughter—"

"Hold up." Shae blinked, twisting her lips. "Are we talking about the same guy? Adrian went from being at the bottom of your list bumped to the top?"

"Oh, no. Not Adrian." Brecee shook her head. "His cousin Dolan. He has a daughter named Laura who might have a heart condition...." Her sisters didn't stop her from rambling on and on until she needed to stop to catch her breath.

"Hmm. I'm not sure if you're more excited about the man or his child," Shari chimed in.

"What did the other Mr. Cole have to say while all this chemistry was mixing?" Stacy asked, then smirked.

Brecee strained her mind to think. "Nothing. But he was sweet enough to bring me coffee and oatmeal cookies. Plus, my car got a free oil change and a wash. Talk about service. He's probably a good salesman."

Everyone was quiet, as if they were disappointed, until Shae smiled. "In other news, my hubby is coming home soon. I can't wait to see him!" Shae looked ready to explode with happiness.

"So, I guess that means you don't need me to go with you to Variety the Children's Charity Dinner with the Stars?" Brecee never liked being a third wheel. "You know I don't mind babysitting Sabrina."

"I already have a babysitter, so, yes, you still need to go. Rahn has a game, but he'll join us afterward. You can keep me company until he gets there."

"I kept you company plenty of times when we shared a bedroom," Brecee reminded her.

They all laughed.

Stacy's husband, Ted, walked into their home office and brought his face close to the camera. He waved at the sisters, then stepped out of view and mumbled something to Stacy.

"Okay, babe," she told him. "Give me five minutes."

Ted was pure entertainment as he counted each finger on one hand, then backed out the room.

Brecee, Shari, and Shae chuckled at their brother-in-law's antics.

"Okay, I'd better hurry," Stacy told them. "Knowing Ted, he's set the timer on me. Let's pray, ladies."

Brecee closed her eyes and bowed her head as Stacy began, "Father God, in the name of Jesus, I thank You for my sisters. Thank You that, no matter the distance between us, our bond isn't broken, just as our bond with You is never broken. Please watch over my sisters and guide Brecee's heart in the man department. Show her who is for her."

Peeking with one eye, Brecee saw each sister with her hand outstretched toward the monitor as they prayed. Smiling, she closed her eye again as Stacy petitioned the Lord for their nation and its leaders, their children, and an endless list of others, until she finally whispered, "Amen."

The next morning, when Brecee returned to work, the emergency department was in chaos after an accident involving a school bus that had overturned. Several more victims were en route via medical helicopter.

As Brecee signed on for her shift, Ashley, the charge nurse, briefed her on the number of trauma patients. Her adrenaline kicked in as she and the staff stabilized the patients and made sure their airways weren't obstructed.

Before seeing any patient, Brecee always prayed that God would allow her to work calmly and effectively, and to reassure frantic parents that their children were in God's hands, as well as in the doctors' good hands. How many times had God whispered, "*Pray without ceasing*"? First Thessalonians 5:16–18 was in full force: "*Rejoice evermore. Pray without ceasing. In every thing give thanks: for this is the will of God in Christ Jesus concerning you.*"

Behind closed doors in the charting room, Brecee conferred with Regina.

"It looks like we have a couple patients with neurological injuries," Regina told her.

"I have an eight-year-old with severe injuries to the left leg and a seven-year-old with penetrating injuries," Brecee said. "I recommend we admit them immediately."

Regina nodded. "I'll have one of the nurses alert the surgical staff."

There was no time to waste; every year, in the U.S. alone, more than seven thousand children under fourteen years old nationally die from severe injuries, and Brecee refused to let that number rise.

"I'm concerned about patient A's blood pressure," Brecee said. "It's normal now, but the residents are monitoring the hemodynamics for any sudden changes." A moment later, she added, "Hopefully, we'll have some downtime to catch up on each other's weekend." Regina nodded as Brecee left to assess a patient in one of the treatment rooms.

By late afternoon, Brecee felt she had worked a double shift. She was tired and hungry. The staff had ordered takeout, and she was glad for the food. She was about to take her sandwich and salad to her office to eat when the night receptionist stopped her.

"Dr. Carmen, you had a delivery." She pointed to the vase of flowers on the counter. "With all the commotion earlier, the day receptionist forgot to tell you."

"Thanks, Mattie." Brecee smiled at God's natural beauty captured in the flowers. The Lord knew she needed them as a calming effect. Shifting her food container into her other hand, Brecee grabbed the vase and tucked it under her arm. Once in her office, she set the flowers on the desk and then ripped the envelope off the cellophane wrapping. It wasn't that she never received flowers, but twice in one week was any girl's delight. She hoped they were from Dolan. He seemed compatible with her, especially with his clear commitment to instill the love of Christ in his daughter's life.

She pulled out the card and frowned.

Thank you.

—Adrian

What he was thanking her for? Brecee wondered, but there wasn't time to solve the puzzle now, though, because her stomach was growling.

Her dinner was consumed before Brecee realized she had eaten it all. She stood and performed some stretching exercises, then returned to the emergency department for the last couple hours of her shift.

Brecee went home with her heart aching for the little ones and their families. She prayed especially for the two boys who were just barely clinging to life. Before she retired to bed that night, she got on her knees and kept praying until the anointed presence of God filled her bedroom and her mouth poured forth His heavenly language in other tongues.

When she stood, Laura Cole came to mind. Since she hadn't heard from Dolan, she decided to call Adrian.

"Hi, Adrian. It's Dr. Carmen."

"Ah, the lovely Dr. Sabrece Carmen," he greeted her crisply. "Why do you always keep me wondering if you've received what I've sent to you?"

How could she have forgotten about the latest floral arrangement? It had lifted her spirits, even if Dolan hadn't sent it. "I'm calling now," she said. "Doesn't that count? Thank you for the flowers. They are lovely, although I don't know why you felt the need to thank me."

"Because you came."

Brecee blinked. His reason was simple, but she found that somehow refreshing, appealing. Brecee liked simple.

And she was embarrassed for failing to properly thank him for all his kindnesses to her. "I also need to thank you for the oil change, the car wash, the tasty breakfast...."

He laughed, and the sound was contagious. "I get it. It was the least I could do, although I wish I could have spent some time getting to know you."

She wanted to ask in what way, but that would have sounded too much like flirting. "Believe me, I wasn't bored," she assured him. "Your little cousin was great company. By the way, I haven't heard from Dolan. How is Laura is doing?"

"She's fine."

That was it? Brecee wanted to ask if they'd gotten a diagnosis and established a treatment plan, but she didn't want to violate patient confidentiality. "Great," she replied. "Please tell Dolan I asked about her."

"I will. Since I have you on the phone, Dr. Carmen—or can I call you Brecee, as you told Dolan to?"

Was that a touch of jealousy she heard? *Nah.* "Of course."

"Thank you, Brecee. Do you have plans for Friday?"

"As a matter of fact, I do." She had committed to letting Shae drag her to that annual fund-raiser dinner—again.

"Then perhaps another time," he said, in a tone that indicated the conversation was over. "I'll make sure my cousins know you asked about them."

"Adrian?" she said softly, not liking the finality in her tone and blaming her aloofness for it. "You have excellent taste in flowers. And I like the scent of the air freshener they used in my car."

"Both remind me of you. I hope we'll talk soon."

The call left Brecee confused. Maybe Adrian was more complex than she'd thought.

She wondered if that was good or bad.

CHAPTER SEVEN

There was no such thing as "business as usual" in the emergency department, but Brecee and her staff welcomed broken bones and sprains over traumas any day. However, every change of season ushered in a new set of problems. With the advent of spring, the staff was sure to see more injuries due to bicycles, skateboards, roller blades, and the like. It was impossible to overstate the importance of helmets to the patients and their parents.

Unfortunately, everything was business as usual in Brecee's personal life. Spending time with Shae filled up her social calendar, usually from Friday through Sunday, unless Brecee went out with some of the other doctors from work.

On Friday evening, after a day of shopping and a hair appointment, Brecee had less than twenty minutes to finish dressing before the limo driver would pick her up for the affair Shae was dragging her to. The ride was courtesy of—or, rather, upon the insistence of—her famous baseball player brother-in-law. Brecee would have been happy to drive herself, but Rahn felt that whenever there was an after-five function, he and his plus-one—or plus-two—should arrive in style.

"Let my husband pamper us until your prince comes along," Shae always argued.

So Brecee had finally stopped protesting.

She stood in front of the full-length mirror on her closet door and admired her gown. The pastel blue number was form-fitting from the bustline past her hips, then flared out in a short train that swished when she walked.

Brecee usually wore her long hair straight or up in a bun, whatever was easier, but she'd had her hairstylist transform it into the mass of curls now swept off her neck and strategically gathered on top of her head.

Peeking out her bedroom window to the street below, she spied the white stretch limo pulling in front of her condo. With one last glance in the mirror, Brecee grabbed her wrap and her clutch purse, then turned off the lights as she made her way to the door. She opened it to find the driver standing there, poised to knock. "Dr. Carmen," he said with a nod. Then he held out his arm and escorted her to the limo.

Brecee climbed in and found Shae sitting there, posing with her smartphone clicking away.

"More selfies to send back home?" Brecee teased.

"You know it!" Shae said, then puckered up for the camera.

Ever since the birth of her daughter, Shae had taken pictures of everything and everyone to text to the rest of the family.

Shae wrapped an arm around Brecee and held her phone at arm's length. "Say cheese and hold it," she said, clicking away.

The driver shook his head as he shut the door.

The ride downtown to the Peabody Opera House took less than fifteen minutes. Seemingly bored with amateur photography, Shae stuffed her smartphone inside her purse and openly admired Brecee's curls.

"You're looking good, Sis," Brecee returned the compliment. "No wonder your husband has bodyguards protecting his cargo."

Shae's face and figure were a tad fuller since she'd had Sabrina. And while Brecee wasn't jealous of that, she wouldn't have minded getting the same glow from a happy marriage.

Slipping an arm through Brecee's, her sister whispered, "You know this isn't just for show. Rahn treats me like a princess at home. I'm so glad God worked everything out between us. I'm in love to stay." Shae wore a whimsical expression.

Brecee had yet to profess love to a man. Rahn had introduced her to some of his teammates, but she didn't want to live in the spotlight like he and Shae did. She got enough of that from spending time with them. "Maybe one day, I'll be able to say that, too," Brecee said with a sigh.

"You need to get out more," Shae insisted. "How else are you hoping to meet the man of your dreams?"

"And miss chaperoning you and Mr. Maxwell? Nah." Brecee stuck out her tongue.

She did get out, usually with colleagues for group activities—parties, staff softball games, and more parties. Shae kept her busy, too, always dragging her along to various events. At first, Brecee had thought it was a fun way to meet people and get to know her new city of residence. Now, she thought she would prefer a simple candlelit dinner with a genuinely Christian man. Unfortunately for her, most of the men at Bethesda Temple were either engaged or already married.

Brecee was the lone Carmen holdout. "Maybe St. Louis doesn't have any exciting eligible Christian bachelors for me." She paused with a sigh intended to produce the maximum effect on her sister's sympathies. "Maybe I should move back home, where all the fine men reside." She smirked as she waited for Shae's reaction.

"Don't even think about it!" Shae snapped in all seriousness. "Shari and Stacy have each other in Philly. I want you here with me—please."

In truth, Brecee had no desire to return home—not yet. She was closer with Shae than with her other two sisters, and she wasn't ready to relocate again. Brecee figured she would give herself five years in St. Louis. Then, at thirty-six, she would reevaluate her options.

After reassuring Shae that she had no intentions of going anywhere, Brecee glanced out the window. The streetlights sparkled on Lindell Street as they traversed the Central West End, passing Forest Park. The scene reminded her of The Oval on Benjamin Franklin Parkway back home in Philly, with its outdoor cafés, vivid night life, and various festivals.

"You're going to love the place where we're going to tonight," Shae interrupted her reverie. "I covered its grand reopening after the multimillion-dollar renovation. It was originally built in the mid-nineteen thirties as the Kiel Opera House. The attached auditorium closed in the nineties and was scheduled to be demolished to make way for Scott Trade Center."

Brecee tried to listen attentively. For Shae, one of the biggest perks of being a news anchor/reporter was having a chance to learn all about the city's culture and history. And she seemed to feel it was her duty to inform Brecee as a recent transplant to the "Gateway to the West." At times, Brecee could take it or leave it.

"Here's a little-known fact I found interesting: It was there that, in the mid-sixties, Frank Sinatra, Dean Martin, and Sammy Davis Jr. performed their only televised concert as the Rat Pack. Remember Johnny Carson? He was the emcee. It closed decades later."

"I'm sure Mother, Auntie and Uncle Bradford would appreciate those ancient tidbits," Brecee mumbled.

"Yep. But the grand reopening featured Jay Leno, Aretha Franklin, and Chuck Berry—at least they were from our lifetime."

"You know Mr. Berry is my idol," Brecee said, patting her chest.

In a sense, he was. When she was first learning how to play the guitar, she'd wanted to mimic his antics, foolishly figuring that if he could get away with them, so could she. Her parents weren't amused and had constantly reminded her that his type of behavior wasn't appropriate when performing for the Lord. Even so, with her rebellious streak, Brecee had tested her limits—with her mother, especially.

When the Arch appeared in the skyline, Brecee knew they were minutes from downtown. Shae transitioned from reporter mode to mommy mode by switching to her favorite subject—Sabrina.

As the unofficial in-house family pediatrician, Brecee always quizzed her sisters on her nieces' and nephews' gross and fine motor skills, making sure they met the expectations with each stage of development. Brecee presented Shae with a short checklist of questions regarding Sabrina's mental development, and Shae beamed as she answered each one with a yes.

They passed the imposing figure of Union Station. The next stop was Peabody Opera House. After parking the limo on Market Street, the driver assisted them out.

Linking arms, the sisters fell into step and entered the lobby together. Brecee was impressed. "This is nice. I love the ambiance." She felt like prancing around like a princess at a ball.

"I told you," Shae said as an usher greeted them and asked for their tickets.

"So, when is Hubby supposed to get here?" Brecee whispered.

Shae took out her phone and pulled up the St. Louis Cardinals app to check the score. "They're in the bottom of the seventh inning against the Texas Rangers, and they're ahead, four to one. If they can hold them off until the top of the ninth, it won't take Rahn long to get here. He'll shower and dress at the stadium."

Once they found their assigned table and Shae snagged a chair for her and Rahn, Brecee wondered if the spot next to her would remain empty. Why were the seats always grouped in twos, with the assumption that every guest would bring a date?

She glanced around, looking for anyone she recognized. Soon she spied some colleagues from the hospital as Shae waved at a reporter and a camera-person who were there to cover the event.

Soon, the musicians onstage began serenading the guests with soft jazz. Brecee tuned out all the instruments except for the guitar. *Perfection.* As she soaked up the music, their table mates began to arrive, all of them coupled off, as predicted.

While the servers delivered their salads, Brecee, Shae, and the others seated at their table took turns introducing themselves.

An older woman who'd identified herself as a jewelry store owner chuckled at Shae's introduction. "Who doesn't know St. Louis' hat lady?" she asked, then gushed about how much she loved watching KMMD. Then she raved about how much she and Shae looked alike.

Early on in Shae's St. Louis television career, she had made headlines by closing out the Sunday newscast wearing a fashionable hat she had worn to church that morning. Now, the viewers tuned in not only for the news but also to see the latest hat trend.

Once the program began, Shae turned her head left and right, checking for Rahn. Over her sister's shoulder, Brecee saw her brother-in-law striding with determination toward their table. He held a finger to his lips, warning her not to alert Shae of his approach.

Rahn pulled out the chair next to Shae and delivered a lingering kiss to her lips before acknowledging the other guests at the table. He winked at Brecee, and she smiled.

What a difference a few years made. Her mind drifted back to a similar event at which Shae had been nominated for several awards. The organizer had invited Shae to kick off the musical entertainment. Of course, her sister had obliged, with the stipulation that her sisters accompany her on stage. It had been a blast, with Shae on the drums, Stacy on keyboard, Shari on tenor sax, and Brecee tearing up the guitar strings as the four sang in perfect harmony.

That was one thing Brecee missed—performing as a family. She and Shae didn't even play in the church band on a consistent basis. Shae had an excuse: She would rather hold her baby and enjoy being a mommy as a member of the congregation. Brecee didn't have a legitimate reason, and God had chastened her. *The gift I've given you is for My glory, not yours!* His voice had seemed to thunder.

Brecee had gotten the message: Use it, or she would lose it. She'd repented, then spoken with the band director, Minister Vance.

"Sister Carmen, although I can never have too many guitarists in our band, I already have three: brothers James, Pride, and Dobson," he'd told her.

Brecee had gnawed on her lip as *Use it or lose it* echoed in her head. Back home, she and her sisters had played in the band every Sunday and for many different church functions. Plus, Brecee had been trained to challenge any musician on string instruments.

"I could put you in the rotation to fill in when members get sick or take vacation," the minister had finally conceded. "Basically, you'll be a substitute. But when I need you, you'll have to come through."

Exhaling a sigh of relief, she'd thanked him and said, "You and the Lord can count on me."

Ever since that negotiation, Brecee had played sporadically at the church. She never turned down an opportunity.

When Rahn put his arm on the back of Shae's chair and scooted her closer, Brecee was brought out of her daze. But soon her mind drifted back to that same ceremony when Shae and Rahn's relationship had fizzled, or so the family had thought. When Shae's name was called for the award, Rahn stepped out from the shadows and escorted her to the stage.

Releasing a sigh, Brecee wondered when—and if—the man God had for her would step out of the shadows.

She tried to clear her mind and focus on the program. After all, it was a fund-raiser to help children with special needs. As she listened to the speaker explain how every donation would benefit the organization, she glanced around. In the distance, a handsome face caught her eye, but then someone else at his table leaned to the side, blocking her view.

Brecee forced herself to turn around. It was rude to stare, anyway. Soon, she was distracted again, this time by the floral centerpiece on their table. It reminded her of the flowers Adrian had sent. Both bouquets were still adding beauty to her dining room. She liked flowers as much as the next woman, but the man who wooed her had to have a different approach. Basically, he had to do something unique that no other brother could copy.

When a round of applause erupted, Brecee reached for the program booklet and realized that the speakers' comments had concluded.

Now, with dinner over, Shae tapped her on the hand. "Rahn and I are going to make a spot on the dance floor. Are you going to be okay?" She was already on her feet with her husband's hand around her waist.

She was about to say her good-byes and catch a cab home or hitch a ride with the limo driver when a presence nearby.

"It's nice to see you again, Brecee." The voice was unmistakable.

Whipping her head around, Brecee sucked in her breath as she stared into Adrian's brown eyes. She'd always thought men looked sexy in suits—she blamed that on her being continually surrounded by male doctors in scrubs—but the tux on this man looked hand-stitched to accentuate every muscle in his body.

"Adrian," she muttered. "Hi."

From the corner of her eye, she noticed that Shae and Rahn had returned to their seats. What happened to their dance number?

"So, a face to go with the name," Shae said. Her tone was so odd, even Brecee couldn't tell if she was being nice or mildly scolding.

"Hello, Mrs. Maxwell." Adrian looked back at Brecee. "You two really do look alike. More so in person."

Rahn extended a hand. "Rahn Maxwell."

"I know." Adrian grinned, and a slight dimple flashed before Brecee's eyes and then was gone. "Adrian Cole. It's nice to meet you. I'm glad the Cards won tonight. I gave away my tickets to the game to be here." He reached inside his breast pocket and pulled out his card. "I'm a transportation problem solver with Broadway Motors."

Brecee wondered if it was always all about business and networking for him.

Her brother-in-law didn't even look at the card. "No need. I remember names and faces." He waved him off. "If it's okay with my wife and Brecee...."

Uh-oh. What is he up to? Brecee held her breath.

"I'd like to invite you to be our guest for a post-game party we're hosting next week after Friday's game."

Shae narrowed her eyes at her husband. "We would?"

Although her brother-in-law was always personable, Brecee hadn't seen that coming. He never invited just anybody to their parties.

Adrian nodded, then faced Brecee. "I accept, if you're okay with that."

"Great," Rahn said, tugging Shae out of her seat again. "Now, if you'll excuse us, we have some dancing to do."

"Would you like to dance?" Adrian asked, a glimmer in his eyes.

She shook her head, trying to figure out what had just happened.

"Then do you mind if I sit with you?" He placed his hand on the back of the empty chair facing her, but he didn't budge.

"I don't."

She observed his every movement, which seemed to be precisely calculated. His expression gave nothing away as he made himself comfortable.

Wow. He was so good-looking, she didn't want to blink. "I didn't expect to see you here."

"I came with some colleagues. Our dealership partners with this organization and a number of other charities." Then Adrian leaned forward and extended his hand. "Let me reintroduce myself. Adrian Cole."

She giggled, but he was serious, his gaze steady on her.

When she reached out, his hand covered hers with ease. Her eyelids fluttered at the feel of his strong yet gentle hold.

"Sabrece Carmen," she said. "But my family and friends call me Brecee." She would play his game.

"I gave Dolan your message, and he says Laura's doing fine." Adrian paused. "Do you want his number?"

Please. Brecee held in a grunt. She didn't call men, especially after she'd given them her number. "No, I don't."

"Good. You won't regret it." He grinned and stood. "Now would you like to dance?"

Feeling as if they had come to some type of terms, albeit unnamed, unknown, and undeclared, Brecee got to her feet. "I think I would like that."

He escorted her to the dance floor, in view of her sister, who was peeping around Rahn's shoulder, shamelessly spying on them.

CHAPTER EIGHT

Adrian smirked. Any other woman would be glad to be wrapped in his arms. Brecee evidently did not, based on the imaginary line she maintained between them. What a shame. With every whiff of whatever perfume she was wearing, the only thing Adrian wanted to do was pull her closer.

"I'm glad you're not taken," he whispered.

"What makes you think that?" She lifted one of her perfectly arched eyebrows in what appeared to be a challenge.

"Well, for starters, you came here alone. There isn't a ring on your finger...." He gave her a challenging gaze of his own. "Should I keep going?"

"Why not?" she asked, calling his bluff.

Chuckling, Adrian gently spun her around, moving to his own rhythm rather than that of the band. "If you were taken, that man would have been right there at St. Louis Bread Company to console you, unless you don't have time for romance and therefore the absence of a significant other."

When she stopped swaying, so did he. Maybe he had hit too close to home. The sexy expression on her face was tempting as she puckered her lips—probably done without her realizing the effect on him. What he wouldn't give to be finished with school and to have more free time to explore a relationship.

She tilted her head upward, seeming to study him. "Are you finished playing guessing games?"

"I don't play games with people. That's not my way. What you see is what you get." He shrugged. "That's exactly what I want in a woman."

"Is that why you're not married yet?" she pressed.

"My parents and my grandparents married for life, and I plan to follow in their footsteps. So, I don't believe in rushing into anything, including relationships," he said, emphasizing the last word. "I do believe in destiny, soul mates, and the perfect woman for me—and that our two hearts will beat as one."

Brecee frowned, then asked, "Where does God fit into your plan? Because my world has been centered on Him as far back as I can remember."

Then she sighed and glanced away, evidently disappointed with something he'd said. He wondered just what.

"I'm afraid we just might not have anything in common, Adrian. I'm a pediatrician. I enjoy childish games and playing pranks. As the youngest of four daughters, I've always been the center of attention in my family; and even with my three sisters being married, that hasn't changed. So, from where I'm standing, I don't see what we have in common. Where's the connection that could possibly lead to two hearts beating as one?"

Although Adrian appreciated her honesty, he didn't care to be dismissed. "I have one request."

She lifted an eyebrow. "Okay...?"

"Show me your world."

She smirked. "Better strap on your seat belt," she said, jokingly.

But he didn't smile. "I'm already buckled in."

Grinning, she appeared to relax somewhat. Moments went by without a word spoken between them as they danced. The imaginary line was still there, but Brecee seemed to be genuinely enjoying herself. Returning her steady gaze, he saw the same disappointment he felt when the organizer stepped up to the podium, called the night a success, and thanked everyone for coming. Wishing for more time together, Adrian escorted Brecee back to her table, where Rahn and his wife were whispering like two lovers deep in a private conversation.

"Do you need a ride home?" he asked.

She chuckled. "Thanks, but unless you have a chariot to trump a stretch limo, I'm good."

"I'm a transportation problem solver, remember? I'm sure I can find you a chariot," he teased back. "But seriously, when can I see you again?"

Brecee shrugged. "I'm off most weekends."

"I work all day Saturday and usually spend the evening studying."

"And you're probably tied up with church on Sunday," she stated.

"Not really, Sunday is definitely my day of rest," he confessed. "I often spend it catching up with Dolan and Laura or visiting my parents. But I am so looking forward to spring break next week."

She shook her head, the disappointment returning to her eyes. "I'm not asking for a lot in a man, except that he be intelligent and confident, and that he take time for God. If you don't do that on Sundays, when do you?"

He didn't have the answer she was clearly waiting for, judging by the way she stood there with her arms folded over her chest. Maybe he'd been premature in asking for a chance with her. He honestly did have a tight schedule, but he also honestly wanted to get to know her.

She rested her soft hand on top of his. "I don't understand your world, Adrian. Before we go any further, may I suggest we be honest about our expectations? Let's each make a list of ten things we want in the ideal mate. We can mail our lists to each other's workplaces."

Was she serious? "In the age of technology, why would we use snail mail?"

"Hey, it keeps the post office in business. And, to stir the pot some more, we can't read what the other wrote until our own list is in the mail." She lowered her voice to add, "If we don't have at least five things in common, let's not try to force something that won't fit."

A woman with guidelines—that was a first. Adrian didn't know what he thought of her terms, but he had nothing to lose, because he sure didn't have Brecee.

"Sure," he finally agreed.

She wiggled her nose playfully. "You're so easy to challenge."

Adrian was relieved. "So, you were kidding?"

"Nope."

Humph. School was back in session. He leaned closer to her. "If I have to play this game, I won't lose." He winked, then stepped back and turned to Rahn. "Thanks for the invite," Adrian told him. "See you Friday." Then he strolled away.

⌒

"Adrian Cole is fi-i-ine," Shae stated while snuggling in her husband's arms inside the limo, as if she had no shame complimenting another man in front of him.

"True," Brecee said, "but it takes a lot more than looks. I should know. I've dated some hunks who were only a shell of a man with no substance."

Shae frowned. "You act like you're unsure about seeing him."

Brecee shrugged. "In one word, he's a mystery."

Shae held up two fingers. "A mystery. Two words."

"Whatever." Brecee rolled her eyes and tugged on a curl that fallen out of place. "I still think I might be more compatible with his cousin Dolan. I mentioned him to you. He has done a great job instilling Christ into his young daughter's life, and you know I love children."

"There's something between you and Adrian," Rahn observed, speaking for the first time since they'd gotten in the limo. "I could tell neither of you knew it yet. That's why I invited him over. God knows I have been in that man's shoes." He turned and inched his mouth closer to Shae's. "I remember being desperate to get my woman back." They kissed.

Brecee looked away to give them a moment of privacy. "I'm not his woman," she mumbled.

Rahn grunted. "Not yet. But when a man has his mind made up, you women are helpless."

Shae groaned. "Please, babe, don't challenge my sister."

"Too late." Brecee beamed. "He agreed to participate in a little unscientific experiment to see if we're compatible."

"And if you're not?" Rahn asked.

"We Carmen sisters don't compromise. Haven't you learned anything from being married to one?" Shae answered for her.

Laughing, Rahn pulled Shae closer. "Yep. Say no more."

Brecee didn't say anything. Shae's mantra sounded good, but she wasn't sure if her heart would cooperate.

When the limo pulled in front of her condo, she kissed Shae and hugged Rahn good night, then allowed the driver to help her out and escort her to the front door. He waited until she was inside and had disengaged her alarm before returning to the limo.

Before climbing into bed, she slid to the floor on her knees. "Lord, I don't know what I'm getting into with Adrian. If he can't love You, Lord, how could he ever love me?" Brecee didn't want to be the Carmen sister who got it wrong when it came to a serious relationship.

Trust Me, the Lord whispered.

After listening a few more minutes for any additional guidance, Brecee ended her prayer with a petition to keep children safe from injuries, predators, and illnesses. "In Jesus' name, amen."

On Saturday, Brecee slept in. Usually, she did something with Shae and Sabrina; but with Rahn in town, Brecee was a faded memory. She wasn't offended at all, however. If she had a husband who was crazy about her, she would be missing in action, too.

When she did step out of bed, Brecee prayed some more for guidance. "Lord, You promise that if I acknowledge You in all my ways, You'll direct my path. I need direction, Jesus," she pleaded, then reached for her Bible and opened it to where she'd left off reading, in chapter 2 of Titus. Her heart fluttered as she soaked in verse seven: *"In all things shewing thyself a pattern of good works: in doctrine shewing uncorruptness, gravity, sincerity…."*

By the time she finished reading the entire book of Titus, Brecee understood the message God had for her. Adrian had asked her to show him her world—to let him enter it. She wanted him to see the benefits of following Christ in a way that would make him want to stay.

Brecee put on her workout clothes and went for a jog through nearby Lafayette Park, admiring all the turn-of-the-century architecture as she crossed the street. While so many people preferred the suburbs, Brecee enjoyed city living. Maybe that was the Philly in her.

The park was considered a historic landmark, something she'd learned from her reporter sister. Shae had taken her on a walking tour the day after she'd moved into her condo, pointing out the pavilion that had survived the Great Cyclone of 1896, which killed hundreds of people in St. Louis. The grounds were spotted with weather-worn cannons fired from a 1776 British warship and other memorable statues of military heroes.

After completing her three-mile course, she headed back home. She thought about Adrian, who would be working right now. Was the transportation specialist, or whatever it was that he called himself, wooing new clients? She prayed that God's will would be done in his life. She also thought about the challenge she'd posed for him that would demand the same transparency from her.

"Right." She figured she might as well get started after she showered and slipped into comfortable clothes to lounge in. After powering up her Tablet, she curled up on the sofa, closed her eyes, and dug deep within herself. Then she began to type.

"Number one…hmm." She already had to pause. After a few moments, it came to her: *Although I don't consider myself vain, he has to be a looker.* "So he won't scare me every time I look at him." She chuckled, but she meant it.

Brecee had always been partial to dark chocolate skin that was free of tattoos and piercings. Adrian reminded her of Philly native actor Kevin Moore, minus his thick beard. Adrian's facial features wowed her: silky black eyebrows, lashes, mustache, and an engaging smile that always seemed sincere. Of course, that slight dimple was an added bonus.

His muscular build reminded her of former football player Will Demps. Brecee hadn't even liked football until she'd caught a glimpse of him playing for the Ravens. She'd followed his career until his final game with the Houston Texans. When Will seemed to be done with football, so was she. Still, the man was not easily forgotten. She wanted a man like that who wasn't easily forgotten—and Adrian couldn't be ignored. He'd definitely gotten her attention last night and, if she was honest, on the first day, when he saw her boohooing. She was just too upset appreciate it.

Number two: He must have a job, unless he plans to be a house husband and a nanny to the children. She didn't like the sound of that. She wanted to be a stay-at-home mom, at least with her first child.

When she got to number three, Brecee became more serious: *He must surrender his will to Christ and trust Him to run the show.* After chiding herself for not making this her first requirement, she scratched out the numbers and changed them accordingly. Then she briefly thought about Dolan. Judging from his daughter, he had probably turned his life over to Christ long ago.

No. She took a deep breath. Dolan hadn't called, and she did find herself attracted to Adrian.

Number four: He must respect me and support me in my commitment to live for Christ—not only on Sundays, but all throughout the week. I shouldn't have to say this, but I want to be clear: I don't sleep around—it's nonnegotiable. God said He is able to keep me from falling, and my desire is to be kept!

Number five: He must understand that family is important. If he can't get along with mine, or if they don't like him, then we can't be together. I won't ask either to pick sides. This is also nonnegotiable.

Number six: He must have a sense of humor. Laughter is better than any medicine I could ever prescribe. He has to be able to laugh with me, not about me or at me. :)

That gave Brecee pause. Adrian seemed so serious, but last night, there had been undeniable vibes between them. She'd felt his pull. He was like water to her oil; his subdued nature counterbalanced the hyperactivity and adrenaline rushes her daily work demanded. Could he deliver the simple things that mattered most to her happiness?

She continued typing.

Number seven: He must consider me more important than everything but God. I want to matter. I want an investment in us.

She realized that number seven was really three requirements in one. *Oh, well. Deal with it.*

Number eight: When he's no longer into me, he needs to tell me and then step aside, so the real deal can come along.

Number nine: He must be very certain that I'm the one before he tells me he loves me, because he can't take it back, and I'll hold him to it.

Brecee gnawed on her lip. She needed one more. It was her game, after all. She'd made the rules.

Number ten: He must want children. I love children—and hope to have my own someday.

Exhaling, Brecee scanned her list. Adrian would either walk toward her or run away as fast as he could.

After proofing it again, she printed it and put it in the mail.

CHAPTER NINE

Less than a week after holding Brecee in his arms at the charity ball, Adrian received an envelope from her at the dealership. He grunted. "So, you were serious." Out of curiosity, he was tempted to open it right away, even though he had yet to start on his own list. How could she possibly find out?

Closing his eyes and rubbing his face, Adrian reminded himself that he didn't operate like that. He earned people's respect and business. Honesty was always at the top of his list. He blamed his temptation on business being slow at the dealership.

Home again after a long day, all Adrian wanted to do was eat some food, take a shower, and hear Brecee's voice. But to call her and admit that he hadn't put ink to paper would not be in his best interest.

He took the envelope from Brecee out of his pocket and stared at it. His fingers itched to open it. Setting it down on the kitchen table, he exhaled, kicked off his Stacy Adamses, and padded across the room to the refrigerator.

"My list," he mumbled, even as he questioned why he'd agreed to this. "Number one: This seems too much like a game to me with no benefits." He took out a covered dish of leftover pasta, scooped a serving onto a plate, and popped it in the microwave. Then he eyed the envelope again. "Why couldn't we do this via e-mail or text?"

Recalling how beautiful Brecee had been the other night—her perfect smile, the singsong sound of her laughter—he smiled. There was his answer. She was worth this silly game, and more. Still, he certainly wasn't going to start on it tonight.

"Tomorrow."

The next morning, Adrian awoke with the list on his mind. It stayed there as he dressed and drove to work. It dominated his thoughts until he reached the dealership, where he switched into work mode.

Wednesday got off to a slow start, especially after one of his potential clients rescheduled. But that never worried him. He didn't look at his position as just a job. He had invested many years—twelve, to be exact—in his work, focusing on building relationships and maintaining them, which was the key to staying in business. The lifestyle he'd created for himself kept him comfortable. He never had to worry about where his next meal would come from.

Adrian grew restless in his office, so he went out to the showroom and began strolling around. It didn't take long for Brecee's list to resurface in his mind. Unable to ignore it any longer, he took out his smartphone and started a dictation.

"Here are the things that are important to me," he began. "Number one: A woman has to look good, smell good, and be of good character. I don't play games."

Kyle Preston, another top-performing salesperson and longtime friend, gave Adrian a strange look as he walked by. Adrian nodded, then decided to head to the parking lot for some privacy.

Outside, Adrian enjoyed the warmth of the bright sun on his shoulders as he walked up and down the rows of luxury cars. "Number two: She's got to be okay with some silence. I'm not much of a talker, unless I'm in a business mode. I prefer to get to know people by watching and listening. Some say I have a poker face, which is good. I don't—"

A beep sounded, indicating the end of the dictation. He must have reached the maximum number of words. Tapping the microphone again, he continued. "I don't like it when people know what I'm thinking. I'm selective as to who I share my thoughts with."

A silver GLA 250 SUV drove into the parking lot, and the driver honked. Adrian squinted and waved at the driver, a longtime client. Another man Adrian didn't recognize was seated in the front passenger seat.

As the driver parked, Adrian walked toward the car, adding number three to his list before he forgot: "She needs to be there for me. I consider myself a patient man, but if I make time in my schedule for a woman, she needs to do the same for me." He tapped the microphone to end the dictation, then slipped his smartphone back in its holder. It was time for business.

Adrian worked on his list over the next several days. By the time it was complete, he'd engaged in plenty of soul searching. He was ready to print it when he made a spur-of-the-moment decision to forgo plain white paper. After work the next day, he stopped at an office supply store and purchased a set of stationery with matching envelopes.

When he returned home, he sat down at his kitchen table with a grin. "You like games? I'm about to one-up you, Dr. Carmen." In the neatest penmanship he'd used since grade school, Adrian rewrote his list for a personal touch. The only thing detracting from it was the line that read "c/o Cardinal Glennon Hospital."

He drove to the Maryland Heights post office on Weldon Parkway to mail the letter. As his hand released the envelope, Adrian hoped he had written the right words to get him to the next level.

To increase his chances to have the winning entry, he had one more stop to make.

It had been days since Brecee had mailed her list to Adrian. She checked in the hospital mailroom twice daily, but still nothing. She was beginning to wonder whether she wanted too much from a relationship and whether her expectations in a man were too lofty.

She hadn't always been overly discriminating in her taste for men. But now that all her sisters were happily married with children, while she had all the time in the world to be single, she was becoming more selective on the men with whom she agreed to go out on an official date. Only a handful had met most of her criteria, yet the chemistry had always fizzled.

She was about to give up hope on Adrian when another stunning floral bouquet arrived from him. An hour later, a decorative envelope showed up in her mail slot. His return address read Maryland Heights.

She couldn't wait for her dinner break to read his list.

Brecee entered the doctors' charting room, having just removed a small piece of candy from the nostril of a six-year-old girl. The things children did.

No one else was in the room except for Regina, who wore a look of expectation. She'd seen the flowers.

Just then, Brecee's smartphone rang. She didn't recognize the number. "Dr. Carmen," she answered.

"Dr. Carmen—Brecee," a deep, rich male voice greeted her. "This is Dolan Cole, Laura's dad."

The look on Brecee's face must have alerted Regina that the call was personal, because she stood and whispered, "I want to know everything," before leaving the room.

Brecee nodded as she took a seat, confused. Why was Dolan calling her now, weeks after she'd hoped he would? It figured he would wait until she held an envelope containing a list from his cousin that spelled out his desires in a woman. Had Adrian passed on her and told his cousin to go ahead and give her a shot?

She chided herself for envisioning a scenario that happened only in cheesy romance novels. Blinking, Brecee refocused on the present. "Dolan! How are you? It's nice to hear from you."

"I was hoping you would say that." He sounded upbeat. "Are you at the hospital now? Laura and I are in the area, and I was hoping we could bring you something to eat, if you haven't eaten already, or take you out for a bite, if you have time."

Wow. On one hand, how thoughtful. But, on the other hand, Brecee wanted to read Adrian's list. *Lord, is this You intervening?* she asked, wondering if it was Dolan who possessed more of the qualities she wanted in a man. He certainly seemed like one who'd probably never missed Sunday school.

Smiling, she decided just to go with it. "Perfect timing. I was about to have dinner." She verified that he knew where the hospital was located. "Come into the main drive on Park Avenue, and I'll stand outside the emergency department doors and wait."

Dolan chuckled. "I can't have a woman waiting, now, can I? We're minutes away." As they ended the call, Brecee heard Laura's high-pitched squeal of delight in the background.

She eyed Adrian's envelope again, then stuffed it into the pocket of her lab coat before hurrying to her office for her purse.

When she breezed outside, Dolan was standing beside the front passenger door of his Audi. As she stepped off the curb, it dawned on her that she knew little about a man she was about to get inside with car. *I don't think so.* Her mother hadn't raised any fools. "Hi, Dolan. We have Café @ Glennon here. Would you and Laura like to join me there?"

He didn't blink at her request. "We accept." He opened the back door and unbuckled Laura from her car seat. The girl hopped out with a worshipful grin and ran into Brecee's waiting arms, giving her a tight squeeze. "Hi, Brecee." She glanced over her shoulder at Dolan, and when he nodded, she said, "*Miss* Brecee."

Beaming at the girl's good manners, Brecee took her hand, and they headed inside while Dolan parked the car.

After he joined them, their first stop was the reception desk. She squatted to be eye level with Laura. "All visitors have to wear identification security badges to keep our children safe." She looked up at Dolan. "This lady will need your driver's license to make them."

Once that task was done, Brecee led the way to the café.

Laura scanned the selection of food, her eyes widening when she spied the snacks. "I like this place, Daddy."

At one of the buffet stations, Brecee admired Dolan's patience with Laura as she weighed her options, trying to decide what she wanted. Maybe that was the reason he hadn't called. His daughter definitely came first in his life—a good sign.

She went to the soup bar and ladled herself a generous helping of beef stew. Dolan filled his plate with vegetables and fried chicken. When they were at the register, Brecee was about to swipe her card to pay, but Dolan nudged her aside and used his, instead.

He grinned—no dimples. Not even a hint of one, like Adrian had. "You may have picked the place, but I'm picking up the tab."

"Thank you." Her father had taught her never to argue with a man if he wanted to pay for a meal.

Laura selected a table, then sat down next to Brecee. "Can I say grace, Daddy?"

"Yes, baby."

Brecee bowed her head and closed her eyes. The prayers of a child were heartwarming—so innocent, so close to God's heart.

"So, what brings you in my neck of the woods?" Brecee asked after they said "Amen." "Do you live close by?"

"We live about half an hour, forty minutes, from here. Laura's class had a field trip at the City Museum. Instead of waiting for her to return to school an hour later, I opted to pick her up," Dolan explained.

Laura stabbed her salad with her fork and bobbed her head. "I liked the museum. They have a tunnel under the ground for kids to go in."

As they ate and chatted, Brecee took note of Dolan's features. Handsomeness definitely ran in the Cole family, because he and Adrian were undeniably fine. But Adrian did have something extra. Maybe it was the mustache, just the right length and thickness. Dolan had a thin beard that looked nice on him, but she wasn't a fan of beards in general. If they grew too thick, they reminded her of cavemen.

Wait a minute. What was she doing, comparing the two of them?

Since Laura appeared distracted, watching other patrons entering the café, Brecee lowered her voice and said to Dolan, "Since I didn't hear from you, I wondered if Laura was okay."

"Yes." He nodded. "Her doctor ordered an electrocardiogram, and it came back normal."

Brecee exhaled a sigh of relief.

"Turns out that some medicine I gave Laura for a fever did something to her heart. They believe it was a onetime occurrence, but I still need to monitor her."

"Arrhythmia," Brecee stated off the top of her head. She didn't need to be certified as a pediatric cardiologist to recognize the signs.

"Yes, that's what she called it."

"What were her symptoms?" Brecee asked.

"She fainted after recess a day earlier. I took her to the pediatrician, and she appeared fine, but the doctor wanted the test done just to be on the safe side. It was scary getting that call from the school."

"I can imagine." It appeared that the situation had resolved itself. "I checked with Adrian to see how she was doing," she said, trying to dig.

"He told me. Sorry. I meant to call you earlier, but being a single father is demanding."

"And I'm sure challenging." Brecee smiled.

"Daddy, can I have dessert?" Laura asked, licking her lips.

"Yes. Jell-O or one cookie," he instructed her, then handed her some money.

"Thank you." Laura skipped away toward the dessert bar.

"You have such a beautiful daughter," Brecee told him.

"Thanks." He grinned.

"You've also clearly done a great job making sure that Jesus is real to her, not like a Santa Claus figure. I like that."

"Now that, I can't take credit for. Lynn, my late wife, planted those seeds in Laura, and they seem to blossom more and more every day."

A humble man. Brecee reached over and patted his hand. "But you're nourishing them."

He shrugged. "I do the best I can." After finishing off his fried chicken breast, he wiped his mouth and leaned back in his seat. "I don't discourage her. My wife's salvation was strong. After we married, she said each day she hoped and prayed that I would come to Christ, as she had. She had so much faith in God and in me. My regret is that she never lived to see it bear fruit." He paused and stared off for a moment before looking at Brecee again.

Brecee blinked back the tears blurring her vision. "I'm sorry." She took a deep breath and gave Dolan an encouraging smile. "At least you came to Christ. How long after her death did you repent and get baptized in water and Spirit, in Jesus' name?"

"Oh, I haven't."

What? Brecee did everything in her power to mask her shock at such a confession. She was so disappointed. This was the one advantage she'd thought Dolan had over Adrian. "How are you nurturing your daughter spiritually?" Her mind was shouting, *Operation child rescue!*

"She has a children's Bible, she attends Sunday school, and I send her to vacation Bible school."

That was probably a couple weeks, at the most, out of her summer. This little girl needed a Christian woman in her life—a committed role model in the faith. Brecee was about to volunteer to be that, and nothing more, but her hospital pager beeped.

Taking it out of her pocket, she read the message: Six-year-old gunshot victim.

Brecee stood. "Listen, Dolan. I've got to go. Thank you for the company and the meal."

Dolan got to his feet as Laura scampered back to the table holding a giant chocolate chip cookie.

"Bye, Miss Brecee," she said. "When are we going to see you again?"

Dolan seemed to be waiting for her answer.

"Soon." Brecee hugged Laura, then hurried to her post, praying that God would continue to nurture the spiritual seeds in Laura's life.

CHAPTER TEN

The child will survive. Brecee praised the Lord with a great sense of relief as she drove the short distance from the hospital to her condo hours later.

When would parents learn that the natural curiosity of children didn't mix well with the toy-like depiction of guns on television and in video games? Gun owners didn't know the facts like first responders. At last year's American Academy of Pediatrics National Conference, the numbers presented had been staggering: more than seven thousand children hospitalized each year with gunshot injuries, hundreds of which proved fatal. There had already been 500 deaths this year alone, and if the Lord hadn't intervened, Jason Kerr would have been gunshot victim number 501.

Turning onto Lafayette, Brecee navigated the narrow alley and pulled into her private garage. Within minutes, she was safe inside her second-floor condo.

She drew herself a bubble bath in an effort to soothe herself after the day's events, including the conversation she'd had with Dolan about Laura's natural hunger for God. Then she thought about Adrian and the letter she hadn't opened. She wasn't sure if she was ready to read it, especially if the contents squashed her hopes for his character.

It was moments like this when she yearned for a hug—from her mother and sisters, from a roommate like the one she'd had while completing her residency in Houston, or from a loving husband who would hold her.

Feeling somewhat refreshed after her bath, Brecee padded barefoot across her bedroom to her makeshift library in search of something funny to read. But her mind kept nudging her to open Adrian's letter.

Resolved that she was a big girl who could handle rejection as well as any three-year-old, she took the envelope out of her purse and studied his handwriting. It was unusually neat, especially for a man, as if he'd spent a minute meticulously fashioning each letter. "You must have gotten an *A* in cursive writing," she muttered.

She opened the seal with her fingernail and pulled out a piece of water-marked parchment paper that had been neatly folded into three. Smoothing it in front of her, she began to read.

1. I don't like games, and I feel like I'm playing one. In that case, I'm playing to win.

Brecee giggled. Maybe she had misjudged him.

2. I'm not ashamed to say I'm attracted to women who look good without flaunting it, smell good, and have a good heart, rather than being mean-spirited.

3. With that said, I'm a people person when I have to be. Otherwise, I'm a private person, preferring to get to know others by observation. Some say I have a poker face. My challenge to you is to read me if you can.

4. In my thirty-three years, I've done things at my own pace to my own satisfaction. I've managed to hold my own without a woman, but I'm willing to make time for one, as long as she'll make time for me.

Brecee raised her eyebrows.

5. I've never married because I've never met a woman I felt I couldn't afford to let get away. When I meet that woman, I'll waste no time proposing, because I'll know that I've fallen in love.

Brecee had to pat her chest a couple of times. "Whew." She could almost hear him say the words. Last week, she'd gotten a glimpse of his intensity.

So, those were the top five on Adrian's wish list. She read on.

6. Faith is important—my parents made sure I knew that—but I don't think that church is necessary. This belief is based on my observations of the way people act during the Sunday service versus all through the rest of the week. I figure I can do without the hypocrisy.

God, how will this this work? was her silent question. A committed, convicted Christian man was a must.

Show him the light, the Lord whispered. *Be the light.*

Brecee smiled at the reminder of Matthew 5:14–16. She continued reading.

7. I want children, plural. Being an only child had its pluses and minuses. I do know there is a Scripture about two being better than one. Does that earn me an extra point?

"Yes, it does." Brecee smiled as she reached for her Bible, then used the concordance to find the passage he was referring to. It was Ecclesiastes 4:9–10: *"Two are better than one; because they have a good reward for their labor. For if they fall, the one will lift up his fellow: but woe to him that is alone when he falleth; for he hath not another to help him up."*

8. *I'm a caring person. You care for children, and I care for damsels in distress.*

The rumble of laughter started deep inside Brecee until it exploded in a thunderous chuckle. Instead of being annoyed by his reference to her crying binge, she found it amusing.

9. *I don't believe in coincidences. I do believe that God has a reason for why and when things happen.*

10. *If you want to know anything else about me, call me. I would love to hear your voice.*

Brecee reached for her phone and did just that.

CHAPTER ELEVEN

No, *no.* Adrian gritted his teeth when he glanced at the TV in the dealership lounge and saw the Cardinals' third baseman hit a home run with two RBIs to take the lead, six to three, over the Cincinnati Reds. He rubbed his neck in frustration. He was waiting on several clients' referrals to come in for a test drive, and he'd need extra innings, like two or three of them, to give him time to get to the Maxwells' for the post-game party.

Adrian missed Brecee like crazy. They had talked on the phone the past two nights, but one topic that hadn't come up was how they were going to make a relationship work with their schedules. That was his main worry. The dealership required only forty hours a week, but, like most transportation problem solvers, he had to meet a monthly quota. For April, the manufacturer was pushing twelve luxury vehicles for extra bonuses and incentives.

The Cardinals held off the Reds, winning the game in the top of the ninth inning. By now, most of the staff had left for the night, but Adrian was still waiting on one client—a restaurant owner who was coming in to test-drive the new Mercedes-Benz E-Class she'd picked out online and to sign the papers. Thankfully, she'd already taken care of getting her credit approved.

Minutes later, she arrived. Once the keys were in hand, the sale would be marked as delivered. Then he would need just three more to meet his quota for the month.

When the lady drove off the lot, her taillights blending with the other cars on the road, Adrian hurried to the restroom to freshen up. He didn't want to look as tired as he felt, so he patted his face with a paper towel dampened with cool water. Then he changed out of his shirt and tie into the dark polo shirt he'd brought. In a sense, he was off duty; but, as a car rep, he was never truly off—not with business cards in his wallet and a bright smile that showed he'd been faithful in maintaining his routine dental appointments for teeth whitening.

Once he'd programmed the Maxwells' address into his phone's GPS, he called Brecee to let her know he was on his way. The sound of her voice made him smile.

Adrian wasn't surprised that the Maxwells lived in Town and Country, an elite suburb of St. Louis, where national broadcasters, CEOs, entertainers, and professional athletes resided in grand estates with acres separating them from their closest neighbors.

When Adrian turned into the long driveway, he recognized Brecee's Lexus under a stone archway that seemed to serve as a bridge from one part of the house to another. He parked behind her car and stepped out.

At the sound of heels clicking against the brick walkway, Adrian turned and gulped at the vision floating toward him. Brecee's beauty immobilized him. Her curls were gone, but her hair spilled over her shoulders and hung down her back. A simple knit top complemented a skirt that flirted at her knees in the front but resembled a wedding dress train in the back. If her slip-on heels were designed to look comfortable, they had the opposite effect. She appeared polished, confident, and ready to strut anywhere at a moment's notice.

He released a low whistle, and Brecee stopped in her tracks. The spotlights against the house gave her a glow. He walked slowly toward her, as if she were a goddess and he didn't want to disturb her majesty.

As if of their own volition, his arms opened within feet of her. Without hesitation, she filled them, and he trapped her in his embrace. The only sound was his breathing as he sniffed the fragrance of her hair. A welcome-home kiss would have been nice, but they weren't playing house yet.

When she stepped back, Adrian reluctantly loosened his hold, then rested his forehead against hers. "You look very pretty."

Brecee reached up and rubbed his jaw. Good thing he'd shaved that morning.

"Thank you," she whispered, then broke free. She linked her fingers through his and led the way to the front door.

The power couple had superb taste, from the manicured lawn and flower beds to the strategic lighting, as if their home were a theater production.

Just before they reached the landing, Brecee paused. "Adrian Cole, you're one handsome man, and I'm glad you want to be here...with me."

Adrian wanted to tell her that he was glad that she wanted him there, but the door swung open, and Shae and Rahn practically tugged them inside.

"It's good to see you again, man." Rahn welcomed him with a handshake, a smile, and a pat on the back. As if he was eager for male company, he immediately steered Adrian away from Brecee and Shae and offered to show him around.

A *tour*? Adrian couldn't deny that the home was a showhouse, but he was here for Brecee. When he looked back at her, she winked, and Shae wiggled her fingers good-bye.

Slipping his hands into his pockets, Adrian fell into step with Rahn. The outfielder had already sent a referral his way, so a relationship had already been established, and Adrian wanted to build on that.

They left the foyer of marble tile and ornate crown moulding. Rahn showed him the entertainment room, the living room, the gourmet kitchen, the family room, the library, the home theater.... Adrian stopped counting. "What's the square footage?"

Rahn shrugged. "Eight thousand, give or take a couple hundred, with six bedrooms—one of which is Brecee's, for the times when I'm on the road."

Too bad Adrian sold luxury cars instead of luxury homes. He could just imagine the commission.

He followed Rahn down a short hallway ending at an elevator. They stepped in and traveled up two levels, and when the doors opened again, Adrian's jaw dropped at the open floorplan of an over-the-top game room. With a pool table as the centerpiece, it also featured a four-lane bowling alley, complete with snack bar, and a children's playroom with chalkboard walls and even a miniature roller skating rink.

Adrian smirked and shook his head.

Rahn grunted. "It's all about keeping my little ladies happy, and the best part is, I have God to thank for blessing me with this all."

That statement gave Adrian pause. Had he ever given God credit for the material possessions he'd accumulated or the accomplishments he'd achieved?

Before he could ponder his answer, Rahn crossed the room, which easily could have been divided into six bedrooms. "Now, this is our home theater-slash-stage," he said, pointing to a raised platform then turned and pointed to a set of French doors. "And Shae's sewing room is through there."

"And I thought customizing luxury cars was meticulous," Adrian said in awe.

They both chuckled, then Rahn patted him on the back. "Have a seat. I don't know if you're hungry or not, but I'm sure those sisters are warming up something to get this party started." He strolled to the bar and grabbed an assortment of bottled waters and sodas.

When Adrian lowered himself into the recliner Rahn had indicated, his muscles practically sighed with comfort as he stretched his legs. Man, he needed one of these in his condo. "How many people are you expecting?"

"You're it," Rahn stated as he passed him a bottle of water and sat down on the sofa.

What did that mean?

Before he could inquire, there was a soft chime, and the elevator doors opened. The sisters stepped out in synch. Shae was carrying her baby daughter, and Brecee held a platter of sandwiches and side dishes.

Getting to his feet, Rahn relieved his wife of the baby, and Shae graced him with a kiss. In that moment, Adrian got a glimpse of his own future as a husband and father.

He stood, as well, and took the tray from Brecee.

"Thanks," she said with a smile—instead of a kiss like Rahn had received from his wife.

"Where do you want this?"

She nodded to the coffee table.

After fulfilling his task, he turned his eyes back to Brecee, studying her expressions, trying to read her body language. He wanted to know what she was thinking.

"I was about to put her in bed," Shae told her husband.

"I can do that, babe. Let Daddy hold his princess for a bit." Rahn spoke to his wife but kept his adoring gaze on the little girl, whose eyelashes fluttered sleepily. As he strolled back to the sitting area, he asked Shae, "Uh, can you give Adrian and me a minute?"

"Sure, babe. Brecee and I will be in my sewing room. I wanted to show her my latest project." Looping her arm through Brecee's, Shae tugged her away and disappeared through the French doors.

Adrian noted the similarities in the sisters' mannerisms as he turned back to Rahn, fully expecting an inquisition, of sorts. *Bring it on*, Adrian thought. He settled back in his seat and waited on his host.

But Rahn took his time, staring at his baby and smiling. There was no doubt the man enjoyed being a father. After a few minutes, it seemed Rahn had forgotten Adrian was even there.

Finally, Rahn glanced over his shoulder toward the sewing room. "We probably don't have long before those snoop sisters return." He chuckled, turning to Adrian. "But I feel that we needed to come to an understanding."

"And what kind of understanding is that?" Adrian asked, reaching for a slider sandwich. He'd just realized how hungry he was.

"First, please don't involve my wife if you and Brecee have any further spats. I can't keep every man in St. Louis from calling my wife, but when I can put a name to a face, it's only fair we have this conversation."

"I'm not interested in your wife," Adrian said calmly. He respected the sanctity of marriage, no matter how fine another man's wife might be.

"I didn't think so, but that's good to know." Rahn nodded. "Listen, the real reason I invited you to my home is that when I saw the way you focused on Brecee when you approached our table at the charity banquet, I was hit with déjà vu. Although I knew very little about you, my heart goes out to any man who falls for a Carmen sister. Shae and I were at a crossroads in our relationship when I attended a similar function in order to ambush her, in a way, hoping she'd talk to me."

Adrian grunted. "I wasn't aiming for drama. I was there to support a client. I didn't even know Brecee would be there. We're still just getting to know each other."

"I'll add you to my prayer list," Rahn told him. "Maybe I can save you some trouble, since you and Brecee are just starting off. The Carmens are a close-knit family, and since she moved to St. Louis to be near her sister, the family is holding me responsible for looking out for her while she's single. If I don't take my role as brother-in-law seriously, then I'll have to deal with an unhappy wife and unhappy in-laws, and that's not happening. I'm warning you: Be afraid."

Amused, Adrian wanted to ask of whom he ought to be afraid. But the man seemed serious, so he kept his poker face while Rahn covered every base and angle, sounding like a father laying down dating rules for his teenage daughter. Despite the absurdity of the discussion, Adrian listened until Rahn ran out of stream.

"I respect this talk and your looking out for Brecee." Adrian leaned back and crossed his legs at the knee. "But Brecee and I have decided to give this relationship a try. I have my own code of ethics that I employ when I date. I have no intention of hurting her; if I do, I'll make amends. As far as disrespecting her, that's not going to happen." He reached for his bottled water, unscrewed the lid, and took a swig. "I haven't known Brecee anywhere near as long as you have, but something tells me you have her all wrong. Just like that Lexus she drives...."

"What's wrong with that Lexus?" Rahn's nostrils flared. "I had that custom-designed and loaded with the premium package features, including an upgraded security system," he boasted. "That was our gift to her when she became board certified in pediatric emergency medicine. Trust me, I did my research."

"And you did good." Adrian nodded. "The Lexus is one of the most dependable luxury cars, It just doesn't fit Brecee's sassy personality. And black?" He shook his head and frowned. "All wrong. I would have put her behind the wheel of a garnet red pearl Audi A6 sedan, where she would be in control."

"Really?" Rahn seemed to give some thought to what he'd said, and Adrian even thought he saw a flash of self-doubt on his face.

⌒

"Can you hear what they're saying?" Brecee whispered as Shae cracked open the door from inside her sewing room.

Shae strained to eavesdrop a few moments. "Girl, they're talking about cars." She sighed, clicking the door closed. "I guess that's what car salesmen do."

"Adrian's a transportation problem solver," Brecee corrected her.

"A what?"

Brecee shrugged and folded her arms. "He takes pride in his work, and that's what he calls his position. I had the same reaction when I first heard him say it." Frowning, she gnawed on her lip.

"What's wrong?"

"I'm just wondering…." She sighed. "I'm wondering if he'll always be on the clock, networking. When I leave the hospital, I'm out of work mode, to a certain extent."

"I hear ya." Shae nodded. "Me, too. Maybe because the reality we're exposed to isn't something we want to constantly talk about." She flopped down in a chair and eyed Brecee. "But if Adrian's who you really want, you'll have to accept that about him." She squinted. "Is he?"

Releasing another sigh, Brecee slid into a nearby chair. "We seem completely different on so many levels, yet there is something about him I can't explain that's pulling me into this comfort zone where I feel I'm supposed to be. Odd, isn't it?"

"No," Shae said softly. "While others saw Rahn's strengths, we were privy to each other's weaknesses. We became prayer partners, in a sense."

"I think Adrian Cole is an open book, too. He's confident, but his occupation—salesman, transportation problem solver, car specialist, whatever—does concern me," she confessed.

Shae reached out and touched her hand. "Vent, Brecee. We're sisters. You don't have to pretend or sugarcoat anything with me."

Brecee sniffed when Shae smiled. "Okay, here's the deal. All my sisters are married. I'm the Lone Ranger without a husband, and I want the status of missus. There's an unspoken expectation among doctors that we should marry among doctors, lawyers, CEOs, or someone making six figures."

"You don't think Adrian makes that much?"

"I think the man is making more than me right now. Clearly, he doesn't have student loans. But sales positions never appealed to me as steady employment. If our relationship moves to the next level, which I would very much like it to, could his unpredictable income support a family if I want to work only part-time, or even be a full-time mother?" She swallowed to stop herself from adding, *I didn't study hard and go to school a long time to live in poverty.*

"It's okay to work through these pros and cons now and not name and claim Adrian like I know some women would," Shae told her, "because it might not be who God has for you."

"Thanks." Brecee nodded. "I guess I'm waiting for God to show me if Adrian is the man He has for me. You said you knew Rahn was the one when he delivered a slice of cake to you at the station."

Closing her eyes, Shae bit her bottom lip and grinned. "Yes. There were so many little things that added up to bigger ones. But don't forget—I stood my ground and held to my convictions when that steroid scandal hit. I trusted God to back me up, and He worked it out!" She high-fived Brecee, then stood. "Come on, let's interrupt our men." Shae opened the door, and Brecee followed her out.

When Rahn and Adrian saw them, they ceased talking and got to their feet. Shae went to Rahn and hovered over little Sabrina as Rahn transferred their daughter into her arms.

Adrian stepped closer to Brecee. "Is this your way of ambushing me?" he asked with a grin.

Brecee jutted her chin. "My sister Shari taught me to plead the fifth, whether I'm guilty or not."

He reached for her hand and wiggled his fingers as he entwined them with hers. "I can hold my own. Plus, my mother can be a frightening inter-rogator. Why do you think I'm still single?" He shuddered.

Laughing, Brecee gave him a playful nudged. "Humph. I don't scare easy, either."

"Oh, but you haven't met Mrs. Cole. My mother can be a fierce cheetah and a lioness rolled into one when it comes to her only child."

"A momma's boy, huh?" she teased.

Adrian stared, daring her to blink. Then, speaking softly yet with great intensity, he said, "If being a momma's boy means that I respect and care about the woman who gave birth to me and sheltered me from the storms, then I'm a proud card-carrying member of the momma's boys club. I'm also the son of Grover V. Cole, who reared me to be a man and taught me how to treat women. I'm confident in both worlds."

That statement took her breath away. It wasn't something he'd read in a book and memorized but something he lived. And she found that attractive. "I like you, Adrian Cole—your strength, your confidence—you. But your mother wouldn't chase me away if I wanted to stay. Trust me."

He squinted. "Is that so?" He leaned closer. "Will you always challenge me?"

"Always. You can thank Saul and Annette Carmen for that."

"Saul? And I thought Grover V., or G.V., was different."

Brecee hadn't realized she had lost track of time, learning more about Adrian until Rahn got their attention.

"Hey, you two." Rahn glanced at his watch. "Stay as long as you want, but it's getting late, and my family and I are heading to bed. Set the security alarm when you leave, okay, Sis?" He wrapped an arm possessively around Shae's waist as they walked toward the elevator.

Late, huh? Since when was eleven thirty late for grown folks? Brecee held in a chuckle as she looked back at her guests.

Adrian stifled a yawn. "I better call it a night, myself. Saturdays are busy."

Rahn turned around. "Oh, and I'll see what I can do about sending more business your way." He pushed the button to call the elevator. When the door opened, he and Shae stepped inside. As the door was about to close, Rahn added in a whisper, so as not to wake Sabrina, "Hope you can make it to Family and Friends Day at the ballpark. Good night."

Left alone with Adrian, Brecee looked beyond his handsome features for signs of exhaustion. Although she hadn't asked him about his day, she was sure it had been long. At least she could look forward to sleeping in tomorrow. The only thing she could do was hug him and silently pray that God would give him strength.

Finally, she wiggled free and stood. When Adrian got to his feet, she guided him toward the spiral staircase leading from the third floor to the second-floor landing, where the baby's nursery was located. They waved to Shae and Rahn, who were putting Sabrina to bed, before continuing downstairs. On the way to the side door leading to the driveway, Brecee grabbed her sweater and purse off the counter.

Outside, a cool breeze gave her goose bumps, making her shiver. Immediately, Adrian put his hands on her shoulders and rubbed her arms.

"Where's your SmartAccess key to start your vehicle?" His voice was husky.

She pulled the key card out of her purse and tapped the start button. The headlights flashed, and the engine purred. She loved her Lexus.

When they reached her car, Adrian leaned against the hood and stared at her with an unreadable expression. "I wouldn't be a gentleman if I didn't make sure you got home safely." He opened the door and waited for her to slide behind the wheel.

She looked up at him. "How about I call you once I'm safe and sound in my condo?"

Adrian shook his head. "How about I follow you home to see for myself, and—"

Without warning, Brecee's defense mechanism kicked in. Her male cousins had taught the Carmen sisters well: *Men think with their pants, so women better use their heads.* Victor's voice was loud and clear at the moment. "And what?" *God, please don't let him say the wrong thing. I'm not ready to write him off my list,* she silently prayed as she waited.

"And make sure you don't get another speeding ticket." He winked. "I know how to tease, too."

She laughed. "You got me on that. But I've gotten my first and last ticket, so no worries there. I live on the South Side. Twenty minutes in the other direction. I'll be fine."

"You are fine, but I insist, because I care about you. I have no other motives. Momma taught me well. I won't disrespect you."

Lord, he says the right things. Can I trust him? Tilting her head, Brecee studied his expression, trying to gauge his honesty. She was sure Shae and Rahn had taken down his license plate number, and their home security system was videotaping them at the moment. "All right," she said, exhaling.

She waved at the security camera, then shifted into drive.

Adrian pivoted on his heel and turned toward the house, evidently look-ing for signs of her sister or brother-in-law, before heading for his Audi.

As Brecee crossed Lindbergh to I-40 eastbound and exited onto the highway, she mused that it had been a long time since she'd been treated with such chivalry. And she liked it. "Lord, please let him be the one."

CHAPTER TWELVE

The next day, Adrian was slightly off his game at the dealership. He was still two sales shy for the month, so he hoped to snag some prospective customers walking into the showroom.

He worked the smile and the handshake, but his mind wasn't on building customer relationships; it was on Brecee and what she was doing on this sunny day in April. Since she lived across the street from a park, he wondered if she was there, perhaps taking a walk or riding a bike?

It had pricked his heart to see traces of doubt in her eyes last night when he'd offered to tail her home. Brecee mattered to him. Despite the other demands in his life, whether work or school, she was becoming his number one priority. It would take some time, but Adrian planned to prove it to her.

"My credit is on the rebound," Mr. Sikeston said, leaning on Adrian's desk and pulling his mind back to the business at hand. "I had some bad investments," he said, glancing at his wife, "but it should still be okay for us to get the Mercedes."

"Let me talk to my financing department and see what kind of interest rate we can get you." Adrian stood and walked out of his office.

There had been plenty of lookers that morning, but if their credit score didn't hit a certain number, getting the key into their hand was a moot point.

It wasn't long before they learned that his score wasn't high enough, after all. So, the Sikestons settled for a preowned car. "Whenever you're ready for an upgrade, I'll be here for you," Adrian told them.

By the time the dealership closed its doors, Adrian had handed out five business cards to potential clients who'd promised that they would be in touch. He planned to follow up with them on Monday with a thank-you note and a gift card to Starbucks or Applebee's.

Adrian was mentally drained as he drove the short distance home. The game face of a transportation problem solver had to be consistent, hiding disappointment and desperation to meet monthly goals. But Adrian liked the adrenaline rush of a challenge, which brought Brecee to mind, so he called her, but it went straight to her voice mail. He smiled anyway. "Hi. I didn't want anything, just to hear your voice. I miss you."

He had never opened himself to a woman this early on in a relationship. But this was Brecee's game, and he was a willing participant.

As he parked in the lot outside his condo, the only things on Adrian's mind were a hot shower and steaming plate of food. At least he could look forward to Sunday, his day of rest. He stepped out of his car and stretched before taking the short pathway to his door. His brain and his body needed the downtime before classes resumed this week, and he went back to the grind.

In his kitchen, it didn't take long for Adrian to fulfill his cravings. Then he caught the end of the evening newscast with Shae Maxwell. He thought about Rahn's invitation to Family and Friends Day at the ballpark the following weekend. Hopefully, he could fit it into his schedule.

Adrian began to doze when his smartphone rang, jarring him awake. Eyeing the caller ID, he saw that it was Brecee.

"You sound tired," she said when he answered. "Did I wake you?"

"I was sleeping," he confessed, "but I like the sound of my wakeup call." He chuckled. "What did you do all day?"

"Oh, a little bit of everything: cooking, cleaning, strolling through my neighborhood, discovering more sights…." Her voice was chipper. "But I thought a lot about you, wondering how your day was going. If you made any sales. If you were hungry."

That comment gave him a burst of energy. "The next time you think of me while you're working in the kitchen, I'll take a personal delivery of a home-cooked meal."

"Personal delivery, huh? Are you telling me you don't get many home-cooked meals?"

"Only when I stop by my mother's. Even Laura cooks eggs better than Dolan, so, suffice it to say, the Cole men can't cook. Mom seems to have a deep freezer full of meals ready to thaw when my key turns the lock at her house."

"Sounds like my mother," Brecee said. "Only she would always send me home with leftovers."

"I think God broke the mold on my mother," Adrian told her. "She's always scheming."

"Really? In what ways?" Brecee pressed him.

He didn't have to rack his brain. His life had been full of examples. "I had a nervous stomach when I was young. So, if I wanted to get sent home from school, I would just eat anything at lunch to make myself throw up, which meant the nurse would call Mom. After the second time, she had the nurse put me on the phone. She asked me why I didn't eat what she had packed. If she wasn't satisfied with my answer, she'd tell the nurse to give me some 7 Up and to send me back to class."

When Brecee burst out laughing, Adrian couldn't help but join in.

"Clever lady," she said. "I remember when I went to senior prom, my mother had my cousins pay their friends to act as undercover bodyguards. I didn't know until the night was over…." She paused. "I miss home. How long as it been since you visited your parents?"

Adrian exhaled. "A few weeks. But, as a good son, I do call routinely to check on her and my pops."

"If I could fly home to see my mother and my other two sisters every weekend, I would," Brecee said. "But Shae is here, so I am, too. When I finished my residency, I could've taken a position at The Children's Hospital of Philadelphia, but then Shae would've been here without any family. One of our male cousins had even considered relocating to St. Louis, just so we would have a bodyguard."

"I gotcha." Adrian nodded to himself. "Why did you think I wanted to make sure you got home safely last night?"

She was quiet for a moment. "I'm getting the message that you care."

Good. Adrian grinned. "I admire your tight family bond. Dolan is my closest cousin here. Most of our relatives live in either Detroit or Oklahoma City."

"Why don't you make a special trip to visit your parents tomorrow?" she suggested.

"I will, if you're ready to come along and meet them," Adrian blurted out, without considering how his mother—or Brecee—would receive that. He held his breath. That's the kind of thing that happened when he played with Brecee. Had he made a bad move?

"I'm giving you a chance to take that back," she said softly.

"I can't."

"Then I would love to come with you. I promise to be on my best behavior."

"Why does that scare me?" he teased, recovering. "I'm surprised you weren't with Shae today."

"That's because Rahn's in town," Brecee explained. "On his weekends at home, I step back into my place and let her be his wife." Her whimsical tone made him curious.

"So, you're the only single Carmen sister left, huh?"

She released a soft grunt. "Yep. I'm still waiting for that special someone to come into my life."

"You're beautiful and caring. That's a dangerous combination for a man not to be smitten."

"Ah, that's sweet." He imagined she was blushing. "I've been holding out for the right one."

Even though he was about to take her home to meet Mom and Pops, he still had to take it slow. "I'm not trying to send mixed signals, so let's take our time and see if you've found the right one."

"I'd like that," she said. "I'll be back from church around one thirty. Be here at two. Until then, get some rest."

⌒

The next morning at church, Brecee got down on her knees to thank God for the privilege of His presence, then stood and slid into the pew next to Shae and Rahn.

She whispered into her sister's ear that she wouldn't be joining them for dinner. Shae asked why, and when Brecee told her, one of her eyebrows lifted like their mother's with a "You'd better explain yourself" expression.

"You're going to meet his parents?"

Brecee reached for Sabrina, then smothered her niece's neck with soft kisses. "We were joking around, and the invitation slipped out. I actually felt bad for him and offered him a way out, but he didn't back down. Maybe he just didn't want to hurt my feelings. We both agreed to wait and see where our relationship is going." She paused as the members of the praise team picked up their microphones.

"Then go along for the ride." Shae nudged her. "Get it? He's a car salesman."

Rolling her eyes, Brecee exhaled. "He's a transportation problem solver," she reminded her.

When Sabrina reached for her mother, Brecee handed her back and stood to join in the sequence of songs about the blood of Christ: "The Blood Still Works," "The Blood," and "I Know It Was the Blood."

Before long, the praise team yielded the floor to the person tasked with reading the weekly announcements. As Brecee took her seat, her mind drifted to Adrian. Was he still in bed? Rahn had an afternoon game that day, but at least he was committed to spending an hour at church with his family before going to work. There was no doubt she wanted what he and Shae had, and she was willing to wait for it.

Pastor Archie began to preach from Romans 5, beginning with verse 4, which he summarized: "Patience produces character, and character produces hope."

Help me, God, to trust You in all things, was Brecee's silent prayer. *You've been with me through all my tests, so please give me patience to trust You and to exercise patience with this new relationship.*

God ministered to her soul throughout the sermon. Many others seemed just as affected when they walked down the aisle for the altar call and requested baptism in Jesus' name.

Minutes after the benediction, Brecee barely took the time to hug Shae good-bye. "Got to go."

She hurried home, careful of her speed. The attorney she'd hired had taken care of one ticket; she didn't plan on using her services again. Once at her condo, she took off her hat and heels, changing out of her stylish suit into a simple knit dress with a coordinating cardigan and open-toe wedge shoes—comfortable and casual, yet classy. After all, she was meeting his mother.

Ten minutes to two, she peeked out the window and saw Adrian drive up. He parked but didn't get out right away. Frowning, she continued to watch. "He better not be about to honk and expect me to come down," she muttered.

She checked her makeup and overall appearance in her bathroom mirror, then glanced out the window again. What was he doing?

A few minutes later, her doorbell rang. She took her time answering, but her frown vanished at the sight of him. Even casually dressed in a polo shirt and jeans, he was an eye-catcher.

"Hi. On time." Adrian beamed, showing that hint of a dimple, and his eyes sparkled as he handed her a bag from St. Louis Bread Company. "I know we're going to my mother's for dinner, and she will kill me if she finds out, but here are your favorite cookies for later."

Brecee's heart melted as she accepted his gift. "Thank you," she whispered. She looked up at him. "I saw you pull in ten minutes ago. When you didn't get out, I thought you were expecting me to come down on my own."

Chuckling, he took her hand and kissed it. "Not on my watch. I respect you and will always treat you as a lady. C'mon. Once my mother sets the table, she likes to serve on time."

"Okay." In the back of her mind, she could hear her own mother scolding her: *Let him be a man.* She locked her door. When she slid into the passenger seat of his Audi, she relaxed. "Ooh, this is nice."

"I thought you would like it." After shutting her door, he came around to the driver side and got in, then clicked his seat belt.

"Is this a loaner from the dealership?"

"This is my own car that I purchased from the dealership. The days of loaner cars are mostly gone."

When Adrian's smartphone rang, he ignored it.

"Aren't you going to answer that?" she asked.

"No." Keeping his eyes on the highway, he squeezed her hand. "It's not my mother...or you. My clients have to accept boundaries. Sunday is my only day off, so I turn myself off, too. Besides, who wants to talk business when I have you to speak with about anything else?"

So, he could separate business from pleasure. That earned him a few brownie points. She appreciated that as they chatted about music, family—everything but work. There were no predictable days in the emergency room, and she didn't relish reliving the heartbreaking cases when she wasn't on the clock.

Soon, Adrian turned into a neighborhood of spacious houses with well-maintained lawns in the suburb of Black Jack. He parked in front of ranch-style home. As they made their way up the front path, one of the black double doors opened, and a woman about the same height as Brecee stood there. Her silver-gray hair enhanced her beauty. Her features were delicate, her frame small but not thin. And her facial expression was unreadable until they got closer. There was no smile on her lips nor a sparkle in her eyes as the woman seemed to size her up.

Adrian kissed Mrs. Cole on the cheek before making the introductions. "Mom, I'd like you to meet Dr. Sabrece Carmen."

Her given name had never sounded so sexy on a man's lips. Hearing him say it even the few times that he had made Brecee consider ditching her childhood nickname that most thought was her real name.

Finally, his mother's face brightened with a smile.

"And this is my mother, Marsha Cole."

Brecee nodded. "Hello, Mrs. Cole."

"My word, you sure do favor Shae Maxwell on KMMD." Stepping back, Mrs. Cole waved them into the house.

"Thank you." The comment never bothered her. It was a compliment, after all. Shae was gorgeous, so Brecee accepted it with pride, because she loved her sister dearly.

Brecee glanced around the house. The dark hardwood floors were so glossy, they looked like they could serve as a skating rink.

"Dinner is almost ready," Mrs. Cole told them. "Sabrece—"

"Please, call me Brecee."

"Brecee it is," she agreed as a handsome, distinguished-looking gentleman stood from his chair in the family room. Even with his salt-and-pepper hair and mustache, he could definitely compete with his son in the looks department. Adrian definitely had good genes.

"Dad, this is Dr.—"

"I heard, Son." His father chuckled and extended his hand. "I'm Grover. Welcome to our home."

Soon, they all sat down in the family room. Brecee thought that the space would be picture-perfect on a winter night, with a warm fire roaring in the large fireplace. Unlike at Shae's house, Adrian stayed by her side.

"So, Brecee, tell us about yourself," Mrs. Cole began.

Both men groaned.

"Well, I work at Cardinal Glennon Hospital as a pediatric emergency department physician. I completed my residency in Houston, then moved to St. Louis to be near my sister Shae and her family. I'm originally from Philly, where my other two sisters and my mother live. We're still extremely close, despite the distance between us."

"And your father...?" Mrs. Cole asked.

"My father died when I was a teenager."

"I'm so sorry. And your mother never remarried?"

"Oh, no." Brecee shook her head. "When we were older, our mother told us, 'With four lovely, almost grown daughters, I wasn't about to bring another man into my house for him to be tempted.'"

Mrs. Cole nodded. "I like her already."

"Thank you." Brecee grinned. "Although no one could ever replace my daddy, my mother sacrificed her personal happiness time and again for our well-being."

"You said you're from Philly?" Mrs. Cole queried. Wrinkles creased her forehead, as if she were straining to recall something.

"Yes, ma'am."

"My mother was born in Jersey, but her family moved to Philly when she was young. My daddy was from Chicago. By the time I came along, they had moved to St. Louis."

Before Brecee could ask her more about her Philly connection, Mrs. Cole said, "So, why aren't you married?"

"Mom!"

"Marsha!"

Both men seemed embarrassed by her boldness, but Brecee waved them off. "This is nothing compared to the interrogation Adrian will get from my family when they come to town at the end of the month." She winked at Adrian. He didn't flinch, and his intense expression made her shiver. She cleared her throat and turned back to his mother. "To answer your question, Mrs. Cole—"

"Call me Marsha." When she smiled, Brecee saw a hint of Adrian in her expression.

The woman was playing with her. "Thank you. I'm waiting for that special someone, and I'm prepared to wait until the dots are connected. God doesn't approve of divorce, and my family certainly doesn't view it as an option for when trouble brews. They believe in a couple working it out as God gives them guidance." So far, that was the only area where Adrian was striking out.

"Good answers." Mrs. Cole smiled. "Dinner's just about ready. Won't you come to the dining room?" She stood and strode out of the room.

Adrian reached out and took Brecee's hand. "She's not finished, you know. At least you're on a first-name basis already."

"She loves you. It's normal for her to desire a say in your life choices."

Once they were gathered around the dinner table, Adrian's parents seemed interested in hearing about her job, so she indulged them.

Overall, Mr. Cole was a quiet man. He let his wife play the interrogator, while he seemed more trusting, taking what Brecee said at face value rather than suspecting her of having a hidden agenda to snag his son.

Brecee was having a good time, especially when Mrs. Cole pulled out an album of Adrian's baby pictures. Some of the photos included Dolan. They were both adorable as infants, but then, all babies were cute to her.

"Well, Mom and Dad…." Adrian got to his feet. "Brecee and I better head out. We both have to work tomorrow, and my classes start back up on Tuesday."

Mrs. Cole turned down her lips with unveiled disappointment. "You could've been finished with school already if you had started with Dolan. Then you would have more time to visit." She turned to Brecee with a smile. "Brecee—I should call you Dr. Carmen—it was nice meeting you. I hope my son will bring you to see us again."

"Thank you." She wasn't about to put pressure on Adrian to say he would, but she would gladly accept another invitation.

His parents walked them to the door and waited as they stepped down to the front walk.

"She might work," she heard Mrs. Cole whisper to her husband.

Adrian must have heard her, too, for he turned around at the same time as Brecee and looked at her.

Folding her arms, Mrs. Cole leaned against the doorpost. Her expression was blank again.

Despite the mask, Brecee had her figured out. Adrian's mother was trying to guard her son's heart, just like her family would do for her.

What his mother didn't know was Brecee would have no problem calling it off if their incompatibility outweighed the things they had in common—most important, faith in God.

CHAPTER THIRTEEN

Brecee's sisters peppered her with questions during one of their phone chats that week. For once, the focus was on her love life.

"I can't believe you met his mother already," Stacy mused.

"Relax." Brecee chuckled at the expressions on Stacy and Shari's faces. "It wasn't a 'taking me home to meet the parents' type of moment. Adrian and I were playing around, and the invite kind of slipped out of his mouth, but he made good on it."

Stacy twisted her lips. The attitude was hanging from her face. "And just what does that mean, exactly? Either the man wanted you to meet his parents or he didn't."

Once Brecee had recounted the conversation, her oldest sister snorted. "Served him right. He was messing with the wrong sister. Hasn't he learned by now that my baby sister is fearless?"

Shari, Brecee's most soft-spoken sister—unless she was in the court-room—jumped in next. "It was hard for me not to fall in love with Garrett after meeting his family. Grandpa Moses had pegged me as his grandson's wife well before he asked." She smiled.

Garrett's mother's family, the Porters, had a lot in common with the Carmens. They were musically inclined and committed to living in holiness before God.

"I can't wait to meet him." Stacy had mischief in her eyes. "I hope he's able to come to the ballpark for Family and Friends Day. I wish the Cardinals were playing the Phillies, but they aren't, so I guess we'll root for our brother-in-law and his teammates."

Brecee noticed that Shari was wearing a mischievous smile of her own. Was she pregnant again? Judging from her expression, she was ready to spill the beans about something.

"Guess who's dating?" Shari said in a singsong tone.

Dating? Brecee was the one dating! Wasn't her love life supposed to be the main topic of conversation? If it was one of their two male cousins, Victor and Dino, that was nothing new. They had been dating since they'd gotten their driver's licenses, and they always complained that there weren't any good old church women left.

"Who?" Brecee asked, in unison with Shae.

"Mom!" Shari and Stacy both shouted.

Brecee's jaw dropped. Shae's did the same.

Finally, Brecee blinked and closed her mouth. "It's been almost twenty years. Who and when? But mostly who?"

"Marcellus," Shari said, with pride in her voice.

Brecee swallowed, her next question forming.

But Shae beat her to it. "Marcellus? As in, your husband's uncle?"

"Yes." Shari nodded.

"Wow." Brecee had to give her mother credit for good taste. The older gentleman was an attention grabber. Any woman of any age would admire his looks. But she never would have paired her mother with Garrett's uncle. Wow. The word seemed to be stuck on Brecee's tongue and in her mind as she tried to comprehend this new development. Of course, Uncle Marcellus's best asset was his Christian faith—the man knew how to pray tirelessly. Garrett looked to him as a role model.

"Okay, I can see them as a couple," Shae finally said. "Stunning."

But Brecee couldn't see that. Or maybe she just didn't want to. If their dating led to marriage, she would have a stepfather. She frowned. "I, uh, didn't know Mom was looking."

She and her mother definitely needed to catch up. When she excused herself from the chat, her sisters knew why. "Tell Mom hi," Stacy and Shari harmonized.

"I'm next after you," Shae said, pointing at her computer screen.

Nodding, Brecee at Shae, Brecee said her goodbyes and immediately called her mother.

"Is it true?" she asked when her mother picked up. "My mother, Annette Carmen, is dating? Isn't there a rule against dating in-laws or something?" she teased, even though she didn't see anything funny about the situation.

"Marcellus Porter is truly a godly man." The excitement in her mother's voice was undeniable. Actually, it was so heartwarming, Brecee's own heart fluttered. "I hadn't realized he had been practicing self-restraint since we first met," her mother gushed like a teenager. "I had no idea. Then, during one of his weekend visits to see Garrett and Shari, I don't know what made me notice, but he had removed his wedding band. He was straightforward about his attraction and asked me if I would be willing to explore it. I told him I would think about it."

How long did you think about it? Brecee wondered.

"I spent a few days in prayer, reflecting on my life since your father's death," her mother said next, as if she'd read Brecee's thoughts. "With no daughters left at home, I asked myself if I was content without a special someone in my life. And then, for the first time in seventeen years and nine months, I removed my wedding ring."

Evidently, her mother's decision hadn't been easy to make. Brecee's eyes teared, and she sniffed.

"Marcellus is the persona of what Saul would be if he still were alive today—charming, incredibly good-looking, and a godly family man."

Was it possible for Brecee to be happy for her mother and sad for herself at the same time? She had never used the word "love" with a man. How was it that her mother found a relationship so quickly after opening herself up to one, while the same process had moved so slowly in her own life? Since moving to St. Louis almost two years ago and witnessing Shae and Rahn's happiness, Brecee had adopted a different outlook on casual dating. She wanted to be in a relationship that went somewhere, that developed into something special, like the relationship every other woman in her family was experiencing.

"You've been single so long, I honestly thought you would never marry again," she told her mother. "I mean, you never seemed lonely to me."

"Sweetie, loneliness isn't always an outer garment. The heart can long for someone without anyone else's knowing it."

"I guess so." Brecee got up from her bed, walked into her bathroom, and grabbed a bunch of tissues to wipe her tears.

"Sweetie, it's all right." Her mother's smooth voice was soothing. It engulfed her with almost as much comfort as her actual presence would have. "Marc is a good man."

Brecee nodded. She knew that, but her mind was still in shock as she glanced at the clock. It was almost eleven o'clock on the East Coast—well past her mother's normal bedtime. But Brecee needed answers. "So, how serious is this?" she asked. "Man, that's the disadvantage of living far away from home. Not only are Shae and I always the last ones to know, but I can't give him a hard time."

Her mother laughed. "Your cousins and my brother-in-law have been sufficient stand-ins."

"Is this casual dating, or...." She held her breath. After so many years, she couldn't imagine her mother being anything else but a Carmen, "Do you think you'll marry Garrett's uncle?"

"If he asked me to marry him today? No. Tomorrow? No. But sometime in the future...maybe. The Carmens marry for life, and I'm too old for any drama."

For life. That's what God wanted, and generations of Carmens had been able to make it happen.

"I want to hear about you," her mother said next. "What's going on with you and Mr. Cole, besides meeting his parents?"

Brecee rolled her eyes. "I don't even want to guess who told you."

"Stacy texted me right after you signed off from the conference call."

Shaking her head, Brecee smiled. Some things never changed. "I went with no expectations, really," Brecee confessed. "My first impression of his mother was that she's hard to read. Her expressions made it hard to guess what she was thinking."

"Well, it's our turn. We'll put the fear of the Carmen clan in Adrian when we visit later this month."

Brecee exhaled. "I'll be glad when you all get here. I definitely need a third, fourth, and fifth opinion. Shae wants to investigate him as if he's a suspect in a crime story she's covering on the news."

"Better yet, Shari might ask him to consent to a criminal background check," her mother said.

Brecee giggled. "Well, I'd better go. Mondays are always busy in the emergency department."

"Okay, sweetie. When it comes to Adrian, stop trying to figure out what the Lord has already worked out. Good night. I love you."

"Wait, Mom." Brecee cleared her throat. "One small request: Can you hold off getting remarried until I'm at least engaged? How would it look for every Carmen woman to be married except for me?"

"I know you're joking," her mother said. "I'm almost sixty, and you're almost thirty-two. Do the math, honey. I'm not getting any younger. Good night."

When the line went silent, Brecee did the math. Unless Adrian was the one, she was going to be an old maid.

⌒

Adrian was surprised to see his cousin walked through the dealership door on his lunch break. They shook hands and Adrian guided Dolan back to his cousin and they took a seat.

"What's up?"

"I heard you took Brecee to meet Aunt Marsha. And the doctor hasn't dumped you?" Adrian roared.

Adrian didn't see the humor. His mother had earned a reputation for being picky when it came to women for her son and her nephews back when they were teenagers. Lucky for Dolan, she'd approved of Denise, his late wife.

"Granted, it wasn't one of my calculated moves, but I think Mom found a kindred spirit with Brecee," Adrian told him. "Neither one is easily intimidated."

"Brecee's got me thinking..." Dolan confessed.

Adrian eyed his cousin warily. "I don't know what you're thinking, but leave my lady out of it."

"I'll ignore your threat." Dolan massaged his beard. "After seeing how clingy Laura is around Brecee, I think I need to open myself up to another special woman. My little girl needs a permanent female figure in her life."

"What are you saying?"

"That height, shape, skin color, and hair length no longer determine my definition of a woman's beauty. 'Sweet' and 'loves my daughter' are at the top of my list."

"Congratulations." Adrian patted his cousin on the back. He'd always believed that a child needed both parents, but who was he to tell Dolan that he ought to look for love again? "Any prospects?"

"No, but I'm sure if I mention it to Laura, she'll start praying for one."

CHAPTER FOURTEEN

Brecee had begun counting down the hours until the Carmens would land at Lambert–St. Louis International Airport. It was showtime. Adrian was about to meet his mother's match.

Ever since she had started seeing Adrian, Brecee had been confiding in her colleague and sister in Christ, Regina, about her concerns. Regina's response was always, "What did God say?"

Brecee was learning that either she had an answer, or she'd better get back on her knees and wait on God to give her one.

Regina was invaluable as a friend and prayer partner. She had even been nice enough to trade her one of her Friday daylight shift with Brecee's midday shift so that she could start her weekend early. Of course, her friend wanted something in return—baseball tickets when her family came to town. Thankfully, it was easy calling in favors from Brecee's brother-in-law.

"Enjoy your family," Regina told her when she showed up to take over Brecee's patients. "I'm in Adrian's corner. Hope he wows them."

Soon, Brecee and Shae were riding in one of two limos Rahn had sent to the airport to pick up their sisters, their brothers-in-law, their nieces and nephews, their mother, and her beau. Would Brecee ever get used to saying that? Then, there was the other Carmen family: Uncle Bradford, Aunt Camille, and cousins Victor and Dino. The two families had grown up as one. Saul and his four daughters and Bradford and his two sons had always been inseparable.

Brecee had been fifteen when her father died. Uncle Bradford had stepped in and never missed a beat, providing the Carmen girls with the same guidance his brother surely would have during their teenage years. This would be a true family reunion, complete with a mini concert, compliments of Shari and her husband's habit of toting their saxophones wherever they went.

After stepping out of the limo at the airport, Brecee and Shae thanked the driver, then headed to baggage claim to serve as the welcome committee.

As they waited, two businessmen gave them seductive glances. Brecee stared them down, while Shae did the mother thing—arched one eyebrow in a way that would put the fear of God into any child.

"Does the rock on my finger need to be any bigger?" Shae stated none too softly.

Brecee giggled. There weren't many men who could afford the diamond gracing her sister's ring finger.

That thought turned her mind to Adrian. "Do you think everyone will like him?"

"Nope." Shae didn't hold back. The Carmen sisters rarely did. "I hope his networking skills are up to par, because you know the family is going to force him to earn their approval."

"I'm sure they will, after he finishes telling them about the best features of their cars."

They chuckled, then continued chatting, keeping an eye on the board of arrivals. When the board showed that the plane had landed, it wasn't long before travelers came spilling out from the terminal. Impatient, Brecee peeked through the crowd. It would be hard to miss the group of ten adults and three children.

"There's Mom," Brecee and Shae said at the same time.

When their family saw them, they hurried toward one another like magnets. Babies were being exchanged for kisses and hugs. Tears welled up in Brecee's eyes. She'd missed her family so much.

She froze when she spied Uncle Marcellus at her mother's side. He didn't wait for her to come to him but rather reached out and engulfed her in a warm embrace that broke the ice.

"You've made a good catch with the queen bee," she told him. "What am I supposed to call you now? Still Uncle Marcellus, or Mr. Nash?" Once Garrett married Shari, he became their "uncle," too.

"Whatever makes you more comfortable."

His deep, rich voice and gentle tone made Brecee reconsider speaking her mind, as she was known for doing. She would have liked to tell him that she wasn't comfortable with him dating her mother, but she held her tongue.

As if he had read her thoughts, Marcellus smiled and said, "Give me a chance."

After taking a few moments to let his affections for her mother digest, she mouthed, *Okay.*

"Where is Mr. Cole?" her mother asked. "I was hoping he'd be here to greet us."

Again, Brecee had to refrain from speaking her mind. *Rahn's not here. Why call Adrian out? God, help me. Why am I reverting to a childish mentality?*

Almost immediately, God imparted a peace that settled her spirit. She smiled. "He's at work. Everyone will meet him tonight."

"At least he has a job," Uncle Bradford stated, winking at Brecee before giving her another hug.

"But a car salesman?" Dino, the younger of her two cousins, smirked.

"Sales drives our economy," Garrett said, holding Saul in his arms.

"C'mon, let's get your bags," Shae suggested. "Rahn has two limos waiting. He's at home with Sabrina, barbecuing."

The men gathered the luggage, and everyone walked outside to wait by the curb. After getting the women and children settled in the first limo, the men piled into the second one. The only exception was Stacy's son, T.J., who wanted to ride with his dad and uncles.

Brecee was always in awe of how the men in the family were so attuned to the women's desires and preferences. She wanted that in her man.

As they cruised to Shae's Town and Country mansion, Brecee just soaked up the love she felt from being surrounded by the most important women in her life. Her mother, a former beauty pageant contestant, had always looked youthful for her age, but today, she glowed. Now that they were all together with no men around, Brecee revisited her mother's love life. "I can't believe my mother is dating!"

Stacy chuckled. "Believe me, the idea took some getting used to." She nudged their mother.

"I found a jewel in Garrett," Shari said. "So, I was more than all right with the idea."

"After she got over the shock," their mother added.

The ride seemed too short as Brecee and Shae got caught up on what was happening back home. As the limo made the turn into the Maxwells' driveway, Stacy looked at Brecee. "So, do you think Adrian might be the one?"

"That's for us to determine," her mother butted in, earning nods of affirmation from her sisters and aunt.

Rahn greeted them at the door, along with the housekeeper, Miss Vera, who worked only when extra help was needed. With a home full of guests, she was there to get everyone situated.

After the meal, the men started talking baseball. It wasn't long before Rahn had to leave for the ballpark to join the team for the pregame warmup session. Dino and Victor accepted his invite to watch the last game in the series against the Atlanta Braves. Stacy's husband, Ted, and Uncle Bradford tagged along, too. "We're going for a sweep," Rahn told them.

Hours later, Brecee became anxious for Adrian to meet her family, but she didn't want to nag him. He was at work, and he knew they were in town.

She texted him. Do you think you'll be able to make it here later tonight? Rahn BBQ'd earlier, so there is plenty.

I'm finishing up with my last client, he replied. See you soon.

She exhaled.

"Nervous?" Shae asked, watching the children help themselves to toys and games in the playroom. They got a kick out of watching Sabrina fight sleep to play with her cousins.

"I am. Do you think he'll pass?"

Shae shrugged. "He's charming and good-looking—superficial qualities. The only thing our family wants to know is the way he feels about you and how he's going to treat you."

"Don't forget to see if there are any skeletons in his closet," Stacy added.

"Should have done a background check," Shari said.

"Stop playing." Brecee shook her finger. "You wouldn't risk getting disbarred."

Brecee eyed the clock on the wall. The dealership should be closed by now, and Adrian was probably on his way. She gnawed on her lips. The last thing she wanted to do was nag a grown man, but she found herself wishing she had planted a GPS tracking device on his car, so she would know how close he was. She got up from her chair in the playroom and walked down the hall to the massive window overlooking the front yard. There were no car lights in sight on the road.

"Hey." Shae came up beside her. "Why don't you call him? Or try texting again?" Even she looked concerned.

"He should be here any minute. Maybe there was some traffic," Brecee said, trying to convince herself.

"Maybe he was in the middle of making a big sale," Shae said, giving voice to Brecee's fear.

She folded her arms over her chest. "I don't want to be in constant competition with cars," she said softly.

"Hey, I'm in constant competition with road trips and spring training," Shae reminded her. "I can see my husband on TV but can't touch him for more than a month at a time. But when Rahn comes home, even if it's for just a day or two, I'm always the center of his attention. And that's all that matters to me. When we're together, it's us."

"What are you saying?"

"I'm saying, how does he make you feel when it's just you two? If he's focused on you, then the other stuff doesn't matter." Shae squeezed her shoulder.

When her mother and some of the other older adults started yawning fifteen minutes later, they started preparing the children for bed. It was then that Brecee knew Adrian had earned a strike against him. There was no sense in keeping her family awake any longer. She was about to call and tell him not to come when he sent a text.

Sorry, babe. I thought everything was a done deal, but then the customer had second thoughts. My manager and I went back and forth with negotiations in order to clinch the deal. We couldn't get it to happen. It's too late now for me to come over. Forgive me?

Her heart sank with disappointment for his loss. Yes, was all she typed before going to inform her sisters and mother. "Adrian got tied up at work," she told them. "He apologizes, and he'll see you tomorrow."

She turned and took the steps to the second-floor bedroom, which she used whenever she spent the night. The bedroom was big enough to be considered a suite, and her mother was sharing it with her for this particular visit.

Sitting in a rocker, Brecee stared out the window into the night. She heard someone come in, but she didn't turn around. She could see her mother's reflection in the window.

Her mother settled herself down on the bed. "Sweetie."

Her presence reminded Brecee of being home. Whenever there was a problem, it seemed like her mom always had the last word before Brecee said her prayers.

"Why are you upset?"

"Why shouldn't I be?"

"It all depends on why. Adrian sounds like a hardworking man. Don't worry about us. We'll check him out soon enough. Get some rest. God's mercies are new every morning, so why don't you extend that mercy to Adrian, rather than storing up what didn't happen tonight for tomorrow? You can't always have your way."

Annette's pearls of wisdom—how Brecee craved them. She nodded, then stood and gave her mother a hug and kiss on the cheek from her.

"Now, I've already said good night to Marcellus. Why don't you send Adrian a sweet text while I take a shower?" Her mother got to her feet and went to the corner where her suitcase sat, then glanced over her shoulder. "Sweetie, if you'll pray without ceasing, God will reveal all He wants you to know about Adrian."

"Okay." She smirked and texted Adrian: I missed you today, but I'm excited about tomorrow. Good night.

Almost immediately, he responded: Sorry. I missed you, too. Tomorrow.

"Tomorrow," she whispered to herself. Closing her eyes, she took a deep breath to help release the unnecessary stress. Then she said her prayers. First, she repented of negative thoughts, bad attitudes, and deeds done that day that hadn't pleased the Lord. With that out of the way, she thanked Him for the blood Jesus shed on Calvary, then interceded for others who were going through trials. Before saying amen, she tagged on a personal request: "Jesus, I really want to know if Adrian and I are meant to be. Please show me."

The next morning, the Maxwells' mansion was a madhouse with the children carrying on in the playroom while her mother and aunt commandeered the kitchen, preparing a buffet of scrambled eggs, pancakes, and fresh fruit.

Rahn had already said hi and bye before heading to the stadium. When it was time to get dressed for the game, Shae was fully decked out in Cardinals gear to show her team spirit. Everyone else wore either a Cardinals hat or a jersey Shae liked to send home.

"Is Adrian going to make it?" Shari asked Brecee.

"Yes, he is." She had to be positive. Despite Saturday being one of the busiest days for car dealerships, she hoped Adrian would make his monthly quota—and the game.

"He'd better," Dino mumbled as the group climbed into the limos parked in the driveway.

⌒

One rule of Adrian's work ethic was never to rush a client. Today, however, he'd make an exception. He needed to get downtown to the ballpark where Brecee and her family were expecting him.

Walking out of his office, Adrian shook hands with Dave Gleason and his wife as he discreetly steered them toward the door. Getting their financing had been a major holdup. He'd had to talk to the sales manager about upping the trade-in amount, then stretching out the Gleasons' payments for them to afford the E-Class Benz Coupe.

Once the Gleasons drove off the lot, Adrian's quota would be met, evident with a corresponding mark beside his name on the sales board. He escorted them outside the showroom, where their brand-new luxury vehicle awaited them. After waving good-bye, Adrian spun on his heels with his mind set on getting out of there.

"Adrian."

At the sound of his name, Adrian almost cringed. When he turned around, he saw a distinguished-looking gentleman walking toward him with his arm outstretched. Adrian obliged him with a handshake and learned that Mr. Russell was a walk-in referral from Rahn. *Of all days.*

Still, this was Adrian's livelihood. Even if Mr. Russell didn't purchase a car that day, he was still a prospective client, with the potential to refer friends and family members to Adrian.

Showing Mr. Russell to his office, Adrian sat down across from him to chat, his object being to get to know the man and his transportation needs.

"I'm retired from Boeing, and the house is paid off. My wife and I thought we would do some traveling and in style. What would you suggest?"

"The Lexus is the most dependable luxury car on the road. Of course, the Mercedes-Benz symbolizes our dominance of land, sea, and air. Behind the wheel of any Benz, you're making a statement. Your status will show before you step out in your Stacy Adamses."

Mr. Russell's eyes danced with excitement.

"Now, I drive the Audi because—"

"No, let me see your selection of Benzes."

"Sure." Adrian stood. "We have sedans, coupes, convertibles, hybrids, SUVs. I guarantee that we have something that will hypnotize you." He led Mr. Russell outside to the lot. The sun was shining brightly, offsetting the chilly breeze. "It's a great day for a test drive," he said as Mr. Russell admired one model after another.

The thrill of the thought of making another sale overrode his desire to get to the ballpark. Still, he discreetly checked the time. The game had started at one. It was now almost two, so he had some wiggle room. Some.

"That two-seater Roadster is calling my name." Mr. Russell was almost salivating as he pointed at the vehicle.

"Excellent choice—until your wife sees it." Adrian would love for the man to drive off the lot with the eighty-thousand-dollar car, but taking a convertible home to an unsuspecting wife was like a child bringing home a dog and expecting to be allowed to keep it. Adrian should know. He'd stopped counting how many times his parents had told him no. Mrs. Russell would definitely want a say in choosing a luxury model. "Let's set up a time for you to bring her in and see if she would like it," he suggested.

Mr. Russell looked thoughtful for a moment. "You've got a point," he finally agreed. "But if Mae could get that mink she wanted, I'm getting a convertible. Do you think I could take it for a test drive? I can bring Mae back on Monday morning for her to see the new addition to the family. How does that sound?" Adrian nodded. "I'll go get the keys."

The man ignored Adrian as he inspected the car's bumper.

When Adrian returned to the showroom, Kyle stepped into his path. "What are you getting ready to do?"

Adrian frowned. "Isn't it obvious? We're taking that beauty for a spin."

Kyle looked over his shoulder. "Aren't you supposed to be at a baseball game with your lady friend? You've met your quota for the month. You don't always have to be top dog month after month."

One of the two of them usually dominated that spot. To others, it might have seemed that they were fierce competitors, but they both knew the importance of having allies in the workplace. Adrian knew that if he needed someone in his corner, Kyle would be the man. They also had an understanding that they would take care of each other's customers if something came up.

"If I had a beautiful doctor expecting me at a baseball game with great seats, I wouldn't still be here," Kyle told him. "Listen, invest in your personal life. Some things are replaceable—things. You told me yourself she's special. Don't be like me. I alienated my children because I was chasing the money, and I lost my wife because she wasn't my priority. Learn from my mistakes. Now, get out of here. You know I got your back on this. No fifty/fifty split. The commission is all yours."

Kyle had taken away any argument Adrian might have raised. He nodded. "Thanks, man. You're right."

"I know." Kyle snickered.

Once Adrian got the keys to the car and handed them to Kyle, both men walked out of the door toward Mr. Russell. Adrian made the introductions, then excused himself.

Taking the quickest route downtown, Adrian hopped on Highway 64. As he drove, struggling to keep within the speed limit, he thought about his mother and smiled.

Days earlier, she had asked about Brecee. When he'd mentioned that her family was flying in from Philly, the comment seemed to trigger something within her.

"I remember your granddaddy mentioning Momma worked for a bakery called Tastykake," she'd told him. "I don't know if it's still there. Ask Brecee or her mother."

Adrian's grandmother had died young, so his mother knew very little about her own mother's life. After rambling on for a while, she'd ended the call by saying, "Son, make time in your life for something else besides working. Dr. Carmen doesn't seem like the type of woman who will settle, and no woman should."

The wisdom of Kyle and his mother played in his mind until he arrived at the ballpark. Fans were swarming around Busch Stadium. Adrian turned on the radio broadcast of the game—why hadn't he thought to do that before?—to see how late he was.

It was already the seventh-inning stretch, and the Cardinals were beating the Pirates, six to one.

Adrian pulled into a nearby lot and paid an outrageous price for what would probably amount to an hour at most. He hurried to the gate where Rahn had told him his ticket would be waiting. When he reached the assigned section, an usher helped him locate Brecee's family.

Shae occupied the aisle seat, with Brecee seated beside her. Although Brecee's family members were on their feet, cheering and screaming, they all stopped and turned his way, as if they sensed his presence.

Not one to scare easily, Adrian was still surprised by the number of men in the group.

Shae smiled at him. "Glad you're here," she whispered before stepping aside.

"Me, too," he said with his eyes on Brecee. He gave her a quick hug, even though he wanted to linger.

She seemed to exhale in his arms before pulling back. "You made it." Her eyes misted. "I didn't think you were going to come. Again."

Brecee had no idea how close he'd come to not showing a second time. Thank goodness Kyle had talked some sense in him, because selling himself to Brecee's family was just as crucial to selling cars to pay bills. He smiled sheepishly. "Have I missed a lot?"

She nodded. "Yes."

Adrian was tempted to ask her if she was talking about the game or her family, but he didn't. Instead, he slipped his fingers through hers.

She grasped his hand. "I want you to meet my mother." She gestured to the woman standing on her other side.

How had he failed to notice the beautiful lady until now? Clearly, when he was with Brecee, she made him forget about everything else around them.

"Hi," the woman said, smiling warmly, her eyes sparkling. "I'm Annette Carmen. It's nice to meet you."

So, this was how the Carmen women aged—gracefully. Adrian had no complaints.

From there, Brecee went down the row, making introductions. This was one good-looking family. Even the men, minus the scowls on their faces, could have easily generated a following of female admirers wherever they went.

Adrian shook as many hands as he could reach before turning his attention back to Brecee and capturing her fingers again. "You look pretty," he whispered in her ear. She smelled good, too.

While everyone else seemed anxious or excited over the outcome of the game, Adrian's only concern was his outcome with Brecee and her family.

CHAPTER FIFTEEN

If you glow any brighter, I'll need SPF one hundred sunscreen," Shae teased Brecee when they returned to the mansion for a post-game party.

"What can I say?" Brecee didn't try to deny her jubilation. "I'm happy Adrian's here. Now I don't feel like the loner of the bunch." She glanced across the marble foyer into the living room, where the men were gathered, talking to Adrian. "But if it's going to work out between us, he has to pass the Carmens' inspection. I refuse to allow a man to make me an outcast from my family. So, if he doesn't like any of them, he'd better play pretend until he leaves."

"He'll fit in like Rahn did," Shae assured her. "Aren't salesman conditioned to turn any situation into their favor? Plus, from the looks of it, they're all laughing and smiling."

"They'll end up talking about cars." Brecee watched Adrian, noting his calm demeanor that exuded an air of self-confidence. She was drawn to that confidence, but she wanted to be the center of his attention.

"Don't be so sure," their mother said, coming up behind them and wedging herself in between. She wrapped her arm around Brecee's waist, then steered her toward the kitchen. "You're the baby girl. They're going to skin him alive." She lowered her voice to add, "He's probably shaking in his shoes."

They giggled as they entered the kitchen, where Shari was supervising her two sons, Garrison and Saul, snacking on crackers at the kiddie table. The women began warming up the leftover BBQ from the night before, along with the pasta dishes that Miss Vera had prepared while they were at the game. They placed the food on a cart and wheeled it to the elevator for transport to the entertainment room.

They spent so much time there, Brecee often joked that Shae and Rahn could have done without the first floor, as it seemed only to serve as a showpiece.

"Gentlemen?" her mother called them to get their attention. "If you care to join us, then follow the food."

"In a minute, Annette," Uncle Bradford replied, as if annoyed by the interruption. "Brecee's young man is telling us about the newest Benz models."

The women groaned as Brecee rolled her eyes in amusement. When the elevator door opened, they crammed inside with the children and cart.

"So much for skinning him alive." Brecee shook her head, but her heart was doing a victory dance.

"Mommy, I like riding the elevator," little T.J. told Stacy. "Can we get one in our house?"

"Ask your dad," Stacy muttered.

Although Shae and Rahn's house was massive and elegant by Brecee's standards, when the children visited, they thought it was a playhouse. As the family pediatrician, Brecee always reminded her sisters of the importance of proper supervision so her nieces and nephews wouldn't wind up in her emergency department.

Once upstairs, they arranged the platters on the bar, then settled the children in the play area and fed them. Afterward, T.J. went for the chalkboard, while Shari's sons rifled through the toy box. Sabrina lay on her play mat, cooing happily.

Putting her hands on her hips, her mother shook her head. "I think our men are putting in their orders for some luxury cars. Either that, or they're grilling Adrian, and he isn't cracking under the pressure. Good for him." She grinned, then glanced at her sister-in-law. "Camille and I are in the mood for a concert."

Her aunt nodded as the two women helped themselves to the front row of theater seats facing the stage.

"That's what I'm talking about," Aunt Camille said as the sisters took the stage.

Playing their instruments was second nature to Brecee and her sisters. Their parents had always encouraged them to use their talents for the glory of God, and they had, whether participating in a musical competition, performing the opening act at a gospel concert, or playing at church on Sunday mornings.

Whenever the sisters were together, they played. Brecee lifted her guitar from its case near the back of the platform. Stacy pulled out the bench at the baby grand piano. Shari attached the neck strap to her tenor sax. Shae handed Sabrina to their mother, then picked up her drumsticks and got comfortable behind the drums.

Brecee stood in front of their audience and bowed. "We're taking requests, Mom and Aunt Camille."

"'Tomorrow,'" Aunt Camille said.

Shaking her head, Brecee smirked. "Now, why am I not surprised?" She had been a young girl when that gospel song by the Winans—her aunt's favorite—had hit the music world.

"No, 'Grateful,'" her mother insisted. "Because that's the way I feel at this moment, surrounded by my girls, who have such good husb—such good men in their lives."

That was her mother. She always looked for the good in people, while her Uncle Bradford and cousins Victor and Dino tended to be suspicious of every man within ten feet of the Carmen girls, considering him guilty until proven innocent. Since her family didn't follow the "name it, claim it" trend, Brecee wondered if God had revealed something to her mother concerning Adrian. "Sorry, Aunt Camille," Stacy said as she ran her fingers across the keyboard for the prelude to Hezekiah Walker's timeless tune of "Grateful." Brecee picked it up on the guitar as Shari blended in with her sax.

Having the best voice, Shae began softly singing the chorus. Stacy, Brecee, and Shari accompanied her with rhythm and harmony, building the tempo until the Spirit of the Lord filled the room more and more with each repetition of "grateful." They worshipped Jesus as David had with his harp.

As they were finishing, the elevator door opened. Out stepped the tall, dark, incredibly handsome black men. Adrian was the only one who looked starstruck. Brecee had told him that she came from a musical family. Evidently, seeing was believing.

While he stood rooted in place, arms folded over his chest, and watched with an appreciative smile, the other men joined Brecee's mother and aunt in the front row. The only exception was Garrett. As if he had been silently summoned, he made a beeline to his instrument case, assembled his tenor sax, and stepped up on the platform next to his wife.

Brecee was surprised that her cousins and uncle didn't join in, but they seemed content to watch the impromptu concert. It would conclude like every one before it, with a battle of the sexes on the saxes, as Shari and Garrett dueled for dominance on their instruments. Although Shari's husband was very good, she was in her element and often beat out even her male cousins, who had taught her to excel on the tenor sax.

When Garrett gasped for air on the last note, applause erupted. The family cheered Shari on as she sustained the tone. The children clapped and jumped in place. When she finally let up, Shari didn't seem breathless but playfully scrunched her nose at her husband, who winked at her.

Brecee chanced a look at Adrian who seemed to be waiting to make eye contact with her. Thrusting two fingers in his mouth, Adrian whistled. She blew him a few kisses as he took a seat next to Marcellus.

Brecee's mother leaned around her beau and asked Adrian if he could sing.

He grunted. "I doubt to anyone's pleasure."

Everyone laughed with him, including the children who were clueless of the amusement.

After a few more songs, the entertainment ended with Shari and Garrett performing a duet to "Tomorrow" for their aunt.

The family showered the sisters with accolades. Adrian stood and, in a few strides, met Brecee at the edge of the stage. She thought he was about to help her climb down. Instead, he grasped her waist and lifted her to the ground.

"Thank you," she whispered.

"You're beautiful, talented, and, to my good fortune, taken."

She decided to reciprocate his compliment with one of her own. "And you are charming, indescribably handsome, and...." Never one to hold her tongue, she expressed her frustration: "Busy."

"True. But, in my defense, I'm a hardworking man who is trying to figure us out. I'd be a fool not to work at it."

She liked the sound of that.

Her uncle cleared his throat. "Brecee, why didn't you tell us Adrian had a Philly connection?"

"He does?" Her mother squinted at him.

"During *our* chat, Adrian said that his grandmother used to live there," Uncle Bradford continued.

"My mother mentioned it, remember?" Adrian asked Brecee. Linking his fingers with hers, he guided her to a seat, then took the one next to her.

Now that he mentioned it, Brecee did remember, and wished she'd asked her more about it.

"Apparently, our grandparents worked together at Tasty Baking Company," Adrian said.

"Get out of here." Brecee blinked as every mouth dropped open. Questions swirled through her head. "When did you find that out?"

"She mentioned it the other day when I told her your family was coming to town. She told me to ask you if you ever heard of Tasty Baking Company, I forgot all about it while your family had me on the witness stand." He smirked in a calm manner that convinced her he hadn't been fazed by the "talk."

"Wouldn't it be something if our grandparents knew each other?" Brecee murmured.

"The likelihood that they crossed paths is pretty small, Sis," Shae told her. "It was a big company."

Their mother chimed in, "In the day, that bakery was a major employer. Every family in the area had somebody working there. My father-in-law was still working there after Saul and I got married."

"I do remember Granddaddy bringing us Kandy Kakes," Brecee said. She suddenly had a craving for the snack-sized chocolate cakes with cream filling. As she licked her lips, remembering the flavor, Adrian cast her a bemused glance.

"There weren't many women who worked there back then." Uncle Bradford seemed thoughtful. "Before Saul was born—when I was somewhere around five or six—I remember Dad coming home, complaining about a group of ladies who talked about the Bible all day long. They sure annoyed him, for whatever reason. Of course, as a saint of God, I know how seeing a person living right before God has a way of convicting folks. Dad used to say he could quote Scripture without reading a Bible—that's how much those ladies talked about God. It would be a coincidence, Adrian, if your grandmother was one of those ladies."

"I don't know...." Adrian stroked his mustache and frowned. "I never met my grandmother. She died when my mother was young. But if she was so much into her faith, I'm sure it would have rubbed off on my mother, and she's never mentioned anything about going to ch—" He didn't finish his sentence, probably because he'd just remembered he was surrounded by churchgoing folks.

"Our salvation is all about God's timing." Uncle Bradford shrugged. "My dad knew little about salvation back then. Sometime later, I remember Daddy saying he was happy that two of those 'holy rollers' were quitting. One was expecting a baby, and the other was getting married and moving to St. Louis."

It would be romantic if her family and Adrian's had a connection going back several generations, yet Brecee had to admit the idea was far-fetched. Her uncle had always been a great storyteller, and his listeners often struggled to separate fact from fiction. "Uncle Bradford...."

He shushed her as Adrian rested his arm on the back of her seat and nudged her closer to him. Liking the feel, she relaxed against his chest, mouthing *Sorry* to her uncle.

"I had no interest in grown folks' business," Bradford continued, "but I remembered asking if that was the city with the big McDonald's arch. I guess I saw it on TV or in a magazine. My daddy explained that it was a monument symbolizing the 'Gateway to the West.' The rest is history.

"Then, something happened. Shortly before Saul was born, something changed my father. He started going to church and Bible class. We all watched as he got baptized. Years later, after the Lord saved me, I often wondered about that lady who had planted the seed of salvation in Dad's life that we all have grown from." He harrumphed. "There are your clues: the bakery and St. Louis. If I were you, young man, I would want to know if there is a treasure waiting to be uncovered, and I'm not talking about the physical kind."

All eyes were on Adrian, but he seemed preoccupied with his thoughts, staring at nothing in particular. Brecee wondered how different his life might be if his grandmother had been around when he was a child and had talked to him about Jesus.

"Okay," her mother spoke up. "Let's eat." Almost immediately, the women stood and began to lay out the plate settings and dishes for everyone to help himself. The men were the first in line, except Adrian, who remained seated, apparently still lost in thought. Brecee squeezed his hand to rouse him from his reverie, though, truthfully, her mind was just as preoccupied. Had God left a paper trail leading them to their destiny?

"Hungry?" she asked him.

Blinking, he smiled. "Definitely."

Brecee went to the bar and fixed two plates. After delivering one to Adrian, she watched as he ate with gusto.

Although she didn't like to talk about her job outside the hospital walls, Brecee wanted him to know that she cared about his. "Thank you for leaving work early today. Did you meet your quota for the month?"

"Yes. Thank you for asking. That's why I was late, but you probably figured that out." He took a sip from his bottled water.

"I did." She paused. "I want to matter to you, Adrian," she said quietly. "I'm not saying I'm a diva whose needs always have to come first...." She didn't want to hound the man. He was there, after all, and he'd made sacrifices for that to happen.

Adrian wiped his mouth and gave her his undivided attention. "I know number seven on your list. You are important to me, Brecee, and I'm trying to work it out so that you will feel it, even when I'm not there. Plus, according to number eight, 'If we no longer work....' That is not an option, because I don't intend to step aside."

"Thank you." She reached for his hands, and they engulfed hers. "I have a confession. I've been a little stressed out because you are so important to me, and I wanted my family to like you. I think they do, to my relief."

He leaned closer, within kissing range. But she was not going to let that happen in front of her family. Plus, she wanted that first kiss to be special.

"I like them, too." He lowered his voice to add, "And I really like you." He winked, and she felt herself blush like a teenager.

The activity around them seemed to blur into the background as they snacked and chatted about everything and nothing. Soon, her family was all entertained out and began to disperse, but not before her uncle asked if they would see Adrian at church tomorrow.

"I'm afraid not, sir," Adrian said with genuine regret in his voice. "I have to work on a group presentation for my management class."

Brecee almost felt bad that her uncle had put him on the spot, but she knew how important God was to a well-balanced life.

"Well, I'll say my good-byes now," Bradford told him. "It was nice meeting you, young man."

Adrian stood and shook hands with her uncle. "Likewise."

"And thanks for the business cards. If I know of anyone looking for a car and willing to drive to St. Louis for it, I'll send him your way."

"I appreciate it." He nodded. "Our entire inventory is posted on Broadway Motors' Web site."

Did the man ever have a conversation without handing out business cards or talking cars? *Stop that!* Brecee chided herself. His confident aura was a big draw, and attractive.

Christians should leave calling cards with everyone they meet, Jesus whispered to her spirit.

God's chastening, reminded her that she needed to witness more and to be about her Father's business. "Lord, help me to be as diligent in doing Your work as Adrian is about his," she mumbled softly.

Adrian turned to her. "What did you say, babe?"

The endearment seemed to float right into her heart. She didn't want to disturb the moment but to let the feeling linger as he returned to his seat and reached for her hands.

"Nothing," she finally whispered.

"I have to admit, the conversation with your uncle was mind-boggling. As if I don't have enough to do, I wouldn't mind going on that treasure hunt. It's almost like a genealogy search one of my friends at work always talks about."

Brecee nodded. "I think it's interesting that we met in St. Louis but both have Philly roots."

Adrian wiggled a thick, silky black brow.

"What?" She nudged him a couple of times.

"Maybe that's why I crave your presence when I'm not with you because—you belonged to me all this time, and I didn't know it." Standing, he pulled her to her feet, then gathered their empty plates. He placed them on the food cart with the other dirty dishes. "Come on. Walk me to my car."

When Adrian wrapped his arm around her waist, Brecee rested her head on his shoulder. The feeling of contentment made her sigh. She was falling in love.

⁓

Adrian didn't want to leave. Brecee stood to the side of the massive driveway, waiting for him to turn his car around. He wanted to kiss her good-bye, but he merely waved before driving off. Glancing in the rearview mirror, he saw that she hadn't moved. She had looked so cute in her baseball outfit, so mesmerizing on the miniature stage, and so compassionate seated next to him. And there were still so many different sides of her that he had yet to explore.

How could he hope to get any schoolwork done now, thinking about her? He had postponed grad school until he thought he could fit it into his schedule. There were a lot of things he would have to shuffle around in order to be with her, but he would.

His mind wandered to his grandmother Cora Lambert. Surely, she wasn't one of the holy rollers who had bothered Brecee's grandfather. He would have heard those tales as a child and would have been brought up in the church. His family wasn't anti-church; they did go, just not on a regular basis. As a matter of fact, it didn't take much of an excuse for them not to go. But, to his parents' credit, they had instilled him with good morals. Until he'd met Brecee, that had seemed to be enough.

Still, Brecee's uncle had piqued his curiosity. Minutes after he arrived back at his condo, Adrian called his parents.

After a cordial greeting, his father wanted to talk about the baseball game. "That was some game the Cards played against the Pirates. Nothing gets by that Rahn Maxwell…"

Adrian couldn't focus on sports at the moment. "Pops, sorry to cut you off, but is Mom around?"

"Sure, Son. We'll catch up later. Hold on."

His mother came on the line moments later. She surprised him by firing one question after another about Brecee's family. He couldn't recall her ever showing so much enthusiasm over any woman he dated. Then again, she had met only a handful.

When she took a breather, Adrian jumped in. "They were very nice and welcoming. She definitely comes from good people, but"—he paused for emphasis—"can you believe Brecee's grandfather and Grandma Cora worked at the same company?"

"Now, that's a coincidence. Hmm."

He had expected a more emotional response.

"I know Grandma Cora died when you were fairly young. Do you remember her ever taking you to church?"

His mother was silent for a moment. "Hmm. Maybe a few times. I mostly remember her being sick. Papa said it was because she lost so many babies along the way. I'm sorry, Son. Why?"

"Brecee's uncle was under the impression that their paths had crossed, and that she was a churchgoing woman."

His mother laughed. "Now, you know that doesn't run in our family."

She was still chuckling when they said their good-byes, but Adrian wasn't ready to admit that the joke was on him. Suddenly, he had a thirst to know more about Cora Lambert.

CHAPTER SIXTEEN

At church the next morning, after Pastor Archie welcomed the congregation and any visitors, he looked in the direction of the Carmens' pews. Brecee knew what was coming next.

"It's always a pleasure when the Carmens are in town." The pastor paused as a round of amens echoed around the sanctuary. "Sister Shae, will you and your family give us a selection?"

Just like Christians didn't go to church without their Bibles, the Carmens didn't leave home without their instrument cases. They were accustomed to being asked to render a selection whenever they visited one another's churches, so they were never caught off guard but could always sing a song on demand.

One by one, Brecee and her sisters stood and filed out of the pew as the congregation gave them a hearty reception. They were followed by Garrett, carrying his and Shari's saxophone cases, and by Victor and Dino with their saxophone and trumpet.

"'Lord of the Harvest,'" Stacy whispered as she slid behind the organ.

Brecee passed the word to the others, then borrowed a guitar from a church band member and strapped it over her shoulder as Shae positioned herself behind the drum set. Victor and Dino stood in front of microphones with their instruments ready to go.

The expression on the faces of several single women in the front row amused Brecee. They looked as if they were salivating as they watched her cousins, and she mused that they were on the brink of sanctification, with the devil urging them to cross over to the lustful side.

Victor was older by four years to Dino, but both were equally good-looking, with an unusual shade of brown eyes and full, shapely lips. Given their rich dark skin that resembled Shari's, almost everybody who met them at the same time assumed she was their sister instead of their cousin. They had yet to be caught by a woman.

"Praise the Lord, everybody," Shae said, drawing Brecee's attention back to the present. "We stand before you to worship. Won't you join us in singing 'You Are My Daily Bread/Lord of the Harvest'?" The Fred Hammond tune was nonstop energy. Soon, all the saints were on their feet, clapping and singing along.

The Holy Ghost stirred His people in the sanctuary. Soon, it became an encore of the earlier praise and worship segment. And it wouldn't have been a Carmen family performance if it didn't allow space for Shari and Garrett to serenade the Lord on sax in their competitive spirit. Finally, Shae ended the song on her drums to a standing ovation of cheers and thunderous applause.

As they stepped down from the pulpit, the church musicians got back in place and picked up the song. They made their way back to their seats as the congregation continued to rejoice and cry in their worship of God.

"Amen, amen," Pastor Archie said when the music stopped. He stepped up to the pulpit and opened his Bible. "Thank you, Carmen sisters and family. Yes, Jesus is our Daily Bread and the Lord of the harvest. I had prepared a sermon to preach, but I feel led to speak extemporaneously along the lines of the song we just sang. In Matthew nine, verse thirty-seven, Jesus lets us know that His daily bread often goes to waste because we—Christians, the saints of the Most High God—we're leaving food on the table or in the field. We're letting it go to waste. We may witness about God's goodness, but it's God's salvation that we're leaving in the field. Are you representing Christ? Yes? Then why aren't you busy gathering in the harvest of souls? It's self-reflection day here at Bethesda Temple. Let us wake up from our slumber."

Hadn't God convicted Brecee of that very thing just yesterday? And here she was today, listening to a confirmation from Pastor Archie. *Lord, help me to leave Your calling card*, came her silent prayer.

Other souls seemed just as convicted as they shouted, "Help us, Lord," or stood to their feet with a shout of "Amen!"

The sermon concluded with an invitation for salvation. "This is your day," Pastor Archie proclaimed. "Let God pluck you out of the harvest of sin. He is here today to save you. The Bible says to repent and be baptized, every one of you...."

As Brecee prayed for others to make a decision for a lifestyle change, she thought about Adrian. Until he made Jesus his daily bread, then he would stay in the harvest. *Lord, help me to be a light. I know that You alone can feed his soul.*

Blessed are they who hunger and thirst after My righteousness, for I will fill them, God whispered, bringing to mind Matthew 5:6.

Then, Lord, please give Adrian a hunger like no other. Brecee continued to pray until the altar call had ended and dozens had repented and requested baptism in Jesus' name. Before the benediction a half an hour later, many of those candidates for baptism had received the Spirit, with God speaking through them in a heavenly language.

Once the service ended, Shae gave hugs and kisses all around. "Brecee knows the code to disarm the security system at the house, so go make yourselves at home."

Dino and Victor were going with her to the station to change and then go to the ballpark for the afternoon game.

"Having Rahn in the family has its benefits," Victor joked, but was serious. He had said on more than one occasion that he and Dino couldn't get enough of the perks of having a celebrity baseball player as a cousin-in-law.

"The best is, he's my husband." Shae kissed Sabrina before handing her off to Brecee, while their mother grabbed the diaper bag.

Sabrina fretted, which she usually did whenever Brecee took her home on Sundays. That happened a lot during baseball season. Although Shae could have taken off work, her family liked to watch her anchor the news when they were in town. Her career success was a great source of pride and honor for the Carmens.

Back at the Maxwells', everyone changed out of their church clothes, and then the women took over the kitchen while the men flopped in front of the flat-screen television in the home theater, under the guise of watching the children.

With the others coupled off after dinner, including her mother and Uncle Marcellus, Brecee interacted with her niece and nephews, whom she would miss terribly once they were gone.

She tested their memory skills with games and books. When she started singing, the children seemed to take that as their cue to bang on the toy drums and strum the guitar or dance on the miniature stage. Taking a seat in the front row, she egged them on. Soon, Marcellus joined her.

"Can we talk?" he asked, sliding into the seat next to her.

"Sure." They hadn't spoken one-on-one all weekend.

"I'm in love with your mother—a lady of class, beauty, and deep spiritual understanding."

Tilting her head, she observed him. Garrett did favor him slightly. "Does my mother know you feel this way?"

"She does, even though she's not wearing my ring—yet."

So, ring shopping was in his future. Brecee still wasn't sold of her mother getting remarried, especially before Brecee could have her own wedding.

"But I'm protective of everything and everyone she cares about. You possess those same qualities, Brecee, to bring any man to his knees to do your bidding."

Brecee sighed, then glanced back at the stage. "Oh, I've been there and done that with men in my past—they made me the priority. I think Adrian wants to, but he can't…." She was embarrassed to admit it, but she continued, "I have to accept that he is a busy man at this time in his life. I was the same way when I was in residency, working long hours. Dating was a pastime, not a priority. Adrian is trying to juggle things—school, work…."

"I like Adrian," Uncle Marcellus stopped her. "But you're a Carmen. Demand respect without opening your mouth, and you'll get it." He didn't blink as Sabrina wailed. T.J. picked her up and brought her to Brecee. "Never settle in a relationship—never. When you become a priority in his life, he will reshuffle things. If not, I recommend you become the woman who got away."

Why did his words sound like something her father would have said to her in this situation? "Thanks for reminding me, Uncle Marcellus."

His grunt became a chuckle. "I had no problem racking up frequent-flyer miles to see Annette. Let him work for your affection, honey. You're worth it."

"I am, aren't I?" Brecee giggled.

Marcellus maintained a straight face as he nodded. He was serious.

She sobered. "Okay. I got it." After a moment, she couldn't resist tacking on, "You know, it still seems weird…my mother, dating."

"I love Annette. Watch and see if I don't prove it." Marcellus planted a kiss on her cheek and stood. "Now, my lady awaits. I'm here if you need me. Ask your sister Shari or Garrett. If I say something, I mean it."

⌒

Adrian knew Brecee wanted more of him. Frankly, he wanted more of her, too. They had snuck in a few breakfast dates, but grad school was especially demanding as finals loomed. Two more weeks, and then the semester would be finished, only for the summer session to begin three weeks later.

It was Saturday night. He should have been taking her out for dinner and a movie or on a walk through the park, but he couldn't. He had lost too many points for missing the midnight deadline when she'd called him for the first time.

He rubbed his face as he stared at his laptop, trying to review the key points of his business analysis.

It didn't help that his curiosity to know more about his maternal grandmother was building by the day. Had his grandmother been that gung ho for God, and he hadn't inherited any of that yearning? If so, when and why had there been a disconnect?

I'm fulfilling My promise to your grandmother, God whispered.

"What?" Adrian blinked at the computer monitor, then closed his eyes. He heard the voice again and shivered. Was God actually talking to him?

"What promise did You make to my grandmother?"

No response.

Rubbing his neck in frustration, Adrian stared at his computer screen, thinking. He needed answers; but since his mother didn't have them, and God seemed to, he would have to start his treasure hunt in the house of God. As much as he hated the thought of giving up his only day off, he was going to church in the morning. He wouldn't let Brecee know his plan, though, just in case he changed his mind.

After shutting down his computer, Adrian prepared for bed. Hours later, his alarm sounded too soon, and he fumbled around with his smartphone, then hit snooze and rolled over. He repeated this process two more times before finally throwing off his covers getting out of bed.

By now, it was almost nine o'clock. So much for getting in an hour or two of studying before he left for the service.

He showered, ate breakfast, and dressed in one of his designer suits, then headed for Brecee's church. It wasn't long before he turned into the parking lot and found a space. He took a deep breath as he racked his brain, trying to remember the last time he had been inside a church. Probably when he'd attended a friend's wedding last year. Had it really been that long?

Adrian grimaced. "Sorry, God." He stepped out of his car and headed for the entrance. Once he was inside, he realized the church was bigger than it looked. How was he going to find Brecee?

"Hello," a woman in a blue uniform greeted him. "Are you visiting with us today?"

"Yes."

Her smile was warm. "Welcome to Bethesda Temple." She handed him a contact card, on which he quickly scribbled his name, home address, and cell phone number. He almost whipped out one of his business cards but decided against it. "Would you happen to know Brecee Carmen?" he asked the woman.

Her eyes lit up. "Why, of course. She usually attends with her sister Shae Maxwell, the news anchor."

Adrian exhaled. "Would you mind pointing me in the direction of where they—"

"Nonsense, sugar. I'll take you to them, and you're right on time to get in some of the praise and worship before Pastor preaches." She patted him on the arm. "Come with me."

The music and voices pulsated as he peeked through the open doors into the large sanctuary. The music captured his attention, but there was an unexplainable tug on his spirit, he couldn't explain. Everyone was standing. The woman he was following seemed to count her steps with soldier-like precision as she led him down the aisle and pointed at the pew where she stopped.

Brecee and Shae were standing with their arms outstretched, worshipping God. Their eyes were closed, so after a whispered thanks to the woman, he squeezed in next to Brecee, trying not to disturb her.

He did a quick assessment of his lady. He had never seen her look so dainty. Her dress was fitted at the waist, accentuating her slender figure, and flared at her hips before stopping at her knees. Her hair hung down her back in curls, and she'd topped off the look with a hat. So, this was what he had been missing every Sunday? How had the men at this church managed to resist her beauty? *Maybe because she's always been mine.*

This is about Me! God reminded him in a voice that seemed to drown out the singers.

Embarrassed, Adrian quickly apologized and looked away. The moment his foot caught the rhythm of the song, the musicians and singers wrapped it up.

The expression on Brecee's face when she noticed him as she went to sit down would forever be etched in his mind. She looked surprised, then happy, and then as if she was about to cry. He hoped not. He had witnessed her tears before, and he didn't want a repeat performance. "Hi," he whispered as he leaned over and kissed her cheek.

She blushed. "Adrian! You're here." Then she patted his arm and leg, as if to make sure she wasn't hallucinating.

Shae peeked over at him and smiled, so he nodded back.

Brecee sniffed, then linked her fingers through his and squeezed his hand. Her eyes reflected questions—questions that would have to wait, as the minister was now taking the pulpit.

"Good morning, church. For our visitors, I'm Pastor Archie. Please stand so that we can welcome you."

Adrian got to his feet as the congregation gave a hearty round of applause.

"We hope that you will return," the pastor continued. "We want your experience today to be unforgettable. The only way that can happen is if God speaks to your heart, and you listen. God bless you."

Pastor Archie took his seat again as the choir stood and started a song with a fast beat that energized everyone. Brecee released her hold and joined in. "I love this song," she told him. "It's called 'The Blood Still Works.'"

The lyrics were stirring, and Adrian soon found himself singing along.

When the pastor returned to the podium and asked the congregation to open their Bibles to Acts, chapter 2, Adrian gave Brecee a gentle nudge as she reached for hers. "Mind if I share?"

"Of course not."

When she looked at him, Adrian caught the warmth of love in her eyes as he'd never seen it before. Why had he waited so long to come to church?

Glancing down at her Bible, he was surprised to see neat notes scribbled in the margins. Clearly, she did more than just read it. Brecee seemed to study it.

"There should come a point in your life when you want to know if what you have with Jesus is real," Pastor Archie began. "We've heard the phrase 'Every man for himself,' and when it comes to salvation, it definitely applies. Verses thirty-eight and thirty-nine: '*Then Peter said unto them, Repent, and be baptized every one of you in the name of Jesus Christ for the remission of sins, and ye shall receive the gift of the Holy Ghost. For the promise is unto you, and to your children, and to all that are afar off, even as many as the* LORD *our God shall call.*'"

Adrian's heart fluttered at the phrase "*the promise...to your children.*" Was God talking to him again?

Pastor Archie continued, "Verse forty: '*And with many other words did he testify and exhort, saying, Save yourselves from this untoward generation.*'"

Is that the message for me? His mind was still stuck on verse 39 when the pastor asked the congregation to stand.

"There is nothing for you in this world," Pastor Archie said in a warning tone. "Nothing's permanent. People are practicing self-destruction left and right. It's time for you to jump ship and save yourselves. Won't you come to Jesus today? Repent of your sins and be baptized, in Jesus' name."

As others began to walk to the front, where several ministers awaited them, Adrian froze in place, his heart pounding. The pastor's words faded as something stirred within him, but he couldn't leave his seat. The only thing that kept revolving in his mind was the phrase "*the promise.*"

CHAPTER SEVENTEEN

It was a spiritual connection with a man that Brecee wanted most in a relationship. That was at the top of her list. Yet Adrian seemed conflicted in his soul after hearing the message.

She exchanged glances with Shae, then looked at Adrian again. He stood there, gripping the back of the pew in front of them, with his eyes closed and his head bowed.

Don't fight the Lord, she wanted to tell him. *Let go.* But the decision was his alone. At least God had given him a desire to come to church uninvited this time.

He accepted My invitation, the Lord whispered.

When the pastor had concluded the altar call, Adrian turned and startled her by engulfing her in an embrace. He seemed relieved. She hugged him back before they sat and waited for the offertory.

"I'm glad you're here," she whispered. "And that I wasn't playing in the band or in a softball game or something to keep me from enjoying this moment of us together...at church."

He nodded. "Me, too."

If she believed in fairy tales coming true, then she would let herself hope that he loved her as much as his tenderness seemed to convey. She felt like she was about to start sobbing. Maybe it was her hormones. Every time they were together, there was more hugging, more holding hands. Now she was holding out for the kiss.

Once the pastor gave the benediction, Shae greeted Adrian, and even Sabrina gave him a wide grin, displaying a budding tooth and a tiny wave. When he winked at Brecee's niece, the baby tried to mimic him, making all three of them laugh.

Taking him by the hand, Brecee introduced him to a couple of saints who approached her with medical questions. Her responses were courteous yet brief. She wasn't up for the lengthy discussions she sometimes engaged in about children's health, not with Adrian there beside her.

Once they were alone again, she asked him, "Do you have to get back and study?" It was a silly question—of course, he did—but that didn't stop her from wanting to hear him respond on the contrary.

"Yes," he said, "and I want you to come with me." He didn't blink.

But Brecee did. "Excuse me?"

"Work with me on this." Adrian squeezed her hand and rubbed his thumb over her knuckles. "I'm trying to multitask on my only day off. I gave God time—"

"Are you coming back to church again?" She couldn't help but interrupt him. She had to know if this was just a onetime visit.

"And again and again," he said in a low voice. That earned him a smile as he continued, "But I'm also committed to this group project." He paused and gazed into her eyes as if they were the only ones in the sanctuary. And they may as well have been, because everyone milling around them seemed to fade into oblivion. Everyone other than Shae, that is; she came into full view right behind Adrian, unashamedly eavesdropping.

"And I want you to be near me."

Her heart melted at his request. "Ah, that's sweet, but I don't want my presence to serve as a distraction."

Still standing behind Adrian, Shae frowned and flared her nostrils. *Girl,* she mouthed, *you better go.*

"I'm distracted when you're not there," Adrian told her. "It'll help me focus just knowing that I can look up and gaze into your eyes; that if I take a deep breath, I'll catch a hint of your perfume. And when I need to take a break, I might try to steal a kiss."

Brecee was falling in love. And it wasn't just puppy love. All it had taken was this busy man's admission that he needed her. How could she say no to that? "Okay."

"Well, with that settled," Shae said, butting in, "I guess Sabrina and I will head out. Rahn's going to pick her up at the station after the game. Bon appétit." She didn't hide her amusement.

"Sisters," Brecee mumbled, shaking her head. "I have to change first."

"And deprive me of this lovely vision?" Adrian shook his head. "Please, not yet. After dinner?" His fake pout made her giggle. She playfully punched him in his arm and was astounded at the solid feel of his bicep.

As he escorted her to her car, Brecee suggested Red Lobster, since she had taste for shrimp. "You can tail me there," she told him.

"Sure. Just don't drive too fast and leave me." Chuckling, he turned and started across the parking lot toward his Audi.

"You'll pay for that," she yelled after him, knowing he was referring to her speeding ticket.

The Red Lobster in St. Charles wasn't far from the church, and they made it there in no time. Brecee parked, then waited for Adrian to come and open her door. They held hands as they strolled inside. Surprisingly, on a Sunday, the wait time was less than fifteen minutes.

Once they had placed their orders—steak for him, coconut shrimp for her—Adrian reached across the table and took her hands in his. Neither of them said a word as they gazed at each other. Adrian's attention made Brecee feel pretty, and it had nothing to do with what she was wearing. She liked the slow, tender way he studied her.

Feeling herself shiver, Brecee broke the silence. "Why didn't you tell me you were coming this morning? Whatever the reason, I'm so glad you did." He didn't have to know she had been praying for the Lord to give him a desire to come.

"It was something your uncle said."

"Uncle Bradford? What?" That wasn't what God had told her. She leaned back, ready to listen.

"While we were at your sister's house, Bradford piqued my interest about a grandmother I never met and never learned much about. I can't fathom the idea of a big-time religious person in my family without there being any remnants of that. It just seems odd to me."

"Dr. Carmen? Brecee, is that you? Wow."

She turned and recognized Dr. Peter Richards from the hospital. He was staring at her, entranced, as if they hadn't worked together a couple days ago. "You look"—he paused and took a deep breath—"incredible."

"Yes, she does." Adrian's deep voice made his presence known that Dr. Richards had to acknowledge her guest.

Adrian stood up, letting his buff six-foot-something frame tower over her colleague. But Dr. Richards worked out, so it was like stone meeting brick. Brecee didn't know the details of Dr. Richards' ethnic background, but he must have had some Asian and Italian ancestors. He was one gorgeous specimen.

Dr. Richards had never shown more than a professional interest in her, but the way he was practically gawking at her right now made her uncomfortable.

Adrian must have sensed it, because he pumped the man's hand with a scowl on his face. "I'm Adrian Cole."

"Dr. Peter Richards." The doctor yanked his hand back and glanced at Brecee, then looked at Adrian again. "Are you on the medical staff at another hospital?"

"I am not." Adrian slipped his hands inside his pockets. Brecee wondered who was hurting worse from that handshake. "I'm a transportation problem solver."

Her colleague frowned. "I'm not familiar with that occupation. Who's your employer?"

"Broadway Luxury Motors," Adrian stated without offering a description of his job.

It must have dawned on Dr. Richards when his mouth formed an *o*.

Just then, their server appeared with their meals. "Excuse me, gentlemen." She squeezed her way in between them.

"I apologize for interrupting." Dr. Richards stepped back. "I'll let you two eat. Dr. Carmen," he said with a nod, his eyes sparkling once again. "I'll see you at our first softball game next Sunday." He faced Adrian. "Mr. Cole." He walked away with a swagger Brecee had never seen before.

Brecee didn't meet Adrian's eyes but surveyed her baked potato. She couldn't recall ever seeing one smothered so artistically with sour cream. Adrian didn't come across as jealous or insecure, but the testosterone was tangible.

He cleared his throat. "Did you tell me you played on a softball team?"

"I thought I mentioned it."

Twisting his mouth, Adrian went for his smartphone. "What time is the game?"

"One."

"I'll be in the stands by twelve thirty."

Brecee nodded, then reached across the table to take his hands before she blessed their food. First, she had to wipe the smirk off her face, because his behavior was downright funny.

While she was trying to clear her head, Adrian surprised her by saying grace himself. His prayer was brief, but she liked his sincerity.

"Amen," she said before dipping a shrimp in cocktail sauce.

"Do you have any hand sanitizer in your purse?"

"Sure." She found the bottle and handed it over.

"Thanks. A man can't be too careful about picking up germs."

That was the end of her self-restraint. She dropped her fork, shrimp and all, to cover her mouth before she released a hearty laugh that could rival the one Adrian delivered the day they met.

Evidently, Adrian wasn't amused, nor did he inquire about what was so funny. He simply cut himself a bite of steak and shoved it in his mouth. He chewed as if it were as tough as beef jerky.

Once she composed herself, Brecee looked at him. It appeared he wasn't going to broach the subject of what had just happened. She couldn't wait until her next video chat with her sisters. They would roll when she told them this one.

Finally, the lighthearted banter between them returned.

"After this semester of classes ends, I'm thinking about taking a break rather than doing the summer session."

"Why?" Brecee dabbed at the corners of her mouth.

"So I can spend more time with you." His voice was soft.

She should have felt ecstatic, but she understood the dedication and sacrifice it took to achieve one's goals. She knew the study cram sessions, the twelve-hour shifts as a resident, the family events she'd had to miss—yes, she knew what he was going through. "Does this have anything to do with Dr. Richards' rudeness?"

"Maybe." Adrian frowned. "I have a problem with him, and any other man who presumes to have the right to look at my lady like that, whether or not I'm around." He paused and took a deep breath.

He'd spoken with just a touch of possessiveness that made it sound sexy. Brecee pushed back her plate.

"That was my temper talking, baby. I'm sorry." He bunched up his napkin. "However, I am serious about thinking of taking a break, so I'll have time to treat you like the special lady you are."

She leaned across the table and silently beckoned him to meet her half-way. "Say that again," she whispered.

"I'll say whatever you want me to say." He seemed dazed.

"Am I your baby?"

"Most certainly." He reached for her hand and brushing his lips across her fingers. His mustache tickled her. She smiled and pulled back.

Holding his gaze, she lifted an eyebrow. "You stay in school, babe." The endearment had slipped out without her intending it to, but it seemed to please him. "Don't let a woman get in the way of your goals. It took full focus on mine to achieve them." It was contrary to what her heart was yelling at her, but, even growing up a spoiled brat, Brecee had been taught not to be selfish. He waved for the server for the check. "You're not just a woman. You're Sabrece Carmen, the woman I refuse to let get away."

Hadn't Uncle Marcellus said the same thing? She beamed. "You're a smart man."

CHAPTER EIGHTEEN

The man is definitely comfortable in his skin," Brecee gushed, just thinking about her time spent with Adrian yesterday. She and Regina were sipping coffee during some downtime in the doctors' charting area.

"You're in love with him," her friend stated. "That wasn't a question."

"Yes, and I didn't see it coming," Brecee admitted with a smile. "I kept thinking about our differences so much that I didn't stop to appreciate how he made me feel."

"I now pronounce you cured and released from doctor's care," Regina teased.

"Leave me alone." Brecee chuckled. "Adrian was right. I enjoyed being close to him, even when he was busy. His study group met at a historic building downtown that houses the T-REX Incubator."

Regina frowned. "That sounds prehistoric. Is it a museum?"

"No, it's a headquarters for dozens of aspiring entrepreneurs. They can rent space at an extremely affordable rate while they build their business. I was impressed with the concept. There's plenty of open space for networking, as well as small private rooms and booths for telephone conferences and Skype chats."

"You do know you sound like a sales rep and not a doctor," Regina teased her.

Brecee grinned. "I'm glad he invited me along. It was like walking into his world."

"So, what did you do during his group meeting?"

"There was a plush lounge with a flat-screen TV and a bar with snacks and other amenities. He can take me along to a group meeting anytime." She giggled. "Believe it or not, I wanted to sit in and observe, to listen to his ideas, his business strategies.... From what little I could hear, Adrian commanded the discussion, citing examples from his sales experience. But he was also a patient and attentive listener. Sales is his calling, and he's got the people skills for success. He would be comfortable selling just about anything."

Regina drained the rest of her coffee and pitched the cup in the waste can. "Sounds like you've found your prince, Cinderella."

"But?"

"But I'm here to remind you that Adrian is a good fit only if he repents and completes Christ's plan of salvation." Regina smiled as if trying to soften the blow of her message.

"I know." Brecee sighed. "Thanks for keeping me grounded. I was hoping he would begin that process yesterday at church."

"Oh, he did," Regina assured her. "He came willingly, of his own accord, which brings me to my next point. I'm glad you haven't bought into the stereotype that doctors have to marry at their professional level. Love isn't connected to status."

"He hasn't told me he loves me, or even kissed me, so we're nowhere near him asking me to marry him."

Regina rolled her eyes. "We aren't teenagers anymore, Brecee. We're in our thirties and at our age, men know we're dating with a purpose in that direction."

"I hope I won't regret telling him to take a summer course," Brecee confessed. "I just don't want getting married at forty years old to be the new thirty." She wasn't willing to wait that long. She had only 10 percent of her eggs left, and she needed three or four of them for a family.

"Take it from me," Regina told her. "I married a doctor while in my residency. It lasted two years. The divorce took one year. It was that experience that brought me to Jesus. If I have to be single for the rest of my life, then I'm trusting that God knows what's best for me." She swallowed. "I keep telling myself that I'm good."

Brecee ached for her sister in Christ who'd had the misfortune of not choosing her mate wisely. Regina's marriage had been superficial, with the aim of keeping up appearances, and having little to do with love.

Devastating ordeals had a way of putting people on the fast track to salvation. Brecee had understood at an early age that she had been born in sin and shaped in iniquity, as stated in Psalm 51:5. But, praise God, it was her love of music that had drawn her to Christ, prompted her to repent, and brought her through her Nicodemus experience.

Regina still wanted to be loved, but she wouldn't accept it unless it came from a godly man.

Before they could take the conversation further, Ashley, the charge nurse, burst into the charting room and alerted them that three ambulances were on their way.

"ETA is four minutes," Ashley told them. "These end-of-the-year field trips always worry me. About forty students were at the Saint Louis Zoo, and it appears there was more on display than animals. Apparently, there was a beehive hidden from view, but as children do, they can find anything they're not supposed to. Some child disturbed it. If it hadn't been for some quick-thinking parents and zoo personnel, it could have been much worse. In addition to our hospital, Children's Hospital is getting four patients." She continued to brief them with the vitals of the children they'd received from the medics via e-mail.

With any allergic reaction, they were concerned with compromised airways, which could produce shock. Besides the three residents, there was one more attending physician on duty. By the time the medics arrived, the emergency department was ready.

"Ashley, get the EPI to their bedsides," Brecee instructed the nurse. "The sooner we can get them injected to minimize the reaction, the better."

"Dr. Carmen, I assigned the most acute case to bay three," Ashley said as she directed the medics pushing the little girl sitting partially upright on the gurney. She was wearing an oxygen mask, and an IV had already been started in her arm.

Brecee scanned the chart and checked the name. *Laura Cole.* Brecee froze—Adrian's cousin and Dolan's daughter. It was always startling when a doctor knew a patient personally.

Seconds later, she stepped back into her professional role as the hospital social worker walked into the room.

"Has her father been contacted?" Brecee asked the woman. "We need to know if she has any other allergies that might compound her reaction."

"The teacher contacted all the parents. They're on their way."

The medics transferred Laura from the gurney to the bed. Brecee noted her blood pressure. It had fallen since the medics had arrived on the scene, and her oxygen level was low, while her heart rate was accelerating. Brecee was concerned about the possibility of her going into shock.

She rubbed the girl's arm. "Laura? It's Dr. Carmen. Brecee. Remember me? We're going to make you feel better, honey. Your daddy's on his way, okay?"

Laura's only response was a tear falling from one eye as she blinked. Brecee stepped aside as the nurse administered another dose of intravenous antihistamines and cortisone to decrease the inflammation of her air passages.

She began to pray. *Lord Jesus, we thank You for the blood You shed on Calvary and that You nailed all manner of sickness and disease to the cross. Little Laura and all the other children here today need You. We know they are special to You and close to Your heart. Heal the bodies You made, Lord. We thank You, in Jesus' name. Amen.*

As Brecee waited on the Lord's direction, the charge nurse beckoned her into the hall outside Laura's room.

"Medics are en route with a GSW, a fourteen-year-old male with a gunshot to the abdomen. ETA six minutes," she said. "Should I alert the surgeon to stand by?"

Brecee nodded.

Just like the devil to stir up chaos, Brecee mentally snapped. *Satan, I rebuke you. In the name of Jesus, get your hands off of God's children.*

"Senseless," Ashley muttered, shaking her head. "Guns and schools don't mix."

Brecee glanced up and saw Dolan rushing through the doors. When he spotted her, he hurried toward her. "Is my little girl going to be okay?"

"Frazzled" didn't begin to describe him. *I'm trusting the Lord for that outcome,* Brecee thought.

"She's stable," she told him. "We're giving her antihistamines and cortisone to help with the inflammation and her nurse is monitoring her blood pressure. I'm sure the social worker asked you already, but does Laura have a history of adverse reactions to bee stings or bug bites? Or any other allergies that you know of?"

He answered her questions as she led him to the bay where Laura had been assigned. Before leaving him to check on the other children, she encouraged Dolan to call Adrian. She would have done it herself, but HIPAA laws prevented her from divulging any information, even to friends and family members.

From the gunshot wound victim, who would need to be admitted for surgery, to a girl who had been mauled by a pit bull, there was a nonstop stream of patients needing Brecee's attention. Hours passed before she was finally able to check on Laura again. The girl's vitals were better, but Brecee recommended that she be kept overnight for observation. Since Dolan wasn't in the room with his daughter, Brecee walked toward the waiting area. She wasn't surprised to see Adrian sitting with his cousin. Adrian's parents were there, too, along with another couple Brecee could only assume were Dolan's folks.

Family—there was nothing else like it. If a Carmen were admitted to a hospital back home, Brecee would be on the next plane to Philly.

Adrian stood when he saw her. "Is she okay?" He looked just as shaken as Dolan had earlier.

"Yes," Brecee assured him. "Laura is a blessed little girl."

"Amen."

Hearing him say that made her smile.

"I'm so glad you're here," he told her, exhaling. "Whew...now, I can put something in my stomach. Have you eaten? Want to grab a bite to eat?"

"I'm starved." Her stomach grumbled to prove it. "Let me check on Dolan first."

When she turned in Dolan's direction, she was surprised to see Regina sitting beside him, one hand on his shoulder. Her shift had ended an hour ago. Her friend had a superb bedside manner and was especially gifted when it came to calming patients and their parents. Did she know that Laura was Adrian's cousin?

Brecee faced Adrian again. "He's in good hands. Dr. Reed is one of the best."

Grabbing her hand, Adrian squeezed it. "Nobody but my baby is the best."

Adrian's praise made her heart throb. His loving gaze was always intense and genuine...and always made her shiver.

CHAPTER NINETEEN

The Cole men needed wives. That was Adrian's thought after what he had witnessed the previous night at the hospital.

Dolan needed a wife even more than he. His cousin was a wreck, even though Brecee's friend Dr. Reed had done a good job of cheering him up.

Adrian had been scared, too. He'd just hid it better. Of course, seeing Brecee had chased most of his worries away.

After a fretful night, Adrian was up early. Usually, he prayed at bedtime—short and sweet. But last night, he'd mostly prayed rather than slept.

In spite of his fatigue, Adrian dressed and went for a jog at nearby Creve Coeur Park. He needed to clear his head of the previous day's events. His comfort was knowing his little cousin was in good hands where Brecee worked. With each lap, he thought about Brecee and permanency. "Should I propose?" Would she agree to marry him? Adrian nodded at a fellow runner. He was getting ahead of himself, as one who had always believed in taking things slow. He had to first make sure he loved her and, second, tell her so.

When he returned to his condo, Adrian jumped in the shower, then called Dolan. "Hey. How's the little princess?"

"Doing better than me. No telling if a chiropractor will be able to realign my spine after sleeping in what hospitals call an 'extra bed.' Plus, the nurses are spoiling her. Dr. Reed's already been in this morning. She actually took my vitals to make sure I hadn't developed high blood pressure."

Adrian wanted to laugh at his cousin's dramatics, but he didn't think Dolan would take it very well. "Dr. Reed is the cute doctor I saw praying for you, right?"

"Yes. I understand now why nurses are called God's angels."

"And pretty ones, at that," Adrian said, thinking of Brecee. What were doctors called? "Okay, man. I'll check up on her later. I have my final class presentation this evening, but I'll come by the house to see her soon. Give her a kiss for me."

In the background, he could hear Laura saying something to Dolan. "Daddy, the nurses say I can have…." Then he disconnected.

Her cheery voice made Adrian smile. Next, he tapped Brecee's name on his contacts list. When she answered, she sounded sleepy.

"Hey, baby. Did I wake you?" Frowning, he checked the time. She was usually up before him.

"I'm awake, just not up yet," she said with a yawn. "I stayed at the hospital later than usual last night. Laura seemed fine when I left. My professional opinion? Dolan should be admitted down the street at SLU Hospital."

Adrian released the hearty laugh that he had held in while talking to his cousin. Brecee giggled. "Actually, parents are part of our treatment plan. The children get better sooner when their parents are confident about their recovery."

"Makes sense." He wished he could talk to her longer, but he had to get to work. "Wish me luck on my group presentation tonight."

"Luck is for nonbelievers," she told him. "God bless you. I heard your practice discussion. You're incredible. I believe in you."

Adrian didn't know why he choked, but her faith in him gave him a booster shot of desire to do even better just to make her proud.

They disconnected on a good note.

The dealership was busier than normal that day. Word had leaked that hot rides for the summer were going on display in the showroom. Adrian made great contacts and even had a potential sale, pending financing, by the time he left for class.

On Wednesday morning at the dealership, Adrian was signing his way through a tall stack of birthday and anniversary cards to send to clients as a reminder that he was committed to nurturing relationships even after a sale, when Dolan showed up with Laura. His little cousin's eyes sparkled when she saw him. Adrian got to his feet and met her halfway.

Lifting the child off her feet, Adrian gave her a tight hug, then smacked a kiss on her cheek. When he put her back down, she patiently waited for what had become routine whenever she visited him—two dollars to hit the vending machine in the customer lounge.

Digging for his wallet, he obliged, then watched as she hurried off for her treat. When he turned to Dolan, his cousin had a frown on his face. "What's wrong?"

Dolan huffed. "Can you believe Laura's pediatrician has cleared her to resume normal activities? She says children are resilient. I still think she ought to stay home from school for the rest of the week."

Adrian shook his head. "Man, would you stop being a mother hen? Let her be the fearless little girl she is."

Stuffing his hands in his pockets, Dolan resembled the defiant teenagers he and Adrian had both been growing up. "You and the family are a bunch of naggers. Mom and Dad said the same thing."

When his daughter returned, he reached for her hand. "Come on, Laura. Let's go home. I need to make sure your clothes are ironed for tomorrow." He was still griping as he marched toward the doors, with Laura skipping along beside him, waving good-bye to some familiar faces.

Yep, his cousin needed a wife to be the boss. Amused, Adrian strolled back into his office. He exhaled as he slid behind his desk. Once again, everything appeared to be all right in the Cole family, but what about on his mother's side? He was still itching to know more about his maternal grandmother.

Before Adrian could resume his tasks, Brecee's ringtone blared from his smartphone. Grinning, he answered, "Hi, babe."

"Hi. Are you busy?"

"Doesn't matter." Adrian would always make time to hear her voice. "Never for you," he cooed.

"Stop flirting with me." She chuckled. "This is a business call."

"And what kind of business would that be?"

"I have a referral for you! I wanted to give you a heads-up before Dr. Terrence Jordan called about test-driving a new Audi. I told him how much I loved your car."

He closed his eyes and bowed his head. "Baby, you didn't have to do that." As a matter of fact, he didn't know how he felt about referrals coming from her.

"You said you're about building relationships for business."

"Our relationship is very personal and private. I don't want to mix that with business. I can earn my own."

"Listen, Mr. Cole." She sounded serious now. "If I want to be a cheerleader and treat my man sweetly, then it's in your best interest to let me have my way."

Adrian chuckled and gave her a mock salute. His woman was unpredictable, but he wouldn't change anything about her. He was the one who needed to make some life changes. He tried to keep his mind clean as he imagined kissing that sassy mouth of hers. Before that happened, he had to tell her he loved her. He had loved her for a while, but number nine on her list held him back from blurting it out: *He must be very certain that I'm the one before he tells me he loves me, because he can't take it back, and I'll hold him to it.* He had reached the point of certainty some time ago.

"An out-of-control woman…I like it," he told her. "And, speaking of cheerleaders, I can't wait to see your skills on the softball field."

Brecee laughed. "I don't know how impressed you'll be. I'm just a sub, and we play only a couple times a month. It takes me the entire game to warm up." They snickered together. "But seriously, I want to give you Dr. Jordan's number in case he gets tied up and forgets to call you. I believe in you, and I know you'll take care of him."

"Like you take care of children. Dolan just stopped in here with Laura. Her doctor gave her a clean bill of health."

"Wonderful news. That's why I chose emergency pediatrics—so I can have a hand in making children whole again."

Whole again. Adrian didn't feel that he would be whole until he found out the truth about his grandmother. "If you're free Saturday evening, maybe you'd like to go with me to my folks' house for a treasure hunt in the attic. I really want to know more about the possible connection between our grandparents."

"I didn't know that was still on your mind, but I love games, so count me in," Brecee said excitedly.

After they ended the call, Adrian phoned his parents. He chatted with his dad a few minutes before his mother got on the line, and then he told them about his desire to search the attic with Brecee.

"Sure, honey," his mother said. "You can go through all that junk, if you want, while Brecee and I chat."

That wasn't going to happen, but he wasn't about to get in a fight over his girlfriend with his mother right now. She had always been picky about his girlfriends—no exceptions. He was already half expecting to have to fight over his woman at the softball game on Sunday afternoon.

"Mom, aren't you the slightest bit curious to know more about Grandma Cora?"

"Not really. She's been gone so long."

To someone who didn't know his mother, she might have sounded cold, but she was just being honest. If Brecee's uncle hadn't thrown him a bone, Adrian would have let sleeping dogs lie, too. "Okay, Mom. See you then."

On Saturday, the dealership was bustling. There were plenty of lookers but no takers. Adrian was discussing the sale numbers with Kyle when the man started smirking.

"What?" Adrian asked.

"Uh, your lady just strutted in, and I don't think she's here to buy a car."

When Adrian turned around, his heart skipped a beat. It wasn't her first time visiting him at work, but today, she walked with a sense of purpose that got everybody's attention. As far as he was concerned, it had nothing to do with her resemblance to her news anchor sister. She exuded an air of confidence, and that drew him closer. She also looked fantastic in her casual dress with coordinating heels that showed off the results of her recent pedicure.

"Hi." She jutted her chin out, and he wanted to kiss her. "I brought you something."

"Yes. I like what I see." His nostrils flared as he gave her another perusal.

"I'm talking about food—a hoagie, aka Philly cheesesteak sandwich, to be exact."

He accepted her offering without breaking eye contact. "I'd say that you didn't have to do this, but, judging from how great you look and how good this smells, I'm glad you did. You make me feel so special."

"You are special to me. Besides, I didn't want you to have to drive to pick me up and then go to your parents'. I can stick around in the area and tail you."

I don't think so. Adrian narrowed his eyes at her. "No, you can drive your gorgeous self-back home or do whatever else you had planned for the day, but I will provide curbside service." When she looked like she was about to protest, Adrian didn't let her. "Babe, you have no idea how much I appreciate you, but you need to let me be the man...and that includes picking you up at your door. This is not a request and nonnegotiable."

When Brecee pouted, Adrian grinned and kissed her on her forehead. "Come on, Doctor. I'll walk you to your car."

Looking in her rearview mirror at the tall, dark, handsome black man with his arms folded across his chest, Brecee smiled as she drove her Lexus off the lot and merged with the other traffic.

Never one who enjoyed being put in her place, she was amused by Adrian's adamant insistence that she accept his chivalry. She desired that trait in a man, and Adrian Cole was delivering it.

Back at her condo, Brecee reclined on the couch and called her sisters via Skype.

Stacy hooted at the latest update about Adrian. "I liked him even more. You've definitely met your match."

"He's a keeper." Brecee beamed.

"I'm just glad that everything is working out," Shae told her.

"I know I've been a no-show at your house lately—"

"It was time for you to have somebody in your life," Shae told her, cutting short her apology. "We've all been praying for you to meet the right one."

Stacy and Shari both nodded.

"So, you *do* think Adrian is the one?"

"As soon as he surrenders to the Lord, it moves him up a couple notches on *my* list," Stacy said. "Without a commitment to God, you don't know about his commitment to you."

"True." Brecee exhaled. She could always count on her sisters to tell her what she needed to hear instead of what she wanted to hear. Between them and Regina, she stayed grounded in God's Word versus what she commonly heard from her coworkers—that God didn't matter in relationships.

After a while, she signed off to make another family call.

Uncle Bradford answered right away. "How's my favorite niece in St. Louis?"

"You'd better not let Shae hear you say that," Brecee teased, knowing that he'd looked at his caller ID.

"I'll tell her the same thing."

They chuckled together. He played that game with all four sisters.

"I'm going to Adrian's parents' house today to look through his grandmother's things," Brecee told him. "Do you really think there might be a connection, or were you just teasing him?"

"I wasn't teasing. I gave it some more thought when we returned home. Honestly, despite what I told him, I don't know if it's possible to ever know for certain," Uncle Bradford confessed. "It would make a nice story, though. Mom and Dad have been gone for so long." He was quiet for a moment, then added, "Your uncle in New York may have some of his papers, but Adrian needs to find out more about his grandmother. Even so, it may turn out to be a mystery we will never solve."

Brecee agreed as doorbell rang. She hadn't been watching the time. "I've got to go, Uncle Bradford. Love you."

"Love you, too, my niecie Brecee. And remember, just because your young man is searching for one thing, that doesn't mean God is beckoning him to do something else."

"Amen." They disconnected, and Brecee hurried to answer the door, stopping in front of the hall mirror to check her reflection. She adjusted her sweater and slid her feet back in her heels. Just as Adrian buzzed a second time, she opened the door and smiled at the sight of the flowers he carried.

His eyes twinkled. "A peace offering, if you're upset with me. For a second there, I didn't know if you were going to answer the door."

Taking the flowers, she wrapped her arms around his neck and pecked his cheek. "I like you just the way you are." She grinned and stepped back. "Although there are a few things I would definitely tweak...."

"Stop teasing me." His nostrils flared. "I wouldn't change one thing about you, not even that dark toenail polish."

"What's wrong with it?" She peeked down at her deep blue toenails, then looked at the flowers again. "I'll go put these in water. Be right back."

Brecee didn't invite him in, and for good reason. She was grateful he didn't question why. They weren't married, and he wasn't saved. Until those issues were resolved, the quick pecks and long hugs were her limit.

When she returned, Adrian was leaning against a concrete porch pillar. He glanced over his shoulder, then stood at attention. "You're the sweetest woman I know." He reached for her hand and drew her into his stare. She swallowed, watching him watch her. What was wrong? He didn't give her time to ask.

"I love you, Sabrece Carmen."

Brecee blinked as her heart fluttered. When she was about to respond, Adrian shook his head.

"Not yet," he said quietly. "You told me not to say it unless I meant it, and I don't want to take it back. The only thing I want is to keep you in my life. Knowing that you're there makes me happy."

Her vision blurred, and when the first tear fell, Adrian's thumb was there to catch it. There on her porch, with the world going on around her, Brecee froze, noting the very moment, the day, and the time when Adrian spoke the words her heart had yearned for.

She wrapped her arms around his waist and rested her head on his strong chest, sniffing to keep her tears at bay.

"You make it easy for me to love you," he whispered, rubbing her shoulders. "I always will."

Lifting her face to his, Brecee smiled. "I love you, too. So much." The kiss was slow in coming, but, once delivered, completely satisfying.

Suddenly conscious of her surroundings, including the possibility of onlookers from the park across the street, she tried to pull back. But Adrian had her trapped. "One more." He kissed her again before releasing her.

God, save him soon, she silently pleaded. The love between them was strong, and she needed every ounce of her Holy Ghost willpower to stay saved.

I can keep you from falling if you stay focused on Me, God whispered.

With their hands linked, Adrian escorted her down the steps to his car. Once they were buckled in, he went to start the ignition but stopped, turned, and looked at her with such tenderness that she now had a name for it: Adrian's look of love.

"Thank you for the delivery," he said with a grin. "I was the envy of all the other associates, and I'm not just talking about the food, but the woman who delivered it."

Closing her eyes, Brecee leaned back. "You're welcome."

When they arrived at the Coles' house, Marsha was preparing a spread of food. She turned to Brecee. "Why don't you let my son go through those dusty boxes by himself while you and I chat?" She looked hopeful, but so did Adrian. The look of love draped his face. He wanted her with him.

Brecee thought fast. Taking a deep breath, she faced Mrs. Cole. "Why don't we all visit for a few minutes, and then I can help Adrian? Two can work faster."

"'*Two are better than one; because they have a good reward for their labor. For if they fall, the one will lift up his fellow: but woe to him that is alone when he falleth; for he hath not another to help him up,*'" Adrian mumbled over her shoulder. "I need her with me."

Whirling around, she stared into his eyes. "Ecclesiastes four, nine and ten." Her parents had drilled that Scripture into her and her sisters while they were growing up, always reminding them that they were to act as a team and always be there for one another.

"How did you know that?" she asked Adrian, staring into his eyes.

"I started to read my Bible a little," he whispered and her heart soared.

"Marsha, let the two lovebirds go on," his father said, his voice slicing through the moment. "I'm sure that with all those boxes they have to go through, they'll soon work up an appetite." He exchanged a wink with his son.

"Thanks, Pops." Taking Brecee's hand, Adrian led the way through the house and up to the attic.

Boxes of all sizes were stacked everywhere. Some of them were falling apart. Brecee was almost wishing she'd stayed downstairs to chat with Marsha while Adrian went on his merry way.

"Uh, where do we start?"

"Let me get some throw pillows for us to sit on, and then we'll get started." Adrian sounded eager and not easily deterred by the monumental task before them.

"Okay." Brecee rested her purse against one of the boxes, then slipped off her shoes and wiggled her toes. Adrian loved her. She wanted to shout her happiness. Instead, she closed her eyes and held it in.

"You have beautiful feet," he said from the doorway before he disappeared.

"Thank you." A woman could never get too many compliments.

While he was gone, Brecee pulled back the flap of one worn-looking box and peeked inside. It was filled with women's clothes—beautiful dresses, some of them faded. One was velvet with detailed stitching. As she lifted it out, a wave of dust arose. She sneezed as Adrian returned.

"God bless my beautiful lady and I mean that whether you sneeze or not." He grinned.

"Thank you." She pointed to the box. "Look at these dresses. Your grandmother must have been petite. And, judging from the styles and quality of what's in here, she definitely had a life outside of work." *But did it include church?* she wondered.

Several boxes nearby contained hats and shoes. "Shae would love these headpieces," Brecee remarked. "Grandma had good taste."

Adrian stopped digging through the box he'd opened and glanced over his shoulder. He met her eyes, then let his gaze travel down to her feet. "I do too." Then he went back to tearing through one box after another.

Dropping a pair of size six shoes, Brecee went to him and rubbed his shoulders. "Sorry. I should be helping. I got sidetracked with the clothes. Your grandmother had plenty of them. Have you found any 'treasures'?"

"Books, Bibles, and baby clothes. What a combination." He shook his head.

"What kind of books? And whose Bibles?" She sat down next to him and began opening a series of smaller boxes containing yellowed envelopes. "These letters are addressed to your grandmother Cora Nichols from Solomon Lambert."

Adrian dropped the box lid in his hand and started reading over her shoulder. "Wow. They weren't married yet." He grunted. "I forgot Nichols was her maiden name."

Brecee slid out the letter dated September 4, 1947, and started to read aloud.

Praise the Lord, Sister Nichols,

I'm glad you accompanied Brother and Sister Daniels to Chicago to attend Mother Mattie B. Poole's street and healing service. You really rejoiced when the church sang "Sweeping Through the City."

I hope you made it safely back to Philadelphia on the train. I sure did pray for you.

Write me back soon with your favorite Scripture.

Mine is 1 John 3:2: "Beloved, now are we the sons of God, and it doth not yet appear what we shall be: but we know that, when he shall appear, we shall be like him; for we shall see him as he is."

Brother Solomon Lambert

Closing her eyes, Brecee took a deep breath. "These must be all their love letters. How romantic." She opened her eyes to see Adrian looking at her. "What?" She stroked his jaw with the back of her hand.

"I love you." He kissed her, then wrapped his arms around her waist. "It sounds like my grandfather loved my grandmother."

"And they definitely met in a church setting."

"Yep. And it's a history I know next to nothing about." His frustration was evident.

"But you're learning about it now, and that's all that matters." Brecee rubbed his hands. "And this is good stuff—something to be proud of. At least you didn't uncover any unsavory ties to serial killers and such. Those are people the family would definitely want to cover up." When she smiled, so did he.

After going through half a dozen letters, Brecee mused, "Evidently, Bethlehem Tabernacle in Chicago was the meetup place a couple of weekends a month." She sighed. "If I had lived in the nineteen forties and fifties, I would have gone to Chicago every week to see Evangelist Mattie B. Poole in action. Can you believe some of the miracles your grandfather described? Cripples walking, the blind seeing, the deaf hearing, and barren women conceiving?"

"Yeah, I wouldn't have mind seeing that myself," Adrian said.

Brecee shook her head in amazement. "She was definitely one of God's servants. Evangelist Poole must have healed your grandmother's friend Sister Daniels, because Solomon mentions her testimony about being pregnant."

"I thought all those miracles ended in Jesus' day," Adrian said.

"If you attend a testimony service, you'll hear all about the wonders God is still doing today. God is the same today, yesterday, and tomorrow. He healed my mother of migraines, He's healed my friends of cancer...but He works those miraculous healings by the hands of those who serve Him alone."

Adrian nodded. "I'll definitely Google Mattie B. Poole."

They continued going through boxes until they came to one filled with sympathy cards. "Look," Brecee said. "These must be from when she passed."

"She died in nineteen sixty-one. So young." Adrian was quiet.

She squeezed his hand. "You okay?"

After a moment, he asked, "How could their relationship have been grounded in church, and the whole thing be such a mystery to my mother?"

Brecee shrugged. "I have no idea, but the promise has been passed down to her and to you. In the Old Testament, when the reign of each king was passed to his son, some worshipped God, while others discarded Him, even though the seed had been planted."

"There's that promise again." He huffed. "This is a whole new world to me. Do you see anything in that box from this Brother or Sister Daniels? Maybe they're still living."

"That's a long shot. I saw a card from a Sister Sarah Daniels with a Philly address, but we're talking from decades ago."

"Are you up for a road trip?"

"Are you serious?" Brecee laughed. She never needed a reason to go home.

"Drive or fly—you choose."

"Adrian, wait. The woman very well may be deceased. Let's at least check whitepages.com."

"You're right." He seemed to deflate for a moment, but then he grinned. "Still, get ready for a road trip."

"I'm on it."

CHAPTER TWENTY

Whether it was to reclaim a forgotten family tradition or to see a promise fulfilled, Adrian was going back to church this morning for answers, and he prayed that God was listening.

Despite the letters he and Brecee had uncovered the day before, their discovery hadn't seemed to spark an ounce of curiosity from his mother. He wondered if something had happened to Solomon and Cora's love for each other and for church that he had yet to uncover.

After showering and getting dressed, he scarfed down a microwave breakfast that he didn't taste, his mind was so preoccupied with pondering whether God had made a promise to his grandmother concerning her family that hadn't been kept.

An hour later, he arrived at Brecee's condo. She opened the door and stepped outside, purse and Bible in hand, as he was hiking up the steps to her porch. She was pretty, even with the simplicity of her attire: a soft pink suit and some type of headpiece that wasn't quite a hat. His heart pounded at the sight. Was this the way his grandfather felt every time he saw his Cora?

Instead of greeting her with the usual peck on the cheek, Adrian lifted her off her feet.

She screamed as she gripped his shoulders. "Adrian Cole, you're going to drop me!"

"I gotcha, babe. Trust me," he said as he slowly set her back down.

She smiled. "What was that all about?"

"I'm excited about God's promise." He grabbed her hand and started for the car.

"Well, alrighty now."

Adrian couldn't explain the explosive energy he felt simmering within as he walked through the doors of Bethesda Temple less than twenty minutes later.

When they reached the pew where Rahn and Shae were sitting, with Sabrina on her mother's lap, Brecee knelt and closed her eyes in prayer.

Adrian followed suit, even as he whispered, "Why are we doing this?"

Opening her eyes, she faced him and smiled. "Because we're in God's holy temple. It's a sign of reverence we were taught by our parents, who learned it from their parents."

"Oh." Adrian closed his eyes and whispered, "Thank You, Lord, for Your promise. Amen."

He and Brecee got up at the same time and then sat in unison. When she stood and started clapping along with the praise band, he did, too. It was crazy, but Adrian couldn't sit still. But as much as he appreciated the energetic music, he couldn't wait for the sermon.

By the time Pastor Archie stepped up to the pulpit, Adrian had already opened his Bible. It had belonged to his grandparents, and he'd brought it home yesterday after the attic search. He felt like a puppy dog waiting for a dog biscuit.

"Good morning and praise the Lord, saints. The Bible says in Ecclesiastes four, verse nine...."

Brecee exchanged a knowing glance with him. It was the same Scripture he had quoted the previous day. He winked, then redirected his attention to the pastor.

"To everything there is a season," Pastor Archie was saying. "Nothing happens by accident. God has a purpose for all things. But my text for today is Jeremiah one, verse five."

Adrian flipped through the pages, passing through 1 Timothy and then 2 Timothy, when Brecee whispered, "Old Testament," then waited patiently as he found the book. Somehow, he didn't feel belittled by her gesture.

"Thanks," he said softly.

"Any time."

Pastor Archie had paused, as if he had been waiting on him, and now he resumed his message. "The verse says, '*Before I formed thee in the belly I knew thee; and before thou camest forth out of the womb I sanctified thee, and*

I ordained thee a prophet unto the nations.' Like Jeremiah, God formed you with a purpose, too, and you don't have to be a prophet to carry out His will. Maybe it's been dormant for years, or even for your entire life. Don't get your purpose and your talent mixed up. It's possible to use your talent to its fullest extent yet never reach your purpose in life." He began to pace back and forth behind the pulpit. "But," he raised his voice, "if you seek God's purpose, then your talent will manifest itself...."

So, what's my purpose? Adrian wanted to shout across the sanctuary. He needed a one-on-one with the minister.

"You don't have to turn there in your Bibles, but Ephesians one, verse four, says, *'He hath chosen us in him before the foundation of the world, that we should be holy and without blame before him in love.'* That's your purpose—to be holy and without blame."

Holy? Adrian grunted. And how was he supposed to accomplish that, with all the temptation around him—namely, the beautiful woman beside him? Brecee had set clear boundaries for their relationship, and although he was committed to respecting them, it wasn't easy.

The preacher cited more Scriptures to back up his teaching on holiness. When he closed his Bible, Adrian's heart sank. He wasn't ready for the sermon to end. He wanted more. *Tell me how to live holy!* was his silent demand.

"As everybody stands, I want you to ask yourself if you are fulfilling God's purpose for your life. If you're honest with yourself, and you know you aren't, then ask God to forgive you for every sin you've allowed your body to commit. Peter said in Acts two, verse thirty-eight, *'Repent, and be baptized every one of you in the name of Jesus Christ for the remission of sins, and ye shall receive the gift of the Holy Ghost.'* The good news is, this promise is passed down from generation to generation. It's a promise to every person who repents and is baptized in water and in spirit, in Jesus' name." He lifted his hands. "Won't you come today? You can't live holy without the Holy Ghost. The evidence is the heavenly language of God speaking through your mouth."

"God, please fulfill this promise You gave my grandmother," Adrian muttered, then faced Brecee. "It's time."

"I know."

Stepping out of the pew, Adrian joined the others making their way down the aisle to the altar for prayer.

When a minister approached Adrian and offered to pray for him, he answered, "I want to be saved, whatever it takes." He almost added that he wanted the same power God had given his grandmother.

"If you have repented of your sins, then you may be baptized in water and in Spirit, in Jesus' name." When Adrian consented, the man told him, "After prayer, another minister will guide you to the changing room."

Adrian waited his turn to use the dressing room to change out of his designer suit and shoes into a white T-shirt, khaki pants, and crew socks. Next, he was led to the baptismal pool. He thought about his grandmother again. As he descended into the water, all he could think about was the promise.

In the pool, another minister—a short man—instructed him to cross his arms over his chest. Groping his T-shirt, the small man spoke in a loud voice, "My dear brother, upon the confession of your faith and the confidence we have in the blessed Word of God concerning His death, burial, and grand resurrection, we now indeed baptize you in the name of the Lord Jesus Christ for the remission of your sins, and you shall receive the promise of His Holy Ghost and speak in other tongues. Amen."

Adrian was pushed underwater then swiftly pulled to his feet. There seemed to be an explosion of something he couldn't explain being released from his body as praises spilled forth from his lips.

In the background, it sounded like angels were shouting and rejoicing with him, or maybe it was the congregation. It didn't matter. An unending stream of "Hallelujah" erupted from his mouth. Then he heard it—the heavenly language—and felt a power take over his mouth, twisting and manipulating his tongue. It was like an out-of-body experience, and it continued as he was nudged back into the dressing room and asked remove the wet clothes. Somehow, he went through the motions of drying off and getting dressed again while the heavenly language continued.

"Praise Jesus, my brother," a minister said to him. "He dwells in the midst of praise. You are now a new creature in Christ. This is just the beginning of your salvation."

I can't do it, Brecee thought as she entered the church's prayer room. There was no way she could shut down the Holy Ghost to hurry Adrian along to go to a softball game. His spiritual rebirth was a once-in-a-lifetime experience.

She texted one of the coaches, a cardiologist, to tell her she wouldn't be able to make it. You need to find a sub for the sub.

He responded, Don't worry about it. We always have plenty willing to play, whether they can play or not.

Tears streamed down Adrian's face as he lifted up his arms in praise. Brecee had been there and done that. She understood that repentance and praise alike often came with tears. Her heart fluttered as she listened to Adrian speaking to God in a heavenly tongue.

Shae had followed her to the prayer room and now stood beside her. As Brecee began softly singing "How Great Is Our God," her sister harmonized with her.

Soon, several other recently baptized individuals were ushered in, singing praises and speaking with Jesus in His language of heavenly tongues. Somehow, in the crowded room, Adrian found privacy in a corner as he uttered to God nonstop. She and Shae worshipped with him and others from afar.

Suddenly, a thunderous sound of praise exploded in the room, bringing to mind the praise coming from the elders standing around the throne of God, as described in Revelation. Losing track of time, Brecee took a seat and whispered prayers to God until she felt a presence behind her.

Opening her eyes, she saw Adrian wiping his eyes and shaking his head. His countenance had changed. Gone was the proud, self-confident man she'd met weeks ago. God had transformed him, and the expression on his face could be described only as "awestruck."

"Is this what my grandparents experienced?" He looked at her with glazed eyes. "I got it," he whispered. "The Holy Ghost was my promise, just like the Bible said."

"Yes, just like the Bible said," she repeated softly as Shae, now joined by Rahn, stepped closer to congratulate Adrian.

"Now what?" he asked Brecee.

"You keep serving God, reading your Bible, increasing your prayer time, and coming to church as much as you can. Anything else you need to know, the Lord will speak it to you," Brecee said as Adrian wrapped her in a hug.

Shae and Rahn waved good-bye, leaving them to share a private moment. "I thank God for you," Adrian whispered over and over again.

"I thank Him for you, too."

When Adrian finally seemed composed, they left the church hand in hand, with smiles on their faces.

"I've got to tell somebody," Adrian said excitedly.

"I know." She grinned. "When God moves in your life, you can't keep it to yourself."

Adrian helped her into his car, then got behind the wheel. But instead of starting the ignition, he pulled out his smartphone and called his parents. Based on hearing only his side of the conversation, Brecee could tell that they were congratulating him, but they probably didn't understand how big a deal it was that he had received a portion of God's Spirit.

Next, Adrian called Dolan, and the excitement exploded from his mouth. It was amusing to hear him pick up speed with each word, and Brecee almost expected him to start speaking in tongues again. When Adrian faced her, his eyes sparkled, and his face glowed with happiness. *One more minute*, he mouthed.

"Take your time," she whispered with a smile. "This is your day of rebirth."

He seemed to take that as the go-ahead to fill Dolan in on every detail, leaving nothing out. As she watched and listened to him, Brecee was certain her father would have liked him. She'd heard him speak plenty about the importance of finding a godly man. "Don't bring home a man who doesn't love the Lord or listen to Him, because he sure won't listen to you," he'd say, citing the example of Pontius Pilate dismissing the intuition of his wife in Matthew 27.

"Are you serious?" Adrian said with a frown, pulling Brecee out of her reverie.

"What?"

"Dolan wants to know if I'm still going to the softball game." He grunted. "I told him the answer is no. Then he asked if Dr. Reed would be playing, because, if so, he was thinking about going and taking Laura."

Brecee giggled and grabbed the phone. "Hi, Dolan. I got sidetracked today and it was worth it, but Dr. Reed isn't on the softball team. She's busy with a ministry event at her church this afternoon."

"Oh." His disappointment was obvious. "I wanted to thank her...."

"Call her," Brecee encouraged him. "I'm sure she gave you her card."

"You gave me your card, too, but my ugly cousin threatened to harm me if I used it."

"You know I can hear you," Adrian teased.

Brecee leaned over, and he met her with a soft kiss before she got back on the phone. "I'm sure she'd like to know how Laura is doing."

Adrian grabbed the phone. "Just call her, cuz. Right now, my beautiful lady and I are going out to celebrate my new birth. Talk to you later." He ended the call, then gazed adoringly at Brecee. He kissed her hand. "I love you, and I love God. My life is so good right now. The only thing that will make it better is a hearty meal. Suddenly, I'm famished."

Seated in a restaurant booth half an hour later, Brecee could hardly eat as she listened to Adrian express his deep feelings about what had happened at church that morning. Even though she'd barely picked at her food, Adrian ordered a slice of cheesecake for them to share. While they waited for their server to deliver dessert, he reached across the table and took her hands. "Thank you for coming into my life. I don't know if I ever would have come to salvation otherwise. You've changed me."

Tears welled in her eyes. "No, Adrian—God changed you. Thank you for letting me be me. I can't wait to call my family and share your good news with them." She grinned as she envisioned the praise parties over a saved soul that would take place in the various Carmen households that night.

"Why wait?" His eyes took on that sparkle of excitement again. "Let's call them right now, and I'll share the news myself."

How could she deny him the pleasure? She called Stacy and asked her to set up a conference call with everybody, including Uncle Bradford. "I've got some exciting news," she told her.

"That news better not be that you're engaged!" Stacy declared in her typical authoritarian tone.

Not yet, Adrian mouthed to Brecee.

You heard that? Brecee mouthed back, and he nodded.

When the decadent-looking slice of cheesecake was placed before them, Adrian blessed it, then forked off a bite and fed it to her. "Have I told you today that I love you?"

Closing her eyes, Brecee let the words seep into her heart. "Yes, but there's no limit. I love you, too."

"Do you think your family will be excited at the news?" he asked. "Mom and Pops didn't think it was that big of a deal."

Her heart ached for him. "You don't know the Carmens," she told him. "God saved you. Not everybody wants to be saved, and that's the reality. But you made the choice, and it's a huge deal."

When they'd polished off the cheesecake, Adrian paid their bill, then helped Brecee to her feet and escorted her out to his car, kissing her ear repeatedly until she giggled.

As Brecee fastened her seat belt, Stacy texted her the conference call number and ID. She put Adrian on speakerphone, then typed in the number and code, then waited to be announced.

Her family started speaking all at once.

"Brecee, what have you done now?" Uncle Bradford asked.

She grinned at Adrian.

"You said you're not engaged," Stacy put in.

"Excuse me," Brecee said, cutting them off. She'd waited patiently for Adrian to profess his love; she didn't want to put the pressure on for him to propose. "Adrian and I are on speakerphone, and it was his idea to call you."

"It's a little unusual to do this in front of the whole family over a conference call, isn't it?" Uncle Bradford asked.

Brecee groaned. "Uncle Bradford, hush. Okay, Adrian, it's your turn."

She jumped, startled, as he shouted, "Everybody: I received the Holy Ghost!"

The jubilant shouts of "Praise the Lord!" were so immediate that Adrian laughed.

"I told you," Brecee mumbled.

"Congratulations," her mother said with a sniffle. "What wonderful news. You'll never regret giving your life to Christ. My husband used to say—"

"Don't bring home a man who doesn't love the Lord or listen to Him, because he sure won't listen to you," the sisters recited in unison.

"Amen." Adrian nodded. "I've got a lot to learn, but I don't want to disappoint God, my grandmother, or Brecee." He reached for her hand.

How was it that she kept falling more and more in love with this man?

"Even though I've been filled with God's Spirit, I'm still hungry to learn more about my grandparents. Mr. Carmen—"

"You can call me Brother Carmen now," Uncle Bradford said with a chuckle.

"Thank you." Adrian choked. "Are you sure there's nothing more you can find out about the female coworkers your father mentioned? Brecee and I found a bunch of letters and some photos in my parents' attic. Only one lady who lived in Philly was mentioned."

When he sighed, Brecee could feel his frustration. He had received God's promise, but he wanted more.

"My father repented and was baptized in water and by the Holy Ghost at Pentecostal Bridegroom Temple," Uncle Bradford recalled. "Since then, our families have worshipped at sister churches. I don't ever recall him introducing us to the person responsible for leading him to salvation. But God knows all answers, and if He wants to share them with you, He will. In the meantime, praise God that you have your ticket for the rapture."

Adrian seemed to accept her uncle's counsel, but something deep down inside of Brecee told her that the Holy Ghost had just cracked open the door for Adrian's hunt.

CHAPTER TWENTY-ONE

The next morning, Brecee strolled through the emergency department with a smile on her face. She was in love. Adrian was in love…with her. She blinked at the giant floral arrangement on the reception counter. "Wow." Adrian had outdone himself this time.

She reached for the envelope, but Teresa the triage nurse stopped her. "Not today, Dr. Carmen. Those are for Dr. Reed." She winked.

Regina? Huh. Had she been that caught up in her own love life that she'd failed to notice? Or had Regina been holding out on her?

"Do you two have a competition going on or something?" Teresa asked. "No one else in the department has received flowers since Valentine's Day, including me—and mine came from my dad." She rolled her eyes. "Dr. Reed knows they're here, but she's been too busy to pick them up. Do you want to take them back to her?"

Laughing, Brecee shook her head. "And deprive Dr. Reed of your teasing? Nah."

Teresa was right—it was a madhouse in the emergency department. But no surprise there. It was Monday, after all.

As Brecee signed her name on the board to let everyone know that another attending doctor had arrived, the charge nurse, Ashley, quickly briefed her on the current patients and who was supervising their care.

A few hours later, when things finally slowed down, Brecee took a seat in the doctors' charting room. After several minutes, Regina sauntered in. "Guess who sent me flowers." She was actually blushing.

"Let me see," Brecee said, playing along. "Here's a wild guess: Dolan Cole."

Regina's eyes bulged. "How did you know?"

Brecee relayed the conversation she and Adrian had had with him the previous day, then shared the news of Adrian's receiving the Holy Ghost.

Jumping up, Regina had to stifle her shout of jubilation. "Yay! Hallelujah."

Brecee beamed. "Girl, I love that man."

"Tell me something I don't know." Regina glanced over her shoulder, as if to make sure no one was coming through the door. "There's more. Dolan asked me out on a date."

"Are you considering it?" Brecee eyed her friend.

"I am." Regina sat back in her chair and crossed her legs. "His love for his daughter drew me to him, even if it was way over the top, but that's a dad for you." Regina snickered. "He is incredibly good-looking, but…."

Usually, whenever Regina said "but," she was at the point of overanalyzing a simple dilemma. She hadn't made a vow to God, per se, but she might as well have made one to herself about dating an unsaved man.

"I've been unequally yoked once already. Never again. I've held off from fellow doctors and other men, but I really would like to get to know Dolan." She paused. "That scares me, because I can see my feelings getting in the way of my following my Holy-Ghost protocol. But now that Adrian has surrendered to Christ, maybe Dolan will follow his lead."

"That's a hope and prayer," Brecee told her, "but we're still our sister's keeper. I don't want to see you fall any more than you want to see that happen to me. That's why you have been holding me accountable for my behavior with Adrian." She smiled. "And he's been nothing but a perfect gentleman. Not once has he questioned why I won't invite him in. I may be grown, at thirty-one, but I know temptation when I see it, and Adrian is six feet three or four inches of it." She paused. "Would you like to consider double dating while you decide whether Dolan is worth your time?" She glanced up and saw Ashley approaching the room to brief them on their latest admissions. Their respite was over. Any further talk of love and happiness would have to wait. "Just think about it."

~

On Monday afternoon, Adrian found himself with some downtime after a repeat client drove off the lot in a new car. He decided to call Dolan.

Not long into the conversation, he invited his cousin to attend church with him the following weekend. "What do you have to lose, man?"

"For one thing, sleep," was Dolan's response.

Adrian smirked. He could relate to that excuse, because he had been just as stubborn. But there was more than one way to get to his cousin. "Okay, then I guess I'll ask my little cousin if she would like for her daddy to go to church."

"Don't use my kid," Dolan threatened.

"Why? It's worked before." Adrian snickered. "Don't you think God deserves a thank-you for Laura's recovery from that bee sting? She could have…." Adrian didn't want to think about what might have happened, much less mention it.

"I did thank Him," Dolan said. "Hold on. I've got another call coming in."

"Go ahead," Adrian told him. "We'll talk later."

Under an hour later, Adrian received a text from Dolan while he was on the showroom floor, greeting some potential customers. When the couple stepped aside for a private conversation, Adrian read his message.

I'll be at church on Sunday.

Huh? Adrian had to reread the message. *Lord, did You do that?* He had to know what had turned Dolan's no into a yes.

He found out on his dinner break, when he called Dolan from St. Louis Bread Company. "Okay, what changed your mind?"

"Regina."

"Who?" Adrian frowned, and then it dawned on him. "Ah, Dr. Reed. You're on a first-name basis already? That was fast."

"I couldn't tell her no, man. She is some kind of fine." Adrian was amused as his cousin continued to ramble, "She called me and got to the point in the first three minutes of our conversation. She's a practicing Christian, and she doesn't date men who aren't. I told her you'd invited me to church and that I was going."

"Liar." Adrian couldn't keep himself from howling.

"Well, you were persuaded by a woman. Anyway, she suggested a double date with you and Brecee."

"I like the sound of that." Adrian nodded to himself. "You're going down, so you might as well not put up a fight. Your late wife cut you some slack when it came to church attendance, but something tells me any friend of Brecee's isn't going to go for it. Should I send you a list of Bible verses?"

"No," Dolan snapped. "If I want them, I can probably get them from my daughter."

Adrian didn't stop laughing until his number was called for him to pick up his order at the counter. Once he'd blessed his food, he texted Brecee rather than calling, in case she was busy. I heard we're double dating. :) I'm at dinner. Call me if when you can. Miss you like crazy.

His phone rang seconds later. "I miss you, too," she said when he answered. "How's your first day as a new man?"

Her soft voice was soothing. "Incredible. Some of my coworkers were so surprised when I shared my experience and newfound commitment, as if they thought I didn't have any church in me." He sipped his lemonade. "Others were composed, but I just spoke with Dolan. Rumor has it I have to share you on a double date Saturday night."

"Is that okay? I should have asked you." She sounded hesitant.

"Baby, as long as I'm with you, it's fine. I'm thinking about cutting my days back to five."

"Oh, really? That's great." Her happiness was evident, but so was her worry seconds later. "I mean, can you afford it?"

Adrian snorted. "I'll make it work. I need to spend more time with you and with Jesus."

"Ah, that's sweet, but I have to go." She smacked a few kisses into the phone before she ended the call.

As he chewed on his ciabatta sandwich, he stared out into the parking at the customers coming and going. Brecee was one of a kind: gorgeous, talented, kind, reassuring, and lovable. He was ready for a permanent change of marital status. But was it too soon? Would she say yes? Just like she'd wanted him to be sure when he told her he loved her, Adrian needed be sure of her answer before he got on one knee.

After work, Adrian drove home with his mind on what he'd told Brecee. With his monthly sales, he could definitely afford to cut back on his hours. Unfortunately, Saturday couldn't be the day he dropped, since it was the busiest day. But he had to spend more time with her, especially with the summer session starting up soon that would require his focus. Maybe they could start going to Bible class together on Wednesdays.

Lord, lead me.

Once he was back at his condo, Adrian thought about his grandmother. Maybe it was wishful thinking, but it seemed as if she was beckoning him to continue his search—that there was more to uncover. After changing out of his suit and tie, Adrian retrieved the box of letters he had taken from his parents' and sat down at his kitchen table.

He stared at the envelopes again. What were the odds that Grandmother Cora's good friend in Philly was still alive, and still lived in the same house? Was the house even there any longer? He had already searched the name and address on whitepages.com, but there hadn't been any matches. Now, he powered up his laptop and typed the street address into Google Maps.

Ecclesiastes 4:9 came to mind again. He glanced at the time. Brecee would be off work and at home by now. She never seemed to tire of listening to him tell her excitedly about his latest find, however small, in his search for a key to unlock his family history.

He called her. "Hey, babe. Were you busy?" He fingered the edge of an envelope.

"I always want to hear your voice," she told him. "Are you home?"

"Yes." He explained to her what he had been doing. "I'm itching to get up there and knock on the door. Do you recognize the address, babe?"

"That's in the Hawthorne neighborhood." Brecee chuckled. "As much as I would love any reason to go home, let's first see if one of my cousins will do a drive-by and introduce himself."

His spirits lifted. "Do you think Victor or Dino would mind doing me that favor?"

"Not at all."

He breathed a sigh of relief. "Thank you."

"Sweetie, for our first double date, what would you say to a cookout at my condo? We can celebrate the Fourth of July, since I have to work the holiday."

Lifting his eyebrows, Adrian smirked. "My woman is letting me cross the threshold?"

"You know why I haven't let you before," she said softly.

He'd been aware of her reasons, but he hadn't understood them until recently. "I never would have done anything against your will, sweetheart."

"My self-defense training would have made sure of it." She didn't sound like she was joking. "But our flesh was involved, and we both needed the Holy Ghost to keep from falling."

"I'll be your protector, babe—spiritually, thanks to the Holy Ghost within me, and physically. You'll always be safe with me, whether you practice Tae Kwon Do or something else."

Brecee burst out laughing, so Adrian chuckled, too, but he'd meant every word. "I'm serious. I love you."

"I love you, too."

"Thanks for the reminder," he teased. "The couple thing is cool. You tell me the time and what you want me to bring, and I'll be there. By the way, are you sure you're okay if I take a summer course?"

"You know you don't need my permission." She paused. "But I appreciate that my opinion matters to you."

The woman's sweetness was driving him crazy. "It's going to cut into our time together. That is why I asked."

"We'll make it work."

"And I'll make it up to you."

"Promise?"

Promise. The word that had sent Adrian on a treasure hunt for an understanding of something he hadn't yet resolved. "Yes."

She sighed. "You're easy to love. You know that?"

"Yep," he joked.

They exchanged air kisses before disconnecting.

CHAPTER TWENTY-TWO

Dating was an all-consuming business, but Brecee wasn't complaining. Adrian was the piece of the puzzle that had been missing from her life.

She had been so busy with her own romance that she hadn't found time to dip into her mother's. That was bad, considering her mom was now in full-throttle dating. Shari and Stacy kept her posted on the important updates, but that morning, she decided to call her mom as she sipped her coffee.

"Hi, sweetie," her mother answered and, in the same breath, asked, "Are you engaged yet?"

Brecee laughed. "I should be asking you the same question. I'm still trying to wrap my head around the idea of my mother courting after all these years. As for Adrian, he needs time to make God a priority before me, and he's busy—"

"Really? Well, I've got a problem with that. If he wants you, then he needs to refocus." She huffed. The tigress was uncaged.

"Mom, he's working full-time and going to grad school. He did ask me if I was okay with his enrolling in a summer course. I don't want to stand in his way. I know how intense school can be. Plus, he said he would make it up to me." Her argument sounded convincing, but that didn't keep her from wanting to be married to the love of her life, like her sisters were to theirs. She was certain Adrian was the one.

"Well then, sweetie, ask God to give you patience. You'll know when you reach your limit." Her mother paused. "That was the doorbell. It's probably Marcellus, here to take me out for breakfast. I've got to go. Love you." She disconnected without waiting for Brecee's good-bye.

Frowning, Brecee finished her coffee, then grabbed a banana and called Shae as she peeled it. They chatted about the baby, then Brecee recapped her conversation with their mother. "I feel like I should be moving as fast as Mom," she confessed.

"You and Adrian haven't been dating long. Just a few months," Shae reminded her. "You two need more time to really get to know each other."

"I know." Brecee gritted her teeth in frustration. "But, as I far as I'm concerned, Mr. Cole should have known my expectations by the end of the first month."

"This is bigger than you, Sis. The right relationship is larger than life."

Brecee huffed. "Yeah. Leave it to Mom. She would have married me off to Adrian yesterday so that she could proceed with her own wedding. The real question is, how long can Adrian hold out, since saints don't indulge in fornication?" That reminded her of the reason she'd called. "Is your hubby going to be in town this weekend?"

"Nope." Shae groaned. "Seven-game road trip. Why?"

"Regina and I are having a double date at my place on Saturday evening, and I was going to invite you and Rahn."

"A triple date," Shae teased then quieted. "You're going to love the intimacy of sharing the simplest tasks with him—cooking, setting the table, cleaning up the kitchen...playing house. The presence of another couple will definitely ward off temptation." Her sister paused. "Oh, I've got to go. I hear your namesake calling for her mommy. We'll talk later. Smooches."

A few hours later, when Brecee strolled into the emergency department, there was another bouquet of flowers waiting on the reception desk. She blinked. Not wanting to make another erroneous assumption, Brecee asked the receptionist, "Me, Dr. Reed, or another special doctor?"

"You this time. Dr. Reed already picked hers up—same florist. How can I get added to the list?" she joked.

Smiling, Brecee took her vase and detoured to her office. Once there, she read the note.

You're always on my mind.

Love,
Adrian

Brecee took a deep breath and then exhaled. As long as he kept up the sweet courtship, she could wait for Adrian to make a move in God's timing. She texted him a thank-you.

After signing her name to the board and being briefed by Ashley, Brecee entered the charting room. Regina was sitting there, her face glowing with a blush. She looked more excited than Brecee had ever seen her. "I'm looking forward to our double date this weekend," Regina told her.

"Me, too. Looks like the cousins have stock in the floral industry." Brecee pulled out the chart on a little girl Ashley had told her about. The child's pediatrician had referred her to the emergency department for an X-ray of her arm to determine whether it was broken. Satisfied with the resident's assessment, Brecee looked up at her friend.

"I expect you to hold me accountable and not compromise if Dolan is against surrendering to the Lord," Regina said.

Brecee nodded.

Regina twisted her lips. "If a good man is hard to find, then Dolan is going to realize that a great woman is no easy catch, either."

"Amen." They high-fived each other before Regina left to discuss test results with a patient's parents.

By late afternoon, the department had treated mostly bike and roller skate injuries, with a few minor lacerations thrown into the mix.

When Saturday arrived, Brecee counted down the hours until Adrian would be a guest in her home for the first time. He had assured her that he would leave work early to spend time with his baby.

Her condo was clean, the day was sunny, and the Carmen family's famous baked beans were in the oven. It was still early when doorbell rang for the first time.

"Ooh." Brecee blinked when she answered the door and saw Regina. "You're brave, wearing all white to a barbecue. Don't you look stunning!"

They exchanged hugs, and Regina walked in. "It beats wearing scrubs any time."

The airy white sleeveless top pinched her waist, accentuating her slender figure and her gorgeous dark skin, which resembled Shari's. Her shoulder-length hair was twisted up in a ball—a smart choice for the St. Louis heat and humidity.

Brecee had learned early on never to wear white to a barbecue. She didn't care if she was at home and could easily change; she wasn't that neat. Today, she sported a tan top with tiny brown polka dots and a long wrap skirt.

"Here, let me take that." Brecee accepted Regina's special-recipe banana pudding and immediately stashed it in the refrigerator.

Regina set down her purse. "Need any help?"

When Brecee shook her head, Regina made herself comfortable on one of the bar stools. "Perfect day for a barbecue."

"I know. Adrian's bringing the hamburgers and chicken. He seasoned them last night and was going to take them to work. The grill's waiting on him." Brecee glanced at the microwave clock to see the time.

"Aren't we anxious?" Regina teased.

"Can I help it if I miss him?"

Regina stretched. "This will be my first time seeing Dolan again since the emergency room visit. We've talked on the phone, and he's sent flowers, but I'm a little nervous." She paused. "In the back of my mind, I can't help wondering if he just wants a mother for his daughter. His unwavering passion for Laura is undeniable, but is there any love left for another woman?"

They chatted about relationships until Brecee's doorbell rang again. She had lost track of time. On her way to answer it, she checked her appearance in the hall mirror. Her long hair was still neatly gathered atop her head, and her minimal makeup—a bare dusting of shimmery powder—was mostly in place.

She opened the door and stared at Adrian. There had never been a time when he hadn't been eye-catching, but his dark sunglasses always kept her guessing if he liked what he saw.

"Hi." He leaned in and greeted her with a kiss as Dolan strolled up behind him carrying flowers and a covered dish. She waved them inside as Regina stood.

Adrian crossed the threshold and slowly scanned her living room. He released a whistle. "So, this is your sanctuary from the world. Nice." He turned to Regina. "It's nice to see you again, Dr. Reed."

"I'm not on duty, so please, call me Regina." She smiled, and when Dolan gave her an appreciative glance, she glowed.

"Here, let me take that, and I'll give you a tour." She accepted the pan of meat from Adrian and set it on the counter, then took his hand and showed off her décor in every room except her bedroom. That truly was her private sanctuary.

Before they returned to the living room, Adrian kissed her hair and slipped his arm around her waist. She looked up and saw the love radiating from his eyes. "How did your day go?"

"I built relationships," he replied, which she had come to learn was a phrase for when he hadn't made any sales.

"And I'm sure those relationships will yield great fruit." She squeezed him tight.

"Brecee, I turned off the oven," Regina called to her. "The baked beans are ready, sister."

"Great. Let's get the meat on the grill." She returned to the kitchen and uncovered Adrian's dish. "Let's see how your seasoning tastes."

The evening breeze tickled the loose curls at the back of Brecee's neck as she supervised Adrian on the grill. While the meat was cooking, he wrapped his arms around her, and she leaned against his chest, gazing in the direction of Lafayette Park. "I love sitting out here when there's a concert in the park. The free serenades are great, albeit a bit faint."

"Find out when the next one is, and we'll get front-row seats," he told her.

Turning in his arms, she looked at him. "I would like that. I've gone before, with Shae—and her bodyguards. Blame it on my brother-in-law. He did have a security scare before meeting Shae. Sometimes, he can be a little overbearing, but my sister has learned to take it in stride."

"Bodyguards?" He lifted an eyebrow, then whistled. "It's good to know my baby has secret service protection when I'm not around."

"J-E-S-U-S," she spelled, then guided him back inside. Dolan and Regina had set the table and were now relaxing at the kitchen counter, laughing at something.

Adrian rubbed his hands. "So, what else do we have to go with this?" In her kitchen, he and Brecee worked efficiently together to make a salad and a pitcher of fresh-squeezed lemonade. "Add some strawberries and a lime," she told him.

He didn't question the concoction.

Shae had been right about their intimacy outside the bedroom. Brecee did enjoy doing the simplest of tasks with him. His presence made her content.

After the meal, the four of them sat on her balcony and watched the small-time fireworks displays of a few neighbors. One thing Shae hadn't told her was that at the end of the night, she wouldn't want Adrian to leave.

⌒

The next morning, Adrian had a hangover, and it had nothing to do with alcohol. It was Brecee. The woman was drugging him with every sweet kiss and embrace. Even their morning wakeup calls were addictive.

She was a temptation waiting to happen. But as he was leaving her place last night, he heard God whisper, *I can keep you from falling and present you faultless.*

Every reminder, whether sensed in his spirit or read in his Bible, strengthened his resolve to live up to the standard of holiness God and his grandmother had set before him. And he was learning that it took determination.

After showering and getting dressed, he called Dolan. "You still coming to church?"

"Yep. I'm fulfilling the prerequisite for Regina to go on a date with me. Don't expect me to come in one way and go out another. I'm just visiting."

Adrian was glad his cousin couldn't see the smile on his face. "Fair enough. See you there."

His cousin had barely seemed interested when he had shared about his Holy Ghost experience, but last night, when Regina had told them how God had healed her after a series of major disappointments, Dolan had seemed to hang on her every word. Hopefully, her influence would rub off on him the way Brecee's had on Adrian.

He ate a quick breakfast, then got in his car and headed to Brecee's condo. Even though he would have to go past the church to get there, he insisted on picking her up. That courtesy had been ingrained in him by his father since his very first date.

Not surprisingly, she was ready before he rang the bell. She stepped outside in a light gray two-piece suit. She seemed to get a kick out of asking him what he was wearing, then dressing in a coordinating color. He sure didn't mind it when their outfits complemented each other.

"You look amazing," he told her, "but I'm starting to wonder if you have clothes to match all the colors in a sixty-four box of Crayolas."

She laughed. "Only my closet knows for sure." She grabbed her Bible and her purse, then locked her door.

Once they were settled inside his car, the scent of her perfume tickled his nose. "You smell good, too."

Her blush was thank-you enough.

As he drove, he gave her a sideways glance. "You know, babe, I have to thank you. After our double date last night, I appreciate the wisdom God gave you about being alone with me. You have no idea how much you tempt me." He grunted and shook his head. "I tell you, without God's Holy Ghost to keep me from falling, I would have tripped a long time ago. So, thank you."

"Amen." When they arrived at Bethesda Temple, Adrian knew the routine this time: select a row, kneel at the pew to pray and thank God for the privilege of being in His holy place, and then join in the praise service.

Moments later, Laura skipped up to their pew. She looked ecstatic to be there, giving him a hug before stepping on his Stacy Adams shoes to get to Brecee, who doted on her with unrestrained affection. Dolan shook Adrian's hand. He didn't look quite as excited.

Before long, Regina joined them. She seemed flustered. "Sorry I'm running late."

Laura's eyes lit up as she climbed over her father and Brecee to get to Regina. Adrian was able to move his feet out of the way this time before his little cousin could crunch them again.

"Hi, Miss Regina. Like my dress?" She looked hopeful as Regina squeezed into the pew to sit next to Dolan.

Regina nodded. "You and your daddy look very nice." Then she knelt to pray.

"See, Daddy? And I picked out your tie." Laura spoke loudly, but the praise music drowned her out.

Of course, Adrian hoped Dolan would experience what he had, but that was between his cousin and God. *Jesus, please open Dolan's eyes to see You, in Jesus' name. Amen.* But what if Dolan didn't make a change? Adrian was having second thoughts about the whole double dating scenario. If things didn't work out between Dolan and Regina, he wondered how that would affect his relationship with Brecee. More than anything, Adrian wanted her to be happy.

After Regina prayed, she stood with them and joined in the praise music. Dolan didn't budge from his seat. The Cole men didn't fake it for the sake of a woman, and Adrian could respect his cousin for keeping it real.

Adrian enjoyed the choir's selections that morning. Judging from the way Laura hopped to the beat, she did, too. But after his experience with the Holy Ghost, Adrian was ready for the meat of the message. When Pastor Archie approached the pulpit, Adrian grabbed his Bible.

"I'd like to welcome any visitors," the pastor said. "We're so glad you're here to worship with us. If God speaks to you during the sermon, I encourage you to take it to heart. We read in Hebrews three, verse fifteen, *'To day if ye will hear his voice, harden not your hearts.'* That Scripture is so compelling, considering where my text is coming from this morning—Jeremiah thirty-one, verse three: *'The LORD hath appeared of old unto me, saying, Yea, I have loved thee with an everlasting love: therefore with lovingkindness have I drawn thee.'* God is not going to force Himself on you and your lifestyle. He won't do it." Pastor Archie shook his head. "But that doesn't mean He won't try to reason with you to draw you away from danger. He handles our hurts and pains like an overprotective mother. Jesus is kind and gentle. But, one day, He will shut the door and say, 'Time's up.' Don't take God's kindness for weakness and ignore the warning signs. The Bible says hell was enlarged because of sin. Where would you go if you died today?"

Adrian sneaked a glance at his cousin. Now that the music had ended, Laura sat quietly beside her father, flipping through her picture Bible. Dolan held an arm around her shoulder. His body language gave no indication that he felt God was talking to him.

But He was talking to Adrian. As Pastor Archie continued to preach, his words seemed to seep into his soul, until the realization hit that had been on his way to hell and hadn't known it.

Pastor Archie ended his sermon with a warning: "There will be a trumpet, and it will be louder than a tornado siren. And just like that"—he snapped his fingers—"the dead in Christ will rise first, and we who are alive and remain in Christ shall be caught up to meet the Lord in the air. Don't miss it! Don't miss it! Don't miss it! Get the Spirit of Christ today. Repent and be baptized in the name of Jesus for the remission of your sins...." He directed the congregation to stand for the altar call and, with bowed heads, to pray for souls.

As the music played softly, Adrian prayed for his cousin, soon adding his parents to his petition. When he heard Laura whisper, "Daddy, I'm sorry for being bad. I want to get baptized, so I can fly with Jesus," he smiled. He had just read a passage in Matthew 18 about taking on the innocence and humility of a child to be led into heaven.

As he continued to pray, he felt a soft nudge, but he ignored it. The second one was harder, so Adrian opened his eyes and stared directly into Dolan's.

"It's time, man," his cousin told him.

Adrian frowned. "Time for what? Don't tell me you're leaving."

Pastor Archie had preached an incredible message. How had it failed to get through to Dolan?

"The sermon reminded me of Lynn." Dolan swallowed. "She used to talk to me about Jesus' loving kindness. Of course, I ignored her. She seemed to overlook my faults, but I guess I can't hold out forever. If my baby girl wants to be saved from whatever little misdeeds she's done, I can only imagine what I need saving from. It's time to surrender."

Stepping out of the way, Adrian watched as Dolan took Laura's hand and proceeded down the aisle to the front.

He exhaled a sigh of relief. One soul down, two more to go.

CHAPTER TWENTY-THREE

Ⓜy *Yoke is easy, My burden is light.* God reminded Brecee of Matthew 11:30 as she witnessed father and daughter repent and receive the baptism in water and in Spirit. As the dozens of new converts praised the Lord, she could feel God's presence among them.

Hours later after leaving church, she and Adrian were at Longhorn Steakhouse, waiting for their meal. Although Adrian had offered to treat Dolan, Laura, and Regina as a celebration of their new births in Christ, Dolan had declined, preferring to enjoy Regina's company without them— this time.

"Hey." Brecee touched Adrian's hand to get his attention. He was staring out the window.

He blinked. "Sorry. I was just thinking about Dolan and how happy his late wife would be. I guess the Lord made a promise to Denise, too, for her family, because Jesus fulfilled it today." Adrian chuckled, then trapped her hands in his strong ones.

"Yep." Brecee exhaled. "God never breaks His promises."

"I know it. Honestly, the way Dolan fought coming to church, I was shocked that he surrendered so easily. Something held me back on my first visit."

Brecee nodded. "True, but we don't know how many seeds his late wife had planted," Brecee pointed out. "Some people come to church ready to repent, while others need more persuasion by the Holy Ghost. My family in Philly's going to think we've got a revival going on here." She pulled out her phone and sent a group text with the praise report.

Stacy replied first. Excellent!

Praise God! came Shari's response.

When her smartphone rang, she glanced at the ID. *Victor,* she mouthed to Adrian, just as their food arrived. He nodded, then quickly said a silent blessing before tearing into his steak.

"Hey, cuz. That's good news about the salvation report, but I've got one for you," Victor said. "I stopped by that house on Old York Road to see, against all odds, if that woman still lived there or if someone remembered her."

Brecee's heart pounded. "Go on."

"The woman who answered the door looked familiar, and you're not going to believe this, but—"

"Hold on. I want Adrian to hear this." She waved to get his attention, and he immediately got up and scooted next to her in the booth, then slid his plate around. She set the phone on the table between them. "Go ahead."

"I think we crossed paths before. Years ago, on campus."

"Okay, so you had an impromptu class reunion. What about Mrs. Daniels?" She calculated her age in her head. "Is she still alive? That would make her...."

"Ninety-four or ninety-five," Adrian stated.

Victor chuckled. "Impressive. Her great-granddaughter, Judith Pride, says Mrs. Daniel lives in a nursing home."

When Adrian faced Brecee, he looked like he was salivating, and it wasn't over his steak. His heart was probably racing, too.

Their server returned to check on them. "Hold on, Vic," Brecee murmured. "We're still eating—"

"No, we're finished," Adrian said, then turned to the woman. "Can we get our check, please?"

"We'll call you back as soon as we pay the bill and get in the car," Brecee told her cousin before disconnecting the call.

"Would you like some to-go containers?" the server asked them.

"No." Adrian set down a wad of cash—enough for the tab plus a generous tip. "I don't want to wait around for her to return my plastic or any change," he told Brecee. She wasn't surprised when he left one of his business cards behind.

Grabbing her hand, Adrian hurried through the restaurant and out the door. She would have called him out on his behavior, but she understood the reason for his adrenaline rush. At least he opened the car door for her, as always, before sprinting to the driver's side.

Behind the wheel, Adrian took a deep breath, then gave her a sheepish grin. "Okay. Call Victor back," he said as an afterthought, he added, "please."

Laughing, Brecee smacked him in the shoulder, then tapped her cousin's number and put the phone on speaker.

"That was quick," Victor said. "Adrian, you'll be pleased to know I actually spoke with Mrs. Daniels."

Brecee thought Adrian's eyes were going to bug out of their sockets. "How did you manage that?" she asked.

"I explained to Judith that a friend of my cousin's wanted to speak with her, and why, and she agreed to take me to the nursing home for a visit."

Adrian was speechless.

"I couldn't believe Mrs. Daniels' memory. When I strolled into the room behind Judith, she squinted at me, then adjusted her glasses. When Judith told her who I was, she called out our grandfather's name. She said I looked just like Theodore."

"Wow," Brecee whispered, stunned.

Adrian cleared his throat. "Did she say anything about my grandmother Cora Lambert?"

"Ah, ah…sorry, Adrian. We got so busy talking about my grandfather and the Lord, I think I wore her out, and Judith suggested we leave before I could ask."

Adrian squeezed his lips together and exhaled through his nose. Once he seemed to have his frustration in check, he slowly stated, "I'm glad she's up to having visitors, because I'm coming."

Yes! Brecee couldn't wait to take Adrian to visit her hometown.

"Fairview Care Center, Bethlehem Pike," Adrian repeated after Victor, then thanked him. "I guess you'll be seeing Brecee and me next Saturday."

She gave him an amused look.

"Babe, I'm sorry I got ahead of myself," Adrian told her once they'd said good-bye to Victor. "Is next weekend good for *you?*"

"Are you kidding me? Shae and I are always looking for an excuse to go home. Do you mind if I ask her to join us? She will be highly ticked if I one-up her on a trip home."

"Of course not. But I'll want to focus on spending as much time with Mrs. Daniels as I can."

That was fine with her, but she at least had to give him an abbreviated tour of the City of Brotherly Love, with dinner at Geno's Steaks, a visit to her home church, a stroll at Penn's Landing....

"Pack light, babe," he interrupted her agenda planning. "Let me know if I need to order three airline tickets."

"Oh, it's definitely two," she assured him. "Even if Shae joins us, there's no way my brother-in-law will let another man buy anything for his wife."

Nodding, Adrian smirked. "I understand the feeling." He leaned over and sealed his statement with a kiss.

⸺

"If I knew it was going to be like this, I would have repented sooner," Dolan told Adrian during their next phone conversation. "I'm at peace."

Salvation was definitely contagious. "Without Brecee, I don't know if I would have traveled this path, but then I think of my grandmother and how hard she probably prayed for my mother," Adrian mused. "I guess there was no way the power of God would stop cold turkey in the family."

"Regina played a big part in my 'now or never' decision to go to church," Dolan admitted. "And then, once I was there, Laura was ready...."

Adrian stood when he spied a car driving into the dealership parking lot. "Business beckons. I'll talk to you before I leave for Philly."

Barring sickness or death, it was unheard for Adrian Cole to skip a Saturday of work at the dealership. The sales manager at Broadway Luxury Motors had reminded him of that very fact when Adrian informed him that he would be out of town the following Saturday.

Adrian tried not to think about the single sale he still needed in order to meet the manufacturer's quota, which changed from month to month. He really wasn't that worried, because he had never failed to meet it before. He'd always credited his expertise or self-confidence for his success, but now he understood that God alone was responsible for his blessings. "Lord, I'm trusting You."

By Friday afternoon, Adrian had built many new relationships over the week, but he paced the showroom floor, hoping that the financing for the Mulligans would be approved. He'd already had three false hopes this week. He didn't want it to be four. *Trust God, trust God, trust God,* he coaxed himself. He was going to Philly this weekend, no matter what.

Are you sure about that? a small voice from nowhere taunted him.

Briefly, a surge of doubt rose up within him, but he shook it away. Yes, Jesus had saved him, but it seemed like his grandmother had put him on that path. Besides his mother, Mrs. Daniels was the only connection he had left to his grandmother. He had to go to Philly.

Two hours before closing, Adrian learned that the Mulligans' deal had fallen through. As his heart began to sink, he began to pray. After stopping in the men's room, he returned to the showroom just as a gentleman strolled in. He looked somewhat familiar, and it didn't take long for him to remember that he was one of Rahn's referrals. If only he could recall his name.

The man recognized him immediately. "Adrian, it's good to see you again." He pumped his hand.

"Good to see you, too, Mr.—"

"Call me Fred," he said. "No need for formalities. Since test-driving that Benz a month ago, I finally convinced the wife that it was time for an upgrade. So, here I am, ready to sign on the dotted line."

Thank You, Lord! Adrian wanted a private moment to dance before the Lord as King David had done. Instead, he exhaled and smiled. "We can make that happen. Come on into my office, so I can see which model you test-drove."

"No need. I already spotted it in the lot, hidden behind two other models. It's got my name on it."

Adrian loved customers who knew what they wanted. "Then let's go out there and get the model number." They strolled outside. Besides financing, the only thing that could thwart his sale was if another associate had already sold the vehicle. When he saw that the sticker was still on it, he grinned once again.

Only minutes before closing, Adrian dropped the keys into Fred Miller's hand. He waved as another satisfied client drove off the lot. It had been tight, but God had come through for him. "Thank You, Jesus!" Adrian pumped a fist in the air. "Won't He do it?" he asked, repeating a favorite phrase of Pastor Archie.

Now he could finally focus on the trip. It came as no surprise that Shae wanted to tag along. A few hours later, Adrian escorted two lovely Carmen sisters and Sabrina through the airport terminal to catch their flight to Philly. Brecee and her sister talked places of interest for Adrian to visit.

"Babe, all that will have to take a backseat to visiting the nursing home," Adrian reminded Brecee as they fastened their seat belts on the plane.

She scrunched her nose at him, a teasing gesture he had seen her sister direct at Rahn a few times.

Despite the late hour of their arrival in Philadelphia, thanks to a delayed flight and the time difference, there still was a welcome party of Carmens waiting to greet them at the airport.

Mrs. Carmen wouldn't hear of Adrian staying at a hotel. "I'm sure you'll enjoy your accommodations at my nephews' apartment." She nodded toward Victor and Dino. "First, though, you'll come to my house for a snack."

That could work, Adrian thought. Maybe he could pick the man's brain about what to expect from Mrs. Daniels the next day. Adrian was so keyed up, he considered camping out at the nursing home in order to be the first guest on Saturday morning.

After a short ride from the airport, they turned onto a tree-lined street of cottage-style houses. Inside Brecee's childhood home, the hardwood floors gleamed, and the furnishings appeared strategically placed. Nothing appeared out of order, not even a throw pillow. The dining room table was ready to go with place settings for a crowd.

Mrs. Carmen didn't waste any time retrieving platters from the refrigerator, assisted by her daughters. The smell and sight of food made Adrian's stomach growl. In no time, the impromptu party had begun.

When Victor announced that he was heading out, Adrian pulled Brecee to the side, away from prying eyes and curious ears, to kiss her goodbye and whisper, "I love you."

"I love you, too," she whispered back with a tight hug.

Once in Victor's SUV with him and Dino, Adrian regretted bringing up Mrs. Daniels' name. It opened the door for Victor to rave about Judith, the great-granddaughter. By the time they reached the guys' apartment, Adrian was ready for bed. Sleep couldn't come fast enough, if it would mean not having to listen to Victor mention Judith's name again. The morning couldn't come soon enough.

CHAPTER TWENTY-FOUR

So, Mom, what's the latest between you and Uncle Marcellus?" Brecee asked on Saturday morning as she and Shae prepared brunch for the houseful of family they were expecting soon.

"We're in love and waiting on you to get married so we can tie the knot, too," she said matter-of-factly.

Brecee slowly turned around and eyed her mother, who was sitting snugly at the table, holding Sabrina. She nuzzled her granddaughter's neck as if what she'd just said was business as usual.

Shae was the first to respond. She planted her hands on her curvy hips. "So, he's the one? You're really sure that he's the second love of your life?"

Their mother's eyes sparkled. "Yes, he makes me happy." Then she frowned and glanced at the stove. "Don't you burn those eggs!"

Whirling around, Brecee used the spatula to fold the egg over the bits of sausage, onion, and green pepper in the skillet, then faced her mother again. "Have I really held your love hostage?"

When she nodded, Brecee teared up. What mother would put her own love on hold for the sake of her child? "Mom," Brecee said softly, "you sacrificed so much for us while we were growing up. You don't have to do that now. I was feeling sorry for myself when I set those terms. Who knows how long I'll have to wait for Adrian to propose? He's so busy with school, with his job, and, now, with digging up his grandmother's history."

Shae checked the biscuits in the oven, then slammed the door none too gently. "Well, I think my sister should fit in there somewhere!" she huffed.

"I do...." Was it wrong to want more? Brecee cleared her head. This was about her mother right now. "If Uncle Marcellus makes you happy, then you have our blessing, including mine. Go for it."

195

Beaming, their mother stood, still holding Sabrina, and hugged both of them. "Then I officially invite you girls to be two of my four bridesmaids next month in our wedding on the *Spirit of Philadelphia*."

Just then, the doorbell rang. Their mother practically floated out the kitchen to answer it.

Brecee looked at Shae. Neither of them blinked. "What just happened?" Brecee mumbled.

"We're going to be in a wedding," Shae said slowly, then moved in slow motion to check on the biscuits.

Brecee forced herself to take a deep breath. "Okay, so we did hear the same thing."

⌣

When Mrs. Carmen opened the door with little Sabrina in her arms, the tantalizing aroma of breakfast greeted Adrian. But it couldn't compete with the scent of his lady when she finally appeared.

He kissed her lips. "Babe, why didn't you tell me your cousins were late sleepers? I've been ready for hours."

When she didn't respond, Adrian scrutinized her more closely. She looked slightly stunned for a second but quickly offered him a smile. "Sorry about that."

He frowned and leaned in. "Is everything all right?"

She nodded, then turned to greet her other family members as they came through the door.

Taking her word at face value, Adrian thanked Mrs. Carmen for inviting him to brunch.

"Sure," she said, but her attention was on Marcellus as he strolled through the door. Mrs. Carmen handed Sabrina off to the nearest relative. The woman was clearly smitten.

"Good morning, everyone," Marcellus said in a commanding voice without taking his eyes off Mrs. Carmen. After engulfing her in a hug, he smacked his lips against hers.

"Mom Carmen, can you two exchange smooches later?" Stacy's husband, Ted, said with a straight face. "We're starving."

The fathers occupied the children while the women finished the meal preparations. Soon, everyone had gathered around the table. Marcellus said grace and the dishes began their circuit.

Seated beside Adrian, Brecee was unusually quiet. Was she giving him the silent treatment because she wanted to give him a tour of her hometown? True, he had been absorbed with Mrs. Daniels; but Brecee meant everything to him, and her happiness was of prime importance. "Babe, if you want to show me a few sights before we head over to the nursing home, I'm okay with that."

Instead of taking another piece of bacon from the platter, she swiped his and took a bite. "Okay." The light returned to her eyes, but it was dim.

"Make sure you check out the Mural Arts exhibition," Shari's husband, Garrett, suggested as his son asked for more milk.

"But he has to see the Benjamin Franklin Museum first," Ted countered. "And, of course, the Liberty Bell Center."

Brecee said nothing. Adrian was becoming concerned. "Is everything okay?" he whispered in her ear.

She took a sip of juice, a convenient excuse not to answering.

"I'd suggest making no more than one stop before we meet Judith at the nursing home," Victor said, bringing an end to the circus of ideas.

Since she and Shae were visiting, they were the center of attention. Maybe when they were alone, she would talk to him. Until then, Adrian watched the time until Victor suggested they get going.

Her sisters and brothers-in-law gathered the children, and soon the group was headed for the Liberty Bell Center.

While out and about, Adrian doted on Brecee. If he wasn't holding her hand, he had his arm around her waist, until she finally relaxed and opened up as his personal tour guide. The glow, the smile, the teasing were back. But what had taken her joy away in the first place?

He did his best not to keep checking the time until they'd stopped at a vendor's cart for something cold to drink.

Finally, they said their good-byes to the others, then followed Victor back to his SUV. Instead of sitting in front, Adrian slid into the backseat with Brecee. Victor grunted. "I'm nobody's chauffeur," he mumbled.

Too bad, Adrian thought. "Indulge us," he said in his defense. As they drove off, Brecee rested her head on his shoulder. He snuggled her closer, then kissed the top of her hair. "I love you," he whispered.

She nodded. "I know."

When the GPS alerted them that their destination was two miles away, Adrian's heart began to pound. Soon, the nursing home came into view: Fairview Care Center Bethlehem Pike. After they had parked, Adrian helped Brecee out, taking note of the surroundings. The grounds were well-maintained, and the place seemed peaceful.

Taking Brecee's hand in his, he started across the parking lot. A woman was standing just outside the entrance, and she smiled when Victor waved. The man picked up his pace and greeted her with a hug.

"Judith must be a special lady," Brecee remarked. "Victor doesn't fall for any woman. She's certainly very pretty."

Adrian quickly scanned the woman. She had nice legs, a nice face, and a nice figure, but he wouldn't pick her over Brecee—that was for sure.

"Judith, meet my cousin Dr. Sabrece Carmen," Victor said.

"Please, call me Brecee." She smiled, then turned to him. "And this is Adrian Cole. He is extremely eager to speak with Mrs. Daniels."

"Gran likes company," Judith said. "Let's go."

Victor was holding the door open before Judith turned around. Adrian smirked. Whether Victor would admit it or not, he had fallen for Judith. Adrian saw so much of himself in the man's actions.

After signing in at the front desk, they followed Judith down a hall. The nursing facility was fresh and modern. The staff acknowledged them with smiles or waves. Victor patted Adrian on the back. "Ready?"

"I've been ready," Adrian confessed. He just hoped Mrs. Daniels would be ready and able to give him the answers he sought.

Brecee squeezed his hand as if she were in tune with his thoughts. Turning the corner, Adrian swallowed as they walked into a small room that looked more like a tiny furnished apartment. A thin brown-skinned woman with her hair in two long braids sat in a rocking chair, staring out the window.

"Gran?" Judith said. "You have company."

Slowly craning her neck to look over her shoulder, the woman grinned as she peered at them through her thick glasses. For being in her nineties, she had very little gray hair to match the wrinkles marring her face. She scanned each of them before stopping at Brecee. "My, my. If it ain't another kin to Theodore Carmen. Aren't you a pretty little thing."

Adrian's heart nearly stopped as Mrs. Daniels glanced back and forth between Brecee and her cousin. He wanted to scream and fan his arms in the air to get her attention. Instead, he impatiently awaited his turn. Besides, her compliment made his lady's face glow.

Brecee blushed. "Thank you. My cousin told me you remembered my grandfather." She stepped closer to shake the woman's hand. "How exciting."

"Mmm-hmm. That Teddy was something else, too." She chuckled to herself. "Y'all have a seat."

Judith shook her head. "We'll be out here in the lounge." She reached for Victor's hand. "You visit with Dr. Car—I mean, Brecee and Adrian."

Mrs. Daniels didn't even look at Adrian as she leaned forward. "You a doctor?"

"I am," Brecee said softly. She never carried an air of importance. Adrian had been around enough people with money to know they usually did everything in their power to stand out in the crowd, and he was in the business of helping them accomplish that in style. "What kind?" Mrs. Daniels asked.

"A pediatrician."

She frowned. "A what?"

"A children's doctor. I love children."

The woman slapped her knees. "Me, too. I had seven of them after Mother Mattie B. Poole prayed for me during one of her healing services."

Mattie B. Poole! Her name was mentioned in the letters, which made Adrian more eager to dispense with the niceties and get down to the business he came for.

For the first time, Mrs. Daniels made eye contact with Adrian. As she stared, he silently prayed that she would see his grandmother's features in him. She squinted, then turned back to Brecee. "And who is he? Your husband?"

Adrian watched Brecee's body stiffen before she slowly exhaled. "No, I'm not married."

Mrs. Daniels frowned again. "What's wrong with him? A pretty little thing like you? I got thirty grandchildren and...." She paused, tilting her head. "Seventeen great-grands. I even have my first great-great-grand on the way." She shifted in her rocker and puffed out her chest.

Before Mrs. Daniels could marry his woman off, Adrian cupped Brecee's hand in his. "She's taken."

"Is that so? Humph. In my day, when a man loved a woman, he put a ring on her quick. But that was a long time ago. Christians kept themselves pure and married...."

Brecee squirmed in her seat as Mrs. Daniels relaxed in hers. She pointed to Brecee. "I like her."

"Me, too," Adrian said. But he'd had enough of the warm-up exercise. Just as he was hoping to get to the meat of the discussion, Mrs. Daniels invited Brecee to ask her anything she wanted to know about her grandfather.

Adrian began to practice the breathing technique he used when a customer couldn't make up his mind on a car color.

"You gave my cousin a lot of information," Brecee told her. "I want to personally thank you for not being ashamed to talk about the gospel and for being a witness to my grandfather. It's because of you that I'm a third-generation Apostolic."

"Good." Mrs. Daniels seemed tickled. Then she shook a finger at Brecee. "But that man was a hard one to crack. At times, he was downright mean. But we knew it was nothing but the devil messing with his mind. I was glad to hear the Lord had saved him. I reckon God will give me credit for planting the seed in that soul."

Breathe in, breathe out, Adrian coached himself.

"Chile, I couldn't help myself. If you had seen the power of the Holy Ghost back then, through Mother Mattie B. Poole, you'd be foolish not to be a believer."

"Who was she?" Adrian asked.

The woman laughed. "Who was Mother Mattie B. Poole? Only one of God's greatest servants in my young days. She had the gift of healing. My husband and I would travel to Chicago every chance we could to go to Bethlehem Tabernacle.... Wooooweeeee." She shook her head. "No building could hold the power of the Holy Ghost working through Mother Poole.

They had to keep moving to bigger and bigger spaces, and they changed the name to Bethlehem Healing Temple."

Adrian's heart surged when she mentioned Chicago. "Do you remember ever traveling with a woman named Cora—"

"Cora Nichols!" Her eyes widened, and she slapped her bony knees, causing her legs to kick out. "That was my friend!" Then the jubilation seemed to seep out of her body as she slumped back in her rocker. "I made a promise to her that I couldn't keep."

"What kind of promise?" Adrian leaned forward. "Cora Nichols married Solomon Lambert, and I'm their grandson."

Mrs. Daniels gasped, then removed her thick glasses as if she could see better and leaned forward for a better look at him. "You're Cora's grandson?" Tears began to stream down her face. "Well, I'll be. Why didn't you say so?"

As if she'd really given him a chance to do so.

Leaning even farther forward, she crooked her forefinger, motioning for him to come closer. Adrian got up and crouched before her. She reached out and held his face in her hands, turning him from side to side as if examining a head of lettuce.

"You sure are—whew! And handsome—woo-wee. Your grandpa was handsome, and your grandmother was a beauty. We worked at the bakery together."

The pieces were coming together. Adrian had to know if his grandparents and Brecee's had crossed paths. "Do you know if our grandparents knew one another?"

"Who?"

"Cora Nichols and...." Glancing over his shoulder, he reached for Brecee's hand and squeezed it. "Theodore Carmen."

"She's a pretty thing, ain't she?"

Not again, Adrian inwardly groaned. His lady's beauty had already been established, but he answered again, "Yes, she's very beautiful." Adrian didn't need any prompting to express what was in his heart.

Brecee must have felt his sincerity, because her eyes misted.

He had to force his gaze back to Mrs. Daniels. "Did Theodore Carmen and my mother work the same shift?"

"Oh, no, baby. I worked second shift with Teddy, and your grandmother worked the first shift. There were a lot of us colored women who worked there back then, and God provided for our families."

"So, they never met?" Why did he feel such crushing disappointment? Maybe because he'd been chasing a dream.

She twisted her mouth, then scrunched her nose—her gesture wasn't as cute as when Brecee did it—and smacked her lips. "I wouldn't say that. Back then, black folks stuck together and knew just about everybody and their business. If somebody needed help or got in trouble, we knew about it."

Brecee must have felt his disappointment, because she began to rub his back. "I would like to hear how Cora and Solomon met."

Rocking back in her chair, Mrs. Daniels glanced out the window. "George and I wanted a baby so bad, but the doctors said we couldn't have one. This was back in the forties, when I was almost twenty-two. People all over the country listened to Mother Poole's radio broadcast, and many would visit her church on Campbell Avenue in Chicago. That's one place I will never forget! She always said on the radio, 'Why suffer while others are being healed? Why die before your time?'"

"Those sound like bold statements to back up," Brecee said, giving voice to Adrian's very thoughts.

Mrs. Daniels chuckled. "She didn't back it up, chile; the Holy Ghost did. God used her in mighty ways. One mother was raised from the dead simply by Mother Poole's rebuking the devil over the phone. People would walk into Bethlehem Healing Temple on crutches, or ride there in wheelchairs, and leave them behind after God healed them. Last I remember, they were still hanging on the walls. Deaf people started hearing and talking. Mother Poole also prayed for women who couldn't carry babies, and they conceived. My seven children were all products of that miracle."

Adrian whistled. *Unbelievable.* "I guess those train rides to Chicago were worth it."

She nodded. "I got pregnant seven times and never lost one of 'em." Turning away from the window, she looked at them as if she had finished reading from a script. "Once, while Cora and I were in Chicago, an ambulance detoured to Bethlehem Healing Temple. Them workers took patients from the ambulance in on stretchers, and ushers moved them to pews in the church. Mother Poole told them medical people they could leave, because their services were no longer needed. Ha!"

"Wow," Adrian and Brecee said at the same time.

"Mmm-hmm." Mrs. Daniels nodded. "It was something to see back then, God's mighty work as the saints of God spoke with authority."

"I wish that God would raise up a prophet to perform miracles like that today," Brecee said wistfully.

"Oh, He did. Many years later, evangelist Mary Boyd was preachin' in Connecticut when she got the news her son had been killed. She got on a plane and went straight to the morgue. After she prayed, that young man got up. Last I heard, he's still alive."

"Wait a minute." Adrian shook his head. "I knew God was real when He filled me with His Holy Ghost. But these miracles…they're mind-boggling."

"I reckon so, but not to believers. We know Jesus is real, and so did your folks. After your grandparents got married, Cora had the same condition as me—she couldn't have babies; and when she did get pregnant, she lost them. I think she got sick after each baby that wouldn't catch. By this time, Solomon had taken a job at a meat packing company in St. Louis, and they moved there from Chicago. But they took the train back to Chicago and went straight to Bethlehem, where Mother Poole was preaching. She healed Cora's womb, and it wasn't long after that when little Marsha was born. But Cora stayed sickly. They took another trip to Chicago, and Mother Poole was sick herself. A few months later, the evangelist died."

Mrs. Daniels' detailed account painted a picture of Adrian's family history that he might never have known. He choked when he thought about how much his grandmother had suffered.

"Your granddaddy got so bitter against God and church as Cora lay dying," the woman went on. "I tried to encourage him, but he had turned his back on God. Before Cora got too sickly, she made me promise to lead Marsha to the Lord. I promised, but after…." She sniffed. "After my dear friend went home to be with the Lord, Solomon stopped taking my calls. All my letters were returned, labeled 'Moved; No Forwarding Address.'"

"All I ever knew was that my grandparents lived in St. Louis, but now I see that's not true," Adrian said, filling in the dots.

Her shoulders slumped as she bowed her head. "I was never able to keep my promise."

Adrian's heart ached for Mrs. Daniels, who thought she had failed his grandmother. "But the Lord saved me."

The woman's eyes widened. "What about your momma? Did she surrender to Jesus?"

Shaking his head, Adrian whispered, "No."

Mrs. Daniels was quiet for a moment, and then she nodded. "Well, as long as she's alive, there's still hope. You come back and see me if you can, or call me. I'll be praying for little Marsha." She looked drained.

Little Marsha? His mother hadn't been little in more than fifty years.

Adrian stood as Judith and Victor walked back into the room. "Thank you for talking to me today," he said, kissing the woman on the cheek. "I appreciate it."

"Yes, thank you," Brecee echoed, giving her a hug.

As they left the room, Adrian was still processing what Mrs. Daniels had revealed to them. How had his grandfather been that angry with God, even after all he had seen Him do? Adrian was a new convert, yet he knew the Lord was limitless in His power to heal and save.

Once they were in the parking lot, he felt Brecee rub his arm. "Are you all right? You're frowning."

"I'm just processing everything she told me. Wow." While Victor and Judith were saying their good-byes, Adrian turned and surveyed the building again. "How appropriate that she would want to live in a home with the 'Bethlehem' in its name."

Walking up behind them, Judith chuckled. "It was this nursing home, or she wasn't going."

"It seems to fit." Adrian put his arms around Brecee's waist. "I guess my treasure hunt led me to Bethlehem."

CHAPTER TWENTY-FIVE

It wasn't what I expected, that's for sure," Brecee responded on Monday morning when Regina asked about her weekend trip.

"What do you mean?" Regina closed a patient's file.

Brecee leaned on the desk instead of taking a seat. Maybe she needed to get her heart and her head examined. "You know that anytime I'm with family, it's a good time. My mother hosted a lovely brunch, and at my home church, I introduced Adrian to plenty of people—including Mother Ernestine Stillwell, the matchmaker of all matchmakers."

She paused, thinking about the church ladies whose mission seemed to be seeing all the young women married off. Brecee didn't want to dwell on that. "Anyway, it was a treat to meet the woman who was responsible for sprinkling God's seeds of salvation in the life of my grandfather."

Frowning, Regina lifted her coffee cup to her lips. "That sounds like a great trip to me."

"Then, I found out that my mother is getting married—I mean remarried—next month."

Regina leaned closer. "And that's not a good thing?"

"It's great for her, strange for me," Brecee admitted. "My own mother is going for round two, when I haven't even gotten to the starting gate." She sighed. "But it's bittersweet. I can't believe she was actually waiting to see if Adrian would propose first." She chuckled. "When I told her to go for it, she did—literally. She gave us the date and place."

Regina giggled. "Work it, Mrs. Carmen. Then there's hope for us."

"I guess I'm having an 'always a bridesmaid, never a bride' moment, but I feel like I'm losing my best friend. Silly, huh? Maybe I need to have Dr. Young prescribe a drug for my confused emotional state."

"Take two time-outs for praise and prayer, and you'll be fine by morning."

That remark made Brecee laugh. "You're right, but when Adrian and I left the nursing home—I'll tell you about all that later—he made the oddest statement." She frowned, recalling his words. "He said, 'I was hoping that our grandparents did cross paths, so we would have a story to pass down to our children.'"

Regina smirked. "That sounds promising."

"But when I reminded him that we weren't married, he casually said, 'I know.'"

"You're not rushing him to the altar, but make sure you also don't rush your own heart."

Twisting her lips, Brecee had to admit that her sister in Christ was right. "Patience has never been my strong point." She chuckled. "Ask my sisters."

"I don't have to ask them. I know it for myself." Regina smiled. "Seriously, let Adrian learn to love the Lord first, then you. That's what I plan to do if Dolan wants to get serious about us. Being compatible means so much more than being physically attracted to each other. Our salvation and faith walk matter, too. And there are other issues to consider. We've both been married before, which didn't end the way we expected. We both have children in our lives—him, personally; me, professionally...."

Brecee gave her a mock salute. "Got it. So, with all this advice from my big sister.... You are six months older than me," she reminded her with a grin.

Ashley stepped into the charting room. "We've got a pileup near Six Flags. It's bad. Medics are airlifting three with critical injuries." She recited their vitals. "ETA is seven minutes. I assigned them to bays three, seven, and twelve."

Brecee's heart sank as she and Regina whispered silent prayers, then got into position to save young lives.

By the time Brecee's shift ended, her heart was crushed. A little boy the same age as her nephew T.J. had died. The family had been so inconsolable that the social worker had requested assistance. If the ten-year-old girl managed to make it through the night, then her condition would be upgraded from critical, but she was in the Lord's hands. Her family knew that, but it was still heart-wrenching. Excessive speed and inattentive drivers were always a bad combination, especially near the entrance to an amusement park.

On her way out the door, Brecee caught sight of the flowers Adrian had sent her but she had been too busy to retrieve. She loved that man. As she walked to her car, she called him. "Hey."

"I don't like the sound of that," his deep voice purred in her ear. "What's wrong, babe?"

"We lost a young boy tonight, and a little girl is just barely holding on." When a tear fell, Brecee couldn't stop the barrage of others that followed.

Adrian's coos turned into a soft prayer for comfort for the affected families and strength for her.

After she'd echoed his "amen," he asked her, "Are you going to be all right?"

Brecee took a deep breath of night air, then exhaled. "Yes. I think I'm going to read a couple of Scriptures before I wind down."

"Good. While you do that, expect a delivery."

She frowned. "Oh, I'm sorry. I forgot to thank you for the flowers. They're so beautiful...." She began to ramble just to hear herself talk. Anything to clear her head.

"Baby, I'm not talking about the flowers. I'm thinking of another delivery."

Her interest was piqued. "What?"

"You'll see when they get there. In the meantime, why don't you read Philippians four, verse seven? I felt God leading me to read it this morning, but I didn't think it pertained to me. Now I see that God meant it for you."

God, thank You for sending me this man who can comfort me and guide me spiritually. "Can you read it to me?"

"You know I will. Hold on."

Smiling, Brecee got inside her car and fastened her seat belt, then waited for him to get back on the phone.

"Okay, here it is: '*And the peace of God, which passeth all understanding, shall keep your hearts and minds through Christ Jesus.*' I'm praying that God will give you peace. I don't like you upset. Now, drive safely."

"I will. Love you."

"And I love you."

Her whole world had turned around at the sound of his voice. As long as Adrian was in her life, she was happy.

When she got home, instead of indulging in her routine bubble bath, Brecee took a quick shower to give herself time to cuddle up with her Bible before bed. She started with Philippians 2 and was about to begin chapter 4 when her doorbell rang.

Her delivery. Brecee's heart swelled with excitement to see what Adrian had sent her now. Slipping her house shoes on, she hurried to answer it. She checked the peephole and gasped in surprise. Adrian Cole had delivered himself to her door.

The second she opened it, Adrian walked in without waiting for an invitation. She flung herself into his arms, and he trapped her in his embrace, guiding her head to rest against his chest.

The steady beat of his strong heart lulled her. Looking up, she puckered her lips for a kiss, which he also delivered before stepping back.

"What are you doing here?" she asked, knowing he had an exam coming up in his summer course.

When Adrian lifted his hand, she noticed the small bag and the familiar logo. "Delivering your favorite comfort food." He grinned, and that faint dimple winked at her.

She was about to cry again, this time because her heart was filled with joy. The man had stopped what he was doing and driven half an hour across town to make sure she was all right and to bring her some oatmeal cookies. "Thank you so much." She hugged him again.

"I didn't come to stay, but I wanted to show you that you're important to me—more important than my job or my schoolwork. I don't want you to ever forget that." He lifted her chin until their lips met for their sweetest kiss to date. "Lock up," he told her. Then he opened the door and was gone.

Taking a deep breath, Brecee did a happy dance across the floor to the kitchen. She prepared a cup of decaf coffee, then meticulously unwrapped her bag of three oatmeal cookies. Taking a seat at the table, she blessed her treats, then took a bite and moaned with delight. Life was good.

⌒

Now that Mrs. Daniels had painted a clear picture of the great faith his grandparents had had, and how his grandfather had lost his faith, Adrian understood his mother's indifference.

But it was the look of defeat on Mrs. Daniels' face that stayed with Adrian. His next priority had to be breaking through the wall that the devil had erected around his mother and father so they could embrace the promise of God's salvation.

His woman was truly a godsend to help him with that mission. Brecee was in tune with him, and together they prayed for God to intervene. When his mother invited them to Sunday dinner after church, it was Brecee who convinced him to accept, when he would have rather taken her out to dinner.

When they were gathered around the table, Adrian brought up Mrs. Daniels again, ignoring Brecee's clandestine kick to the shin. "Mom, I'm having a hard time understanding why your interest wasn't piqued by your own mother's history. It's as if your spirit is dead or numb."

"I'm not going to deny that God hasn't been good to my family," his mother said, "but I don't feel the need to go crazy with the Bible and church. Jesus knows I love and appreciate Him. I tell Him so every night when I go to bed. I'm fine, Son. Now, stop your worrying about your father and me."

Just as stubborn, Adrian was about to press his point when he heard God speak. *Hold your peace. I will breathe into her soul, and restore her dry bones layer by layer*, the Lord whispered, echoing Ezekiel 37.

Conceding to God, Adrian let the words rest in his heart for now. To make sure he complied, he slid a spoonful of his mother's banana pudding into his mouth.

Moments later, his father asked him about the latest models at the dealership. It wasn't long before his mother and Brecee became bored with shop-talk and began to clear the dishes. He and his father moved to the family room and turned the TV to the Cardinals' baseball game.

"Do you think you can get some free tickets for us?" his dad asked with a hopeful look.

"I'll ask Rahn. If not, I'll treat," Adrian assured his father.

He strained to eavesdrop on what his mother and Brecee were discussing in hushed tone in the kitchen. He stiffened when he heard Brecee use the word "wedding." Then his lady added,

"It's a beautiful yacht, and it should be the perfect venue for the wedding. I'm really happy for my mother. She and Marcellus make a stunning couple."

As long as they weren't planning his wedding, Adrian relaxed. His mother should know by now that he didn't rush anything, especially his love life.

CHAPTER TWENTY-SIX

It was time to say, "I do," and Brecee wanted to double-check with Adrian that he could make the trip to Philly for her mother's wedding. She called him at work. "Have you reached your quota?"

"Not yet, babe," he answered. "For years, I did it on my own with little effort. But ever since I surrendered to Christ, the devil has tried to shake my faith at this time every month."

"The trying of your faith works patience," Brecee paraphrased James 1:3.

"And the last couple weeks have been trying my nerves. But I'm determined to impress God with my faith in Him. I'm sure that's what my grandmother would've wanted."

Brecee smiled. Who wouldn't root for Adrian? He wore his confidence as he did his suits—tailored. "Well, I believe in you and in God's favor." She glanced up to see Ashley heading her way. "I've got to go."

"Okay. I love you, babe."

"I love you, too." She ended the call with a smile and a prayer that she would put smiles on her patients' faces, as well.

As the wedding drew closer, Brecee's mother acted as if she had never been married before. Her excitement was contagious. "Now, you and Shae are coming into town on Friday night, right?" she wanted to confirm during a phone call.

"Yes, Mom."

"And Adrian's coming with you, right? You know that we Carmen women have great legs, and I want to show yours off, so I ordered bridesmaid dresses with a hem that flares at the knees. They're flirty without compromising modesty."

Brecee shook her head. "Then you selected those beautiful peach chiffon and lace dresses for Adrian." The dresses were very feminine, and they would be a comfortable weight to wear during autumn in Philly. Her last two sisters had gotten married in the winter, and she was still thawing out, just thinking about how cold she'd been.

"How else can I get Adrian to either step up or step back?" her mother demanded. "Your sisters can go home to their husbands. He can't touch you until he puts a ring on yours."

I know, Brecee thought.

A month ago, Brecee might have appreciated the tactic; but, as her relationship with Adrian had grown, she had become increasingly satisfied with her status as his lady, with or without a ring. She knew it was coming at some point, according to God's timing. Yet her mother was still playing matchmaker.

"Mom, don't worry about Adrian," she told her. "He's a good man. Just think about your own good man. Marcellus is about to get an incredible wife."

"And I'm getting a passionate man of God for a husband," her mother gushed.

The former beauty queen was the new forty in her mid-fifties. "You'll be stunning in that form-fitting mermaid dress, Mom. You'll look like a young bride."

"I feel young! The wedding dinner cruise is going to be so romantic. Marc and I will see our first sunset as husband and wife."

Okay, Mom. I was doing good. Don't make me jealous.

The Friday before the wedding, Brecee, Adrian, Shae, Rahn, and Sabrina boarded a plane for Philly. Although Adrian hadn't sealed the final sale he needed in order to meet the month's quota, he didn't appear worried. "Mr. Hudson's financing has been approved," he told Brecee. "He assured me he would be there tomorrow. I just need Kyle to put the keys in Mr. Hudson's hand and watch him drive off the lot. Then my deal is sealed."

"I'm glad you and Kyle are committed to helping each other out instead of engaging in cutthroat competition," Brecee said as they settled in their seats on the plane. "Otherwise, you would probably have to be at the dealership tomorrow. Thank you so much for coming with me."

As she snuggled up against Adrian, he linked his fingers with hers. "Always." He winked.

This wedding was expected to be a grand celebration. Marcellus had reserved a block of rooms at the Hyatt Regency Philadelphia at Penn's Landing for the families, conveniently located near where they would board the cruise ship for the ceremony and reception. As a wedding gift to his mother-in-law and new father-in-law, Rahn was picking up the tab.

They arrived in Philly without any delays and were soon riding in the limo Rahn had arranged to take them downtown. Before they had even checked in, it was like a big family reunion in the hotel lobby, with a hundred-plus guests for the wedding: the Beloses, her mother's Portuguese relatives; and Marcellus's family, the Porters.

As they mingled with friends and family over hors d'oeuvres in one of the hotel banquet rooms, which Brecee and her sisters had reserved for a welcome party, she introduced Adrian to one relative after another. "Are you intimidated yet?" she teased.

Adrian grunted. "Nope. My mother may come from a small family, but the Cole side is overwhelming: Uncles Sylvester, John, Vallard, Dolan—my cousin's named after him, Stephen, Tallmadge, Marshall, Herbert...."

"Okay." Brecee nudged him. "I get the point."

The bride and groom had decided to follow tradition and not see each other again until their wedding day, but that didn't stop the cousins from reacquainting themselves, nor did it foil the famed musical duel between the Carmens and Porters. It was a jam session to remember.

After the get-together, as Adrian escorted Brecee to her room, she mused that someday, this celebration would be for her. Outside her door, Adrian kissed her good night.

As she watched him swagger down the hall to the elevators, Brecee thought about her bridesmaid dress and her mother's motive for choosing it. "Maybe Momma does know best."

⌒

The next morning, Adrian awoke completely disoriented. He wouldn't have said he'd had a nightmare until he woke up and found himself alone in bed. It had been pure bliss when he'd closed his eyes last night and dreamed of going to bed with his wife.

After climbing out of bed, Adrian prayed, did his daily push-ups, and then showered. Love had to be in the atmosphere, because he couldn't get Brecee out of his mind. While he had the nerve, he dialed the front desk and asked to be connected with the bride-to-be. "Mrs. Carmen—"

"Not for long," she said in a singsong voice. "Adrian?"

"Yes, ma'am. Sorry if I woke you."

"Nonsense. When a woman is in love, she can't sleep."

"Neither can a man," he mumbled. "I'm calling to ask your permission to marry your daughter."

She gasped. "Please tell me you're not trying to make that happen today."

Adrian chuckled. He wished. "Oh no, ma'am. But soon. I was hoping you and your daughters would be busy this morning, so I could do a little ring shopping."

"Excellent! Consider it done. I would love to have you as my son-in-law, but only if you can commit to making my daughter first in your life after the Lord. I mean it. She's my baby, and she's always gotten plenty of attention. If you're not prepared to give that to her, then I suggest you reconsider your request."

"I'm afraid that isn't an option. Brecee and I fit together, spiritually, and I love her with all my heart."

"Well then, what are you waiting for? The jewelry district on Sansom Street opens soon." Laughing, the future Mrs. Porter ended the call before he could say good-bye.

What had he been waiting for? They had been dating for almost five months. That felt like an eternity for a saved man to be celibate around a woman he loved, and he did love Brecee more than he could ever explain. Was she ready to say yes?

He pulled his Bible out of his suitcase and was reading from Mark 6 when his smartphone rang. He smiled when he saw it was Brecee. "Morning, babe. Have you eaten yet?"

"I'm sorry, but Mom just called and said she thought it would be nice for all the ladies to order room service in her suite. Do you mind hanging out with the boys?"

His future mother-in-law sure worked fast. "I'll be okay, sweetheart."

The line was silent.

"Babe, what's wrong?"

She sniffed. "You've never called me 'sweetheart' before."

Adrian frowned. He hadn't realized that the endearment was something new. He was touched that she'd noticed, but he was always touched by the little things she did for him. "Babe, you're the sweetest thing I've ever met. I love you, and there are many more names I would like to call you as we grow closer every day." *Like "Mrs. Cole."* "You ladies enjoy your day, and I'll meet you when it's time for us to board the ship."

"Okay." Her voice was so soft and seductive, just like in his dreams. "See you later, babycakes," she said, speaking louder, then giggled as she ended the call.

He laughed at her silliness. "And that's why you're going to be my wife," he stated to himself.

Adrian was about to leave when he thought of one more person he should speak to. He picked up the hotel phone. In less than a minute, the operator had connected him to Marcellus's room. After they'd greeted each other, Adrian got to the point. "I know you're not officially Brecee's stepfather yet, but I wanted to ask you for her hand in marriage."

He was prepared to hear a response along the lines of "Sure, thanks for asking."

"She's still mine," Marcellus said. His deep voice held no jest. "Brecee became a part of me when our families were joined by the marriage of Shari and Garrett."

"Yes, sir." Adrian took a seat. He had the strangest feeling he wasn't going anywhere for the next ten or fifteen minutes.

"Sabrece is a lady, Adrian. Always remember that. She's to be protected and loved. She needs to know her heart is in safekeeping with you. I was glad to hear that you surrendered to Christ. That means God will show you how to love her. Disagreements are part of life and marriage, but if you lay one finger on her, we will find out, and I will come after you. I won't need backup. Do I make myself clear?"

Marcellus's warning was over the top. Adrian was exactly the type of man his parents had reared him to be—a protector, not an abuser. But Adrian had to respect a man who cared so deeply about his woman. "I will love her and protect her and make her smile," he reassured him.

"Then you have my blessing. I thank you for respecting me as the man I hope she will feel comfortable calling 'Dad' one day."

After hanging up, Adrian took the elevator to the lobby, where he ran into a small gathering of Brecee's male family members and their children.

Rahn walked up to him, carrying Sabrina who wanted down. Adrian had seen her take a few tentative steps and flop, but with all the children running around, Sabrina definitely wanted to be set free. "We're on Daddy duty while our wives prep for the wedding," Rahn told him, "so we're taking the children to the zoo. Want to tag along?"

Adrian glanced at Garrett's sons, who were horsing around, until Saul smacked Garrison in the face. A dual was about to go down. "Ah, nah." He chuckled. "I think I'll do some sightseeing on my own."

"Good choice."

They parted ways, and Adrian waved for a cab. "There's a jewelry district nearby?"

The driver nodded. "Jewelers' Row," he said in a thick accent. "I take you there."

CHAPTER TWENTY-SEVEN

Brecee could have purred from the pampering. She, her mother and sisters, as well as Aunt Camille, had just returned from the hotel spa after getting their nails manicured, their hair styled, and their makeup applied.

"Don't my girls look stunning?" Brecee's mother took a deep breath and fanned her face with her hand.

"Now, Mom, don't cry," Shae warned her. "You'll mess up your makeup."

Their mother nodded, blinking away her tears. "As I look around at the beautiful women my daughters have become, I'm not ashamed to boast that Saul and I made some pretty babies."

Once the laughter died down, their mother continued, "I want you to know I respect and love each one of you. I appreciate all that you girls have done to make this occasion so special—"

"And on such short notice," Brecee reminded her.

"Yes." She blushed. "After your father, I never dreamed I could love another man, especially at my age."

"Ha! Miss former beauty pageant contestant?" Stacy said. "When we're together, people still mistake us for five sisters."

"I'm glad you all are okay with my marrying an in-law of Shari's."

"We are," the sisters said in unison.

"Besides his good looks, what attracted you to Marcellus, Mom?" Brecee crossed her ankles, careful not to test the durability of her toenail polish.

"What first caught my attention was his carefree stroll, with one hand tucked in his pocket at just the right angle," Stacy spoke up. "His swagger should be patented."

"I call that a confident stride that comes from serving twenty years in the Air Force," her mother said with a smile. "But, for me, it was his directness, his sincerity, and his generosity. He told me that the first time the Porters visited our church, he was struck by my beauty, even though I was hidden behind a big purple hat, and by my graceful walk. But when he saw your daddy's cherry-size diamond on my finger, he shut down all his intentions."

"You should have seen his face when he learned that you were a widow," Shari said, laughing about her husband's uncle. "It glowed like he'd just seen Jesus." The ladies all chuckled, but Shari insisted, "I'm not kidding."

Their mother stretched out carefully on her bed, reclining gingerly on the stack on pillows, so as not to ruin her curls. "I respected Marc so much more for not crossing the line. When you all were small, men still flirted with me despite my little girls and my ring." She scrunched her nose the way her daughters often did, only she did so to show disgust, whereas their duplication of the look always came off as cute.

"But Uncle Marcellus was wearing his band, too, probably to ward off hussies," Shari said, and they all giggled. "I call that a kindred spirit."

"We both had the same mind-set," their mother said, nodding. "When he removed his ring, it was a sign that he was ready to move on." In a whisper, she added, "I'm glad I finally found the courage to remove mine." Staring at her left hand, she wiggled her ring finger, admiring the new diamond gracing it.

"But there is one more thing that made Marc special," she went on. "He asked me to describe my life with Saul. I appreciated that so much, and it was at that moment I knew I could fall in love with him. He wasn't trying to compete with my love for your father but to complement my life with his love."

Brecee patted her chest as her sisters and aunt sighed. "That was so beautiful, Mom. I wish I had been around to witness your courtship."

"You just be an active player in what God has given you and Adrian," her mother mildly scolded her, then capped if off with a glorious smile.

"That man sure loves me, and he shows it all the time." Brecee thought about the night he'd showed up at her door with a bag of oatmeal cookies. She twisted a lock of curls around her finger. "He's so different from me in terms of personality, so I guess opposites really do attract. I'm drawn to the unexpected with him."

"One look into Rahn's soulful eyes, and I was done," Shae gushed. "Whew!" She fanned herself as if a hot flash had crept up her skin.

"Ted's determination wore me down. It didn't hurt that the weird neighborhood kid of our childhood turned out to be a hunk." Stacy grinned.

Everyone was waiting for soft-spoken Shari to chime in. Brecee, Shae, and Stacy considered her to be the most beautiful Carmen sister, with her flawless dark skin that contrasted starkly against their fair complexions. Dimples, lashes, legs—she had it all. Garrett called her his African goddess.

"Garrett's perfect for me," Shari murmured, almost as if she were talking to herself. "He makes me feel special, beautiful, honored…." She smiled.

The ladies continued to share love lessons until lunch was delivered to the suite—a delicious spread of finger sandwiches, fresh fruit, and cheese—compliments of Marcellus. Brecee smiled as she wondered if she would ever be able to view him as a father figure.

When it was time to get dressed, the ladies touched up their makeup and fluffed their curls. Brecee was grateful that the family's longtime hairstylist had been cleared by the hotel salon manager to make an on-site visit to do their hair for the special occasion.

As Brecee studied her reflection in the mirror, she thought about Adrian and wondered what he had done all day. The last time he had seen her dressed up was at the charity banquet where they had had their first dance. Now that she thought about it, that night had sparked the beginning of their courtship. As she scrutinized her attire, Brecee wondered what her appearance this evening might spark. In the back of her mind, she hoped to make Adrian say to himself, *I can't let her get away.*

An hour later, the bridal party stepped off the elevator. In the lobby, Brecee cataloged Marcellus's expression as he glanced over his shoulder and stopped mid-sentence when he saw her mother. The son he'd been speaking to, who was also one of his groomsmen, stood straighter. Garrett's eyes sparkled when he saw Shari.

Brecee scanned the crowd for her special person. Adrian and Marcellus's unmarried son seemed to notice her at the same time, and both were heading her way. Adrian's strides were long and purposeful. She loved to watch his walk. He cut the other man off, intentionally or not. When he reached her, he lowered his head and kissed her as he whispered, "Good evening, sweetheart."

Closing her eyes, she accepted the soft brush against her lips. When she fluttered her eyelashes, and he came back into view, Brecee sighed. Although she hadn't asked him to wear a tux, she was glad he had. If he ever gave up his day job as a car salesman—rather, transportation problem solver—he could hit the runway.

"You are the most beautiful woman I see." Adrian took her hand and twirled her under his arm like a ballerina.

Brecee giggled. "I guess you don't see the bride."

"I'm afraid not. My eyes won't let me look at any woman but you."

When she looked into his brown eyes, she saw the magnitude of her love reflected in them. Or was it his love that she saw? "Thank you." She stroked his smooth jaw. He winked, then held her hand as they got in line behind the bride and groom in an informal procession to the limos that would transport the bridal party to the ship.

Brecee's mother turned around. "Adrian, you're welcome to ride with us," she told him.

"Thank you, Mrs. Carmen. I need to keep an eye on my pretty little lady."

"That you do," her mother replied.

As the wedding party limos pulled out, the rest of the guests took shuttles to the boat. In no time, they were boarding the *Spirit of Philadelphia*. The hostess greeted them and directed to them to the second-floor banquet room, giving them a superb view of the Delaware River.

It wasn't long before everyone was in place for the ceremony. This was Brecee's fourth appearance as a bridesmaid. She tried not to tear up as Uncle Marcellus's voice grew louder and bolder as he professed his love to her mother. She recognized the amorous look on his face.

"Annette, I'm so glad that God says it's not good for a man to be alone. Thank you for filling my empty space."

Brecee couldn't see her mother's expression, but she was sure that it reflected a mirror image. "Marcellus Porter, I don't take love lightly; and when you spoke those words to me, I felt them. Today, I give myself to you to be your wife for as long as God gives us breath...."

Don't cry, don't cry, don't cry, Brecee coached herself. But when she heard her sisters sniffling, the tears began to fall as Brecee's former pastor pronounced the couple husband and wife.

Brecee chanced a peek at Adrian. She was startled to find him watching her instead of the bride and groom. He looked smug and seemed oblivious to the emotions that were stirring within her with every whisper of love.

Applause erupted in the room, along with the catcalls and cheers. The sound must have echoed throughout the cruise liner, even though the room was enclosed. Suddenly, Brecee needed air. As everyone rushed the newlyweds to congratulate them, Brecee made her escape to the deck for some fresh air. She needed to get a grip. Every wedding that wasn't her own took away some of her strength, and if she kept attending these ceremonies as a single woman, there would soon be nothing left except an empty shell.

Lord, help me. She just had to make it through the photo session and the dinner, and then she could regroup. Brecee thought she could do this—be satisfied going at Adrian's pace—but her emotions couldn't be frozen in time. She felt helpless.

Closing her eyes, Brecee allowed the warm breeze to play with her curls. She took a deep breath and opened her eyes to admire the Benjamin Franklin Bridge as the sun began to set.

Soon, good memories began to replace her moments of misery. She smiled, remembering the happy time spent with her mother and sisters in the hotel suite. Those moments had been priceless. She reflected on the accolades her sisters had offered about their husbands and was thankful for how cherished her brothers-in-law made them feel. If their mother could find happiness again at fifty-eight years of age, there was hope for her, right?

Have I not told you that whatsoever things are true, honest, pure, lovely... if there be any virtue, and if there be any praise, that you should think on these things? God whispered bits and pieces of Philippians 4:8.

Brecee swallowed. She had been reading through that particular book, and God was using it to give her comfort when she needed it most.

"There's something beautiful about a woman who loves me." Adrian's deep voice spliced through the serenity she had just embraced.

Sucking in her breath, she shivered as she slowly turned and faced him. To her, Adrian would always be one of God's finest specimens of a man, and she desperately wanted to be his. But it seemed he wasn't ready. Steadying her voice, Brecee tried to sound cheery. "It was a beautiful wedding, wasn't it?"

Adrian walked closer. "It was."

She fought back her tears to ask him, "What are some of the things you love about me?" She needed reassurance.

As he stood before her, the wind stirred up a teasing breath of his cologne. Brecee sucked it in and held it as long as she could before releasing his scent into the wild. As they watched each other, she began to wonder if he didn't have an answer.

When he lowered himself to one knee, Brecee felt faint. "What are you doing?" she choked out as her heart tried to recalibrate. The Lord knew she couldn't take any teasing at the moment.

Whatever is lovely...think on these things, God whispered in the wind.

"I love your inner beauty and your passion for life. And I meant what I said. I love how you love me. Of course, you have the best pair of legs of all the bridesmaids."

She blushed as her eyes misted. "Watching this ceremony confirmed to me that when two people truly love each other, they should be together."

It took a wedding to make you realize that you wanted a forever with me? The devil was attempting to taint her tender moment with vanity.

Whatever is pure! the Lord's voice rumbled in the waves below the ship.

"Sabrece Lynn Carmen, would you do me the honor of marrying me?" Adrian's eyes had a slightly pleading look just before he bowed his head and dug into his pocket.

When he pulled out a small box lined with red velvet, she began to sob. All the questions, doubts, and longings had been a self-imposed torture. Adrian had wanted a forever with her, after all. It wasn't a spur-of-the-moment decision. The ring proved it.

She nodded as he slid the beautiful diamond ring on her finger.

Then he looked up at her. "Sweetheart." He paused and smiled as they both remembered his endearment. "I need to hear you say the words that you will be my wife."

"Yes, Adrian. I want to love you for the rest of my life as your wife."

Brecee blinked as he jumped up and lifted her off her feet in a hug. They sealed their engagement with urgent kisses, until the sound of applause made Adrian slowly lower her to the deck.

When she turned to face the banquet room, she saw all the wedding guests watching them through the windows, their glasses raised in a toast. "Cheers!" they shouted.

CHAPTER TWENTY-EIGHT

With Brecee by his side, Adrian approached the newlyweds during a break in the photography session to apologize for stealing the spotlight. "I just couldn't wait any longer," he explained. It was the truth. Five months was too long when he had found the one woman he couldn't let get away.

"Honey," Brecee's mother touched his hand, "you made my daughter's day. And that's reason for any mother to celebrate." She beamed with happiness, either because she was now married or because her baby daughter was now engaged. Maybe both.

"Nothing can compare to being in love," Marcellus said as he gazed at his new wife. "We were blessed to find love twice. Enjoy it."

Adrian exhaled, relieved that he hadn't offended the newlyweds. "I've never seen Brecee so happy—and I've definitely seen her smile. Of course, that was after she stopped bawling."

Laughing, Brecee elbowed him before taking off to show her ring to another group of friends. The price tag had equaled that of a preowned luxury car, but she was worth every commission check Adrian had earned over the years.

Less than a minute later, a pair of soft, fragrant hands snaked around the back of his head to his face and covered his eyes.

"That better not be anybody but my fiancée," he feigned a threat as he reached around and guided her in front of him with one arm.

Brecee's face glowed as she giggled. "How did you know?" She teased, then puckered up for a kiss, and he brushed one against her lips. Then she turned and faced her mother and stepfather, who stood watching with silent amusement.

"We better get out of the way so that others can congratulate you," Adrian said when he realized the photographer had been snapping pictures of them.

Brecee was about to head off again when Adrian pulled her back and kissed her once more before letting her go.

Left alone, Adrian was waved over by her brothers-in-law. They took turns shaking his hand.

"Welcome to the family, Mr. Carmen," Rahn said with a mischievous grin.

Adrian grunted. "I'm sure my baby will want to take my name."

"Oh, I'm sure she will, too," Rahn agreed. "Our wives all took our names, but that's not what I'm talking about. Those Carmen sisters will have their way with you. Tie your heart into knots...."

"Drug you with their love," Garrett added.

"They are downright hypnotic," Ted put in.

Adrian's laugh escaped before he could trap it. "Tell me something I don't know. Brecee had me wrapped around her finger the day I met her, though I didn't realize it till later. Since I love her, it's only fair I let her have her way with me." He exchanged fist bumps with each one of them, then stuffed both hands in his pockets and went in search of the love of his life, whistling as he walked.

⌒

"Who gets engaged at somebody else's wedding—and her own mother's, no less?" Regina exclaimed when Brecee called her with the news.

"Evidently, I do." She giggled. "It was so beautiful. I wish you had been there." She was filled with so much happiness, she felt as if she might explode.

"I'm sure it was romantic. I've never been on a dinner cruise, much less a wedding on the water."

"I'm talking about Adrian's proposal. The wedding celebration was a blur after that." She giggled like a preteen every time her mind replayed the moment Adrian had gone down on bended knee. She never saw it coming. If she had, she wouldn't have stressed herself out over it. "I'll show you my rock when I get to work, but I wanted to tell you before everyone else."

"I can't wait!" Regina told her. "See you in a few hours."

Staring at her reflection in her bathroom mirror, Brecee lightly applied her makeup before getting dressed for her shift. Although she was right-handed, she enjoyed attempting various tasks with her left hand just to see her diamond reflect the light at different angles.

Since the moment she'd said yes to Adrian, she hadn't stopped thanking and praising God for His blessings. Of course, she'd also done a lot of repenting for her lack of faith and for her impatience. Thank God He'd forgiven her.

Before she had left Philly, she and her sisters had made a list of "must-haves" she wanted for her wedding. First, it had to be in June—good-bye to winter nuptials—because she wanted a rooftop ceremony. "I want the wind to blow through my hair like Beyoncé," she'd said. Her sisters had laughed, but Brecee wasn't joking. She wanted to look like a mythical goddess on her big day. That meant she would have to wait ten months to become Mrs. Cole.

Thanking God for giving her sunshine to start her Monday morning, she bounced out the door to her Lexus for the short drive to the hospital. Once there, she parked and then strutted into the emergency department. Not usually one to speak with animated gesticulations, Brecee couldn't resist waving her left hand in the air whenever she conversed with a colleague. If the individual didn't get the subtle hint, Brecee politely informed him that her status had indeed changed, though many of them had probably learned about her status change on Facebook the night before.

After signing in on the board, she chatted with Ashley and several others at the nurses' station, happy to show them her ring. Then she proceeded to the doctors' charting room, where Regina was just finishing a conversation with another doctor.

After he left, Regina turned to Brecee. "Wow. You're glowing. Let me get my shades so I can examine this ring." She grinned and clapped her hands. "I'm so excited for you!"

Brecee held up her left hand for Regina to inspect. "Fourteen-karat rose and white gold with a halo diamond center." She didn't float back to reality until Ashley interrupted them.

"We have two toddlers with severe lacerations from broken glass. Stitches will definitely be necessary," Ashley advised them.

As Brecee supervised the resident handling one of the patients, she wanted to scold the caregiver for leaving the naturally curious children unsupervised around glass figurines. After that, her shift was relatively quiet, with only a few sprains and fractures.

She was about to take a dinner break when Adrian strolled through the door with flowers and a Styrofoam takeout container, the aroma of which made her stomach growl more loudly than usual.

"What are you doing here?" her mouth asked, but her eyes and nose didn't care.

"I couldn't stop thinking about you," he told her with a grin. "Business was slow, so I left work a few hours early and decided to surprise my fiancée with dinner."

"You can surprise me anytime. Come on. Let's get you a badge, and we can eat in my office."

Once they were alone behind closed doors, Adrian gave her a tight hug. He seemed reluctant to end the embrace. They sat down, and Brecee offered a prayer before digging in. After she sampled Lady Ada Mac & Cheese, she closed her eyes and groaned. "Ol'Henry has some good soul food."

Leaning back in his chair, Adrian smirked. "I thought you would like something different. Also, Mrs. Almost-My-Wife, I'll have you know I started on my guest list."

Brecee stared at him. "Without my having to remind you? I'm impressed."

"Actually, Mom is getting me a list of the addresses of family and friends. My client list is in my file, and I was thinking of inviting Mrs. Daniels. Her presence would be symbolic of my grandmother, in a way."

"I think that's a great idea." Brecee paused from her eating and placed her hand on top of his. "Even though it's unlikely our grandparents ever had a conversation, they both benefited from Mrs. Daniels' faith in God. From witnessing on her job to inviting your grandmother to tag along as she traveled to Chicago for those healing services, the woman was doing God's work."

He smiled. "You're right. It's funny how people are drawn together."

She nodded, then scooped up a serving of her collard greens. Once she swallowed, she dabbed at the corners of her mouth with her napkin. "God really does have a master plan. My sister moved to St. Louis to distance herself after a painful breakup. I followed her here so she wouldn't be alone. Otherwise, I could have remained in Texas or applied at The Children's Hospital of Philadelphia."

"Praise God, my beautiful wife-to-be came to me. Sabrece Lynn Carmen was meant to be loved by me." He patted his chest.

Adrian made this profession with so much awe in his voice, Brecee's eyes filled with tears.

Several minutes later, her pager went off. Frowning, she collected her trash and tossed it in the garbage can, then stood. "I've got to go." When he got to his feet, she wrapped her arms around his neck and kissed him. "Thank you for my flowers and the food, but the best gift was your visit."

Adrian escorted her back to the emergency department. Near the exit, he reached into his pocket, pulled out his wallet, and handed her a credit card.

"What's this for?"

"Shopping. Thanks for being so understanding about how busy I'll be with my classes this fall. I want you to be able to get whatever you want or need. I ordered another card for you with your maiden name on it, to use until we're married."

Brecee lifted an eyebrow. "Are you sure you want to give me a blank check, per se?"

"Oh, it has a limit on it. And I would be crazy to tell you what it is." He winked, then turned and swaggered out the door.

CHAPTER TWENTY-NINE

Perfect. Adrian finished fussing with his bow tie and scrutinized his reflection in the full-length mirror. He and his seven groomsmen were holed up in a makeshift dressing room at the Philadelphia Free Library, waiting to be summoned. It was the venue Brecee had chosen for their rooftop wedding and paid for with Adrian's American Express card.

Dolan, his best man, patted him on the shoulder. "You ready for this?"

Adrian nodded. He wanted to get this marriage thing right, striving to make as few mistakes as possible and to make Brecee happy. *Lord, help me to be the head that You expect me to be,* he prayed silently, then remembered something Pastor Archie had said during one of their premarital counseling sessions:

"Brother Cole, many marriages fall apart because the husband lacks the understanding of the Scripture that tells husbands to live with their wives according to knowledge. Take time to understand her, and love her despite her shortcomings. Honor her as if she were a queen. First Peter three, verse seven, says that wives are the weaker vessel. Weaker than who? Their husbands. That means both of you are to submit to each other and to the Lord for guidance. Love her and take care of her, and she will honor you always...."

"I'm looking forward to forever with Brecee," he said with confidence, forcing back the slight fear at the thought of being responsible, not only physically, but emotionally, for someone other than himself.

"You won't regret having her as your wife," Rahn stated calmly, his arms folded across his chest. The outfielder was in the lineup with Adrian's Cole cousins from Detroit.

He hadn't planned to have so many groomsmen, but Brecee wanted a big wedding; and, since she was the last Carmen sister to get hitched, as well as the baby girl, his future in-laws had spared no expense to make it happen.

Adrian's mother had been supportive. She loved Brecee almost as much as he did. Their families' combined guest list topped two hundred, and most of the invitees had responded affirmatively.

"All you have to do is show up, Mr. Cole," Brecee had teased him when he'd received the first credit card statement for a deposit on something or other related to the wedding.

Adrian didn't care about the money. All he wanted was for Brecee to say yes, then board the plane for their honeymoon in the Bahamas.

The knock on the door made him and all the groomsmen stand at attention. The photographer strolled in with suggestions for their poses. The man was in and out in no time. The next knock came from Victor, who had been instrumental in assisting Judith to get Mrs. Daniels to the church.

"It's almost showtime." He grinned mischievously. "I have to say, my cousin looks gorgeous. Just make her happy, and nobody gets hurt." He cracked his knuckles for emphasis before closing the door.

When Adrian heard more knuckles crack, he turned around. His cousins from Detroit were in a military stance. "We got your back, cuz. If the Carmens don't start none, there won't be none," Tallmadge III said, as if he were the group's spokesman.

"At ease, men." Adrian laughed.

"That's a Carmen threat that every man who marries a Carmen sister gets," Rahn explained, but Adrian's cousins didn't look amused.

When Adrian heard the opening strains of "The Lord's Prayer," he glanced at the time and took a deep breath. Then he waved over his ring bearer—Stacy's son, T.J. He looked handsome in his miniature tux. His counterpart was Adrian's little cousin, Laura, who made the cutest flower girl.

Pulling a small envelope out of his breast pocket, Adrian squatted and looked the boy in the eyes. "Will you go and slide this under the door for your aunt Brecee?"

Seemingly glad to have a mission, T.J. snatched the envelope and took off down the hall to Brecee's dressing room. Adrian stood and wiped the beads of perspiration from his forehead.

"Why don't we have a prayer to calm your nerves?" Garrett suggested.

Adrian nodded, and the men circled around him and bowed their heads. Even his Michigan cousins compiled. "Lord," Garrett began, "in the mighty name of Jesus, we come boldly to Your throne of grace, where we obtain mercy. We thank You for this union that You are about to sanctify. Give the bride and groom peace to enjoy this special day...." Garrett prayed until they heard another knock.

"Amen," they all murmured.

"It's time," the wedding coordinator instructed them.

Thanking everyone, Adrian stepped out of the room with Dolan to join Brecee's former pastor in the courtyard, leaving his groomsmen to escort the bridesmaids up the aisle.

Brecee had been primped to the satisfaction of her mother and sisters. Her long hair had been curled into spirals, and a headband of lace and pearls rested across her forehead.

The door of her dressing room opened a crack. "Aunt Brecee?" T.J. squeaked. "This is for you." He handed something to his mother, then raced out of the room.

"Slow down, T.J.!" Stacy yelled after him. She shook her head. "That boy."

Brecee took the envelope from her sister and slid out the note inside.

You're perfect for me. You bring out my best. I'm ready to make my princess my queen.

The stylist who had applied her makeup to perfection threatened Brecee not to shed one tear after she read Adrian's note.

"Okay." Brecee sniffed to choke back her emotions.

Her sisters and Regina were immediately at her side, hovering over her with fans. They didn't stop until Brecee convinced them that she was okay.

Minutes later, the wedding coordinator summoned the mothers of the bride and groom. Both women gave Brecee a kiss and a warm hug. Her bridesmaids and matron of honor, Shae, followed suit.

When Brecee heard her musical cue, Shae opened the door. There stood Marcellus, waiting to escort Brecee up the aisle. The man was ridiculously handsome at his age. Her mother had good taste.

His eyes twinkled. "If I'd had a daughter, she would've been as pretty as you—a princess," he complimented as he guided her arm through his and rested her hand on his forearm.

A princess. Her eyes misted. "Thank you...Pops." She grinned, and he smiled back.

Marcellus puffed out his chest and, with a stride of military precision, began their procession toward the altar and her groom.

As Brecee got closer to the double doors that opened to the rooftop courtyard, everything blurred—the exquisite decorations her bridal party had created in her color theme of bluish-gray with explosions of fuchsia. Every person, every object, froze as her vision zoomed in on Adrian. Forget her stepfather's good looks—it was Adrian who was ridiculously handsome. She swallowed as she made her way along the white runner that had been imprinted with the text of Ephesians 5:31: *"And they two shall be one flesh."* As she inched closer to Adrian, the words faded from the runner and were implanted in her heart.

With each step, Brecee silently praised God for the Word that would bind her and Adrian together forever.

When they reached the front row of chairs, her mother got to her feet. Both she and Marcellus kissed Brecee on either cheek. That hadn't been planned, which made it even more special.

Adrian shook hands with Marcellus, then kissed Brecee's mother before turning to her and taking a deep breath. "Ready to be my wife?"

"Yes," she whispered, and that's when she saw it—the "look" her sister Shae had alluded to when she'd talked about how special Rahn treated her. Adrian's eyes spoke volumes. He stared as if seeing her for the first time. She hoped it was because of the form-fitting lace dress with its long train. Either way, she had never felt so cherished.

Pastor Underwood, the minister from her family church in Philly, cleared his throat. "You need to bring her closer, young man, if you want to marry her."

"Sorry," Adrian muttered, hustling closer to the makeshift altar.

"Very well." The minister peered at them over the rim of his glasses. "We are gathered here today in the sight of the Lord Jesus Christ and these witnesses...."

Before long, he guided Adrian in the recitation of his vows.

"Sabrece...Brecee, I promise to love you more with every day of my life. You'll never doubt my faithfulness."

She felt every word he boldly proclaimed in front of their guests as intimately as if he were whispering to her alone. Then her own voice shook as she recited her vows. "Adrian, I'm honored to be the woman you have chosen to spend the rest of your life with. I promise to love, respect, and obey you. My faithfulness will be never ending...."

Minutes later, they were pronounced husband and wife. Adrian gathered her in his arms, and they indulged in a sweet kiss.

Exhaling, they faced the crowd. The applause became deafening. Adrian twirled her under his arm and shouted, "My wife!"

Brecee blushed. That declaration earned him another kiss, which she stood on her toes to deliver.

CHAPTER THIRTY

Adrian had had enough of the smiles, hugs, and handshakes. He was ready to start his honeymoon—now! But their flight to the Bahamas didn't leave until six the next morning. He had no problem thinking of ways to occupy their time.

Only for Brecee's sake did he agree to pose for the countless pictures. Every time she looked at him, he thought he'd never felt so loved. And the cameras captured every one of their embraces and kisses.

When he thought they were away from the camera's lens, he pulled her aside. "Thank you for marrying me."

Her lips curved upward and her eyes sparkled as she rubbed his jaw. "Thank you for asking me. It seems like I waited forever."

"I want forever with you." He kissed the ring on her finger as the camera flashed again. He gritted his teeth. "What did you pay for—rather, what did I pay for—the paparazzi?"

Her arms encircled his neck. "Can I help wanting to relive every moment of the fairy-tale wedding you gave me?"

He rested his forehead against hers and grunted. "Whatever you want, babe." Then, linking his fingers through hers, Adrian led her to the reception to a chorus of cheers and shouts of "Congratulations!"

When they were finally seated at the head table, along with the members of the wedding party, Adrian couldn't keep his eyes off his bride. He was so excited that he lost his appetite, even when the plates of delicious-smelling food were set before them. Who could eat at a time like this?

"Do I have to feed you your dinner and cake, too?" Brecee teased as she held a forkful of salad and coaxed him to open his mouth. "You really should eat. You are going to need your strength." She leaned closer for a kiss.

"Flirt." His nostrils flared with passion as he took his fork and began to eat with forced gusto to humor her.

It wasn't long until it was time for the first dance. Standing, Adrian guided his wife to the dance floor, and that's when he noticed Mrs. Daniels sitting at the same the table as his mother. The two were chatting away like old friends.

He whispered to alert Brecee as he spun her around under his arm. Then he dismissed the distraction as he held his bride close and swayed to the band's rendition of BeBe Winans' "I Found Love."

Brecee sang along, softly serenading him in his ear; and by the time the song ended, she had him panting, about to fall to his knees in weakness. If only they could catch an earlier flight to the Bahamas. "Come on, honeymoon," he practically growled.

She giggled and hugged him tighter. Seconds later, the wedding coordinator summoned them to the table where they would cut the cake. Adrian blinked at his first sight of the cake topper: an African-American groom holding his bride in the air and kissing her beside a Mercedes-Benz.

"Wow," he murmured. "Where did you find this?"

Brecee grinned. "I couldn't resist. It was pricey, but it was my way of saying that I respect what you do, and I'll always support you, no matter what the endeavor."

Adrian lifted her off the ground like the pose of the cake topper and kissed her long and hard. They could cut the cake later.

EPILOGUE

Adrian couldn't imagine paradise, but the Sandals Royal Bahamian Spa Resort on the Nassau Paradise Island gave him a glimpse of what heaven might look like. As he and his wife soaked in the sun on the white sand, he didn't care about admiring the clear blue ocean. Brecee's clear eyes fascinated him far more. And the honeymoon suite was their hangout for pillow talks, candlelit baths, and constant whispers of love.

"How about staying another week?" Adrian asked, playing with Brecee's hair. "Or have we maxed out my American Express?"

"I may have left you five dollars," she sassed him. He retaliated by tickling her until she pleaded for him to stop. Then she snuggled close to him. "Honey, our mother taught us how to get the most for the least amount of money. We called in favors and bargained for services. The Carmen sisters did good." She looked at him through her thick eyelashes and rubbed his jaw. "I don't want us to be in debt and put more pressure on you to work long hours to surpass the quota. I want to be your quota."

He grinned. "You already are. Two more semesters of classes, and I'll have my master's degree."

"I'm…." She swallowed. "I'm so proud of you, and I love you."

Those were the last words they spoke for the night.

At the end of the week, when their plane landed in St. Louis, they vowed that their marriage would never be business as usual.

Dolan called them first, as if he had GPS tracking on them and knew they were back at Adrian's condo, surrounded by boxes of Brecee's stuff and wedding gifts galore that his parents had dropped off while they were gone. "Hey, I just carried my bride over the threshold," Adrian told his cousin.

"Mmm-hmm." Dolan chuckled. "Welcome home. I called because I have some news that should make your day."

Adrian sat on the bed and watched Brecee happily unpack their clothes, humming and teasing him with some dance moves as she did. "I have a beautiful wife to make my day."

Brecee threw him an air kiss, and he motioned for her to come closer and deliver one in person. As she was about to, Dolan said, "Your parents attended church with me and Regina yesterday."

Adrian hurriedly smacked lips with Brecee, then gave his cousin his attention. "What?" he sat up straight. He must have alarmed Brecee, because her eyes widened, and she mouthed, *Is everything okay?*

He covered the phone with his hand and repeated what Dolan had just told him. Brecee danced around the room and pumped her fists in the air.

"Yep," Dolan confirmed. "The pastor preached on Ephesians one, verse four: *'According as he hath chosen us in him before the foundation of the world, that we should be holy and without blame before him in love.'* God must have convicted Aunt Marsha's soul, because she was the first one into the aisle, walking to the front. Just like me all those months ago."

Adrian's heart pounded and he repeated the news to Brecee.

"Needless to say, your mother experienced her Nicodemus moment with the water and Spirit baptism, in Jesus' name."

"Amen, amen! Hallelujah!" Adrian and Brecee shouted in praise.

While Dolan was still on the line, Brecee's cell phone rang as if her families had timed their return.

Seeing the frown on Brecee's face, he told Dolan he'd call back later, then disconnected. "What's wrong, baby?"

"It's Victor." She put him on speakerphone.

"Hey, Adrian," Victor said. "You better be good to my cousin—"

"Man, we've already been through this," Adrian reminded him. "You threatened me at the wedding, remember? Anyway, "Right. anyway, Judith just called. She thought you would want to know that her great-grandmother passed away in her sleep this morning. Apparently, all day yesterday, she kept saying, 'I kept my promise.' Do you have any idea what she meant?"

"Yeah." Adrian's heart dropped at the news. It was as if Mrs. Daniels had lived long enough to complete a mission. "Even in her old age, she was still witnessing to my family as she had promised my grandmother she'd do."

Brecee rubbed his back. "Thanks for letting us know, cuz. Please tell Judith she has our deepest sympathy."

After ending the call, Adrian turned around and stared at his wife. "You know, I thought if it wasn't for Mrs. Daniels, our paths might never have crossed. But now looking at you...humph." He grunted. "Woman, there is no way on God's earth that I wouldn't have found you. I would have kept searching until I discovered the jewel that was hidden away in the treasure chest God had for me."

BOOK CLUB DISCUSSION QUESTIONS

1. Discuss your thoughts on the relationship, if any, between a man's suitability as a mate and his salary. Do you believe that the husband should be the primary breadwinner of the family?

2. When Adrian met Brecee, he had a lot going on in his life. What are your thoughts about his justification about moving their relationship along at a snail's pace due to his commitments to work and school?

3. Who first introduced you to the Bible? Was it a parent? A grandparent? Discuss the influence of this person on your spiritual walk.

4. One of the items on Brecee's top-ten list of crucial qualities in a mate was the ability to get along with her family, and vice versa. What's your take on this ultimatum?

5. Discuss Annette Carmen's relationship with her daughters and her decision to put her own marital happiness on hold for Brecee's sake.

6. Did Brecee hold fast to her expectations, or did she begin to settle for whatever time Adrian was willing to give her?

7. Discuss Brecee's struggle between desiring to be married and living happily as a single woman. Have you ever dealt with a similar struggle? How did you handle it?

8. Who was your favorite character, and why?

9. How important is the character of Mrs. Daniels in the story?

10. Do you believe in miracles? If so, share one that God has performed for you or that you have heard someone else testify about.

AUTHOR'S NOTE

My husband's family and mine crossed paths before either of us was even born. As a matter of fact, God had it in the works even before our parents got married.

In the mid-1940s, my grandmother Jessie and my husband's grandfather J. T. both worked for Pacific Railroad in St. Louis. Both were married at the time, but the couples didn't spend much time together. My husband's grandfather later surrendered his life to Christ and was blessed by God to be appointed deacon at the same church my husband, Kerry, attends now. Kerry is a third-generation Apostolic (Pentecostal) follower. I don't recall my grandmother attending church, but she was a wonderful woman, and everyone who knew her, including my husband's uncle, Jerry Downer, remembered her as being a hard worker, as he told me when he learned that I was Miss Jessie's grandmother. It is indeed a small world!

Fast-forward some forty years and two generations. My husband and I met at church and fell in love. I had a Catholic background, so when God saved me, I became the first-generation Apostolic. It wasn't long after my walk with the Lord had begun that I heard the testimonies about Mother Poole's gift of healing. I made up my mind that I wanted a strong walk with the Lord and to use whatever gift He bestowed on me.

It just goes to show you that you never know how a person who crosses your path—whether at work, at church, or even at a department store—may touch your future.

Thank God for Grandma Jessie and Deacon J. T. Deacon.

If you enjoyed Adrian and Brecee's story, please post an honest review on Amazon or Goodreads. Also, consider joining my street team to help me promote my work.

Until next time, happy reading!

ABOUT THE AUTHOR

Pat Simmons is a self-proclaimed genealogy sleuth who is passionate about researching her ancestors and then casting them in starring roles in her novels, in the hope of tracking down any distant relatives who might happen to pick up her books. She has been a genealogy enthusiast since her great-grandmother, Minerva Brown Wade, died at the age of ninety-seven in 1988.

Pat describes the evidence of the gift of the Holy Ghost as an amazing, unforgettable, life-altering experience. She believes God is the Author who advances the stories she writes.

Pat holds a B.S. in mass communications from Emerson College in Boston, Massachusetts. She has worked in various positions in radio, television, and print media for more than twenty years. Currently, she oversees the media publicity for the annual RT Booklovers Conventions.

She is the multi-published author of several single titles and eBook novellas, including the #1 Amazon best seller in God's Word category *A Christian Christmas*. Her award-winning titles include *Talk to Me*, ranked #14 of Top Books in 2008 that Changed Lives by *Black Pearls Magazine*. She is a two-time recipient of the Romance Slam Jam Emma Rodgers Award for Best Inspirational Romance, first for *Still Guilty* (2010) and then for *Crowning Glory* (2011). Her beloved Jamieson men are featured in the Guilty series: *Guilty of Love, Not Guilty of Love,* and *Still Guilty*; the Jamieson Legacy series: *Guilty by Association, The Guilt Trip,* and *Free from Guilt*; and the Guilty Parties: *The Acquittal* and *The Confession* (coming 2015). Given the success of the Jamieson men, Pat was elated to introduce the Carmen Sisters series from Whitaker House. *Driven to Be Loved* wraps up the trilogy, which also includes *No Easy Catch* and *In Defense of Love*.

In addition to pursuing such hobbies as researching her roots and sewing, Pat has been a featured speaker and workshop presenter at various venues across the country.

Pat has converted her sofa-strapped sports fanatic husband into an amateur travel agent, untrained bodyguard, GPS-guided chauffeur, and administrative assistant who is constantly on probation. They have a son and a daughter.

Readers may learn more about Pat and her books by visiting her Web site, www.patsimmons.net; connecting with her on Twitter, Facebook, Pinterest, or LinkedIn; or by contacting her at authorpatsimmons@gmail.com.

Welcome to Our House!

We Have a Special Gift for You ...

It is our privilege and pleasure to share in your love of Christian fiction by publishing books that enrich your life and encourage your faith.

To show our appreciation, we invite you to sign up to receive a specially selected **Reader Appreciation Gift**, with our compliments. Just go to the Web address at the bottom of this page.

God bless you as you seek a deeper walk with Him!

WE HAVE A GIFT FOR YOU. VISIT:

whpub.me/fictionthx

WHITAKER
HOUSE